MOUTHWATERING PRAISE FOR NANCY
COCO'S CANDY-COATED MYSTERIES!

### *Oh Say Can You Fudge*

"Beautiful Mackinac Island provides the setting for a puzzling series of crimes. Now that Allie McMurphy has taken over her grandparents' hotel and fudge shop, life on Mackinac is good, although her little dog, Mal, does tend to nose out trouble. . . . Allie's third offers plenty of plausible suspects and mouthwatering fudge recipes."
—**Kirkus Reviews**

"WOW. This is a great book. I loved the series from the beginning and this book just makes me love it even more. No one can make me feel like I am in Mackinac Island better than Nancy Coco. She draws the reader in and makes you feel like you are part of the story. I cannot wait to read more. FANTASTIC is the only thing I can say further about this book."
—**Bookschellves.blogspot.com**

### *To Fudge or Not to Fudge*

"*To Fudge or Not to Fudge* is a superbly-crafted, classic, culinary cozy mystery. If you enjoy them as much as I do, you are in for a real treat. The setting of Mackinac Island immediately drew me to the book as it is an amazing location. The only problem I had with the book was reading about all the mouthwatering fudge made me hungry."
—**Examiner.com (5 stars out of 5)**

"We LOVED it! This mystery is a vacation between the pages of a book. If you've never been to Mackinac Island, you will long to visit, and if you have, the story will help you to recall all of your wonderful memories."
—**Melissa's Mochas, Mysteries and Meows**

"A five-star delicious mystery that has great characters, a good plot and a surprise ending. If you like a good mystery with more than one suspect and a surprise ending, then rush out to get this book and read it, but be sure you have the time since once you start you won't want to put it down. I give this 5 Stars and a Wow Factor of 5+. The fudge recipes included in the book all sound wonderful. I am thinking that a gift basket filled with the fudge from the recipes in this book, along with a copy of the book, some hot chocolate mix and/or coffee, and a nice mug would be a great Christmas gift."

—**Mystery Reading Nook**

"A charming and funny culinary mystery that parodies reality show competitions and is led by a sweet heroine, eccentric but likable characters, and a skillfully crafted plot that speeds towards an unpredictable conclusion. Allie stands out as a likable and engaging character. Delectable fudge recipes are interspersed throughout the novel."

—**Kings River Life**

### *All Fudged Up*

"A sweet treat with memorable characters, a charming locale, and satisfying mystery."

—**Barbara Allan**, author of the Trash 'n' Treasures mysteries

"A fun book with a lively plot, and it's set in one of America's most interesting resorts. All this plus fudge!"

—**JoAnna Carl**, author of the Chocoholic mysteries (NAL)

"A sweet confection of a book. Charming setting, clever protagonist, and creamy fudge—a yummy recipe for a great read."

—**Joanna Campbell Slan**, author of *The Scrap-N-Craft Mysteries* and *The Jane Eyre Chronicles*

"Move over, Janet Evanovich—there's a new kid on the block. Nancy Coco's *All Fudged Up* is a delightful mystery delivering suspense and surprise in equal measure. Her heroine, Alice McMurphy, owner of the Historic McMurphy Hotel and Fudge Shop (as much of a mouthful as her delicious fudge), has a wry narrative voice that never falters. Add that to the charm of the setting, Michigan's famed Mackinac Island, and you have a recipe for enjoyment. As an added bonus, mouthwatering fudge recipes are included. A must-read for all lovers of amateur sleuth classic mysteries."

—**Carole Bugge**, author of *Who Killed Blanche Dubois?* and other Claire Rawlings mysteries

"You won't have to 'fudge' your enthusiasm for Nancy Parra's first Mackinac Island Fudge Shop Mystery. Indulge your sweet tooth as you settle in and meet Allie McMurphy, Mal the bichon/poodle mix, and the rest of the motley crew in this entertaining series debut."

—**Miranda James**

"The characters are fun and well-developed, the setting is quaint and beautiful, and there are several mouthwatering fudge recipes."

—*RT Book Reviews* (3 stars)

"Enjoyable . . . ALL FUDGED UP is littered with delicious fudge recipes, including alcohol-infused ones. I really enjoyed this cozy mystery and look forward to reading more in this series."

—**Fresh Fiction**

"Cozy mystery lovers who enjoy quirky characters, a great setting and fantastic recipes will love this debut."

—*The Lima News*

"The first Candy-Coated mystery is a fun cozy due to the wonderful location filled with eccentric characters."

—*Midwest Book Review*

Also by Nancy Coco

**The Candy-Coated Mystery Series**

*All Fudged Up*

*To Fudge or Not to Fudge*

*Oh Say Can You Fudge*

*All I Want for Christmas Is Fudge* (e-book)

# All You Need Is Fudge

## Nancy Coco

KENSINGTON PUBLISHING CORP.

http://www.kensingtonbooks.com

KENSINGTON BOOKS are published by

Kensington Publishing Corp.
119 West 40th Street
New York, NY 10018

All Kensington titles, imprints and distributed lines are available at special quantity discounts for bulk purchases for sales promotions, premiums, fund-raising, and educational or institutional use. Special book excerpts or customized printings can also be created to fit specific needs. For details, write or phone the office of the Kensington Special Sales Manager. Kensington Publishing Corp., 119 West 40th Street, New York, NY 10018. Attn: Special Sales Department. Phone: 1-800-221-2647.

Kensington and the K logo Reg. U.S. Pat & TM Off.

ISBN-13: 978-1-4967-0162-6
ISBN-10: 1-4967-0162-3
First Kensington Mass Market Edition: August 2016

eISBN-13: 978-1-4967-0163-3
eISBN-10: 1-4967-0163-1
First Kensington Electronic Edition: August 2016

10 9 8 7 6 5 4 3

Printed in the United States of America

*This book is for my family.*
*Thank you for your years of support and love*
*and for giving me the freedom to follow my dreams.*

# Chapter 1

I don't find a dead body every time I take Mal—my bichonpoo puppy—for a walk. Really. In fact, it had only happened once. But finding dead people seems to be a theme for me since I returned to Mackinac Island to run the historic McMurphy Hotel and Fudge Shop. It was no surprise to anyone that I had 9-1-1 on speed dial on my cell phone.

"9-1-1. What is your emergency?"

I could tell it was Charlene on the phone. She worked long hours. In fact, so many hours I had begun to think she was a workaholic like me. "Hi Charlene," I said as brightly as possible. Water dripped down the side of my face and I wiped it away.

"Allie McMurphy, is that you?" she asked.

"Yes, it's me," I replied, trying to slow my heavy breathing. I was soaked and my muscles shook from the stress of dragging a dead weight out of the water and over the three foot marina wall.

"Who's dead now?" Charlene asked.

I think she was kidding. I wasn't. "I'm not quite

sure," I said and stared down at the purplish face of the woman I had just pulled from the lake. Something was vaguely familiar about her, but it was hard to tell. People looked different when they were dead.

"But there *is* a dead person," Charlene stated. "Seriously?"

"Yes, I'm afraid so. Can you contact Rex?" Officer Rex Manning was my go-to guy whenever I found trouble . . . which seemed to be often.

"Where are you?"

"I'm at the marina off Main Street near the coffee shop."

"Allie, it's yacht race week. A dead body in the marina would be disastrous."

"Well, I didn't put it there." I stifled a shiver. Yacht racing happened a couple times on Mackinac Island. It was the first of the season and people were gearing up for the influx of boaters and boat enthusiasts. In fact, just yesterday I was at the yacht club with my best friend Jenn Christensen helping to coordinate an event.

Jenn was the event planner, not me, but I went along for support and because I was doing everything I could to gain access into Mackinac Island society. Small business was about community and I was working hard to become a part of the tight knit community that was Mackinac Island.

"Rex is on his way," Charlene said, "along with a crew of first responders. Are you sure the person is dead?"

I noted the pallor of skin and that the open eyes looked glazed over and colorless. "I think she's been dead a while." A shiver took me. It was a cool morning. The sun had just started to come up when I began the walk and now that I was soaked through, the wind felt cold against my skin.

"Okay," Charlene said. "I'll stay with you until Rex gets there."

"Thanks." I brushed my currently seaweed-like strands of hair out of my face. Mal was having a good time sniffing the girl I'd managed to drag mostly onto the grassy knoll in front of the marina. I hugged my lake water–soaked, legging-covered knees to my equally soaked shirtdress-covered body. "Mal, come here."

I snagged my dog away from the dead girl and held Mal to me. Her warm little body was a comfort. It was still early. The first ferries had yet to arrive with their boatload of tourists. It was quiet. Some of the maids and groundskeepers had started their walk from the workers' quarters to the hotels to start their day. The shops would not open for at least another hour and a half.

"Your puppy is with you?" Charlene asked. "Is there anyone else nearby?"

I looked around. "No. The marina is pretty quiet. Mal alerted me there was something in the water. As soon as I saw the woman, I jumped in to save her, but it was too late. She really is quite cold and stiff."

"She's most likely in rigor," Charlene said. "I never thought I'd ever say that out loud in my life. But I've been brushing up on my dead body terminology a lot since you moved here."

I winced at the tone of her voice. "Like I said, Mal

found her." I looked at my puppy. She was nearly six months old and wagged her little stub tail at the sound of her name. "She has a good nose."

"You two are quite the pair," Charlene said.

The first time I ever called 9-1-1 Charlene had not believed me. She thought I was a prank caller. Now all I had to do was say my name and she assumed the worst. In fact everyone on the island assumed the worst.

"What were you doing near the marina?" she asked.

"Mal needed her morning walk and I wanted to see the yachts that came in for this weekend's race." A glance over my shoulder showed me that the marina was full of large sailing boats. Some people on the boats had begun to stir. A gentleman in shorts and a T-shirt came out on his deck with a coffee cup in hand. I watched as he stretched and looked at the lake then did a slow turn. I shuddered when he did a double take at the sight of me and Mal and the pale bloated body of a woman wearing a bright blue and orange, color-blocked dress. Her feet were bare. She had painted her toenails robin's egg blue.

"A guy on his yacht spotted us," I told Charlene and waved at the guy who stared with his mouth wide open. I suppose seeing a dead body first thing in the morning would be a bit of a shock for anyone.

"Don't let him get close," she warned. "We don't need a crowd messing up the crime scene."

In the distance I heard the siren of the ambulance. The state of the art ambulance and fire truck were the only motor vehicles allowed on the island. Other transportation on the island that time forgot was limited to horse and carriage, bicycle, or foot traffic.

"Is everything okay down there?" the man hollered from the deck of his yacht.

"Things are under control," I called back and pointed at my cell phone. "I've called 9-1-1."

"What happened?" Police Officer Rex Manning had pulled up on his bike, hit the kickstand, and walked carefully toward me.

Mal, of course, having no respect for possible crime scene evidence, wiggled out of my embrace and raced up to greet him with a twirl and a nose bump. Rex absently patted Mal as he walked to where I sat next to the body.

"I pulled her out of the water," I said and trembled. "I tried pushing water out of her lungs, but she was already gone."

"Long gone from the looks of her," he said as he squatted down beside me. "She was in the lake?" He didn't look at me as he took a pen out of his pocket and lifted the hair away from her face. Rex wore his uniform well. He had the chest and shoulders of a man who worked out regularly at the gym. I always thought of him as having that action hero kind of look with his shaved head and gorgeous eyes.

"Yes, she was in the water near the pier where the coffee shop is." I pointed toward the spot. "I didn't see her at first. Mal pulled me to the edge so I went to see what she was fussing about."

"Your pup has a good nose for death." He frowned. "I think I know who this is."

"Is that good or bad?" I asked and bit down as my teeth started to chatter.

He glanced at me. "You need to get warm." Standing, he waved down the EMTs.

George Marron came down to where we were with a blanket in one hand and a med kit in the other.

"She might have hypothermia," Rex said to him.

George draped the blanket around my shoulders. "Whenever I get a call with Allie involved, I automatically bring one." He was a little taller than me and Rex. He had high cheekbones, long, black hair that he wore in a braid down his back, and black eyes that spoke of his native ancestors.

I huddled in the warmth. "I don't think it's shock this time," I said with a touch of pride in my voice. "I'm soaked."

"The water's still cool this time of year," George agreed. "Even for mid-July." He checked the pulse at my wrist. "Your lips and fingers are a little blue, but you're right, you're not shocky."

"I'm fine." I smiled at him to reassure him that I didn't need an exam, and huddled into the blanket. "Just wet." My teeth chattered as if to emphasize my words.

Rex stood and waved the second EMT with the stretcher over toward the body. "You pulled her out of the water all by yourself?"

"Yes, mostly," I said as Mal curled up in my lap. The woman's legs still dangled over the retaining wall. "I didn't have the strength to finish the job,

I'm afraid. I wanted to get her far enough that I could try to push water out of her lungs and start CPR."

"Okay, tell me exactly—step by step—what you did." His cop's gaze noted all the details of the marina as it started to wake up.

George and the other EMT pulled the body all the way over the retaining wall. A pair of squawking gulls swooped by. Officer Charles Brown showed up and stayed near the road to keep back the slowly gathering crowd.

"I knew the yachts were coming in for race weekend and thought I'd take Mal for her morning walk down here. The coffee shop was open and Frances had told me that she likes the blueberry scones they serve so I figured I'd stop in and pick up a few for the staff."

"What time did you leave the McMurphy?" Rex asked.

"I finished my last batch of fudge around five forty-five and left right after that. So however long it takes to put Mal's halter and leash on and stroll down here." The marina was across from the yacht club and the Island House Hotel about half a mile from the McMurphy on Main.

"So around six AM?"

I nodded. "That sounds right." I hugged Mal. She wanted to greet everyone and help the EMTs with the body.

I, on the other hand, knew she'd be in the way so I hugged her to hold her in my lap. "We walked down this way. I didn't see anything unusual, just the boats and the sunrise. We walked the lower path near the retaining wall and headed down the dock to the coffee shop. About halfway, Mal started barking and pulling me toward the water."

"She must have smelled the body."

"Something," I agreed. "When I saw the girl floating, she was faceup. I thought maybe she was swimming. Then I noticed how pale she was. I called out, but she didn't answer."

"And?"

"And I jumped in. I didn't think about it much. I thought she needed help. I was a lifeguard in high school and instinct kicked in. I put my arm around her torso and swam to the wall. When I could stand, I put my hands under her arms and pulled her over the wall. It's harder than you'd think."

His blue gaze twinkled. "I know. I'm still trying to picture how you did it."

"Honestly? I sat on the wall and grabbed her and pulled. When I got her up high enough, I scooted back. I was able to bring her far enough onto the grass that I knew she had solid earth beneath her. Then I used my palms to push water out of her lungs, but it didn't help."

"She was dead."

"Yes." I pushed my slowly drying hair out of my face. "When I realized she was stiff, I took out my phone and called 9-1-1."

He tilted his head and drew his eyebrows together. "Didn't your cell phone get wet?"

"Yeah," I said and lifted it up. "But it's water-proof. You know I'm pretty clumsy and have a tendency to answer my cell phone when I'm in the bathtub."

He grinned. "Yeah, I know."

I felt the heat of embarrassment rush up my cheeks, but worked to ignore it. "Jenn made me buy one of those waterproof, cell phone covers. I can't take the phone diving, but it will survive getting wet."

Thankfully, Jen had come up for the summer to help me manage my first season at the McMurphy. My Papa Liam was supposed to be here to train me, but earlier this year, he'd gone nose down while playing cards at the senior center and they hadn't been able to revive him. Jenn came up to fill the void. She was actually better at making friends on the island than I was. All in all, she took good care of me.

"Huh," Rex said. "It's a good thing, then, I guess."

"Yes."

"Mal seems relatively dry," he pointed out.

I made a face. "She didn't follow me into the water. She stayed on the pier and barked. Then she raced over here when I managed to pull the girl up on land."

"Smart dog."

"Should we call Shane?" I asked. Shane Carpenter was the local CSI guy who also happened to be dating Jenn. I liked to think that I was the one who introduced them. In fact, if the relationship worked out in the long run, I would claim that it was all my doing.

"Charlene already did. The body has clues," Rex said. "He'll want to know the water temperature and see what else is floating in the water. And he may need those clothes you're wearing."

"Oh, right." I glanced down at my dress and leggings. My white Keds were gray from water. "Wait. Is it okay to move the body?" I pointed at the guy holding the stretcher. It was folded up so that you couldn't see the wheels. A body bag was on the ground beside the body and open, ready for them to roll her onto it.

"You pulled her out of the water so she has already been moved," Rex pointed out. "I don't want to leave her out here for gawkers." His eyebrows were drawn together and his mouth rested in a flat line. He was a handsome man and had two ex-wives to prove it. His hands were large, square and efficient as he did a simple check of the body. He motioned for the EMTs to bring over the stretcher. "You said she was faceup in the water?"

"Yes. It seems weird, right? I mean usually when you think of dead bodies in the water you imagine them facedown."

"Sure." He eyed the surrounding area and made notes on his notepad. "Maybe she was dead when she hit the water and floated up."

"Maybe." I watched as they rolled the dead woman over carefully, inspecting her back for contusions or anything else that might tell us whether it was a simple drowning or something more sinister before they would tuck her into the body bag and roll her onto the stretcher.

Gail Hall from the coffee shop walked down from the pier with her hands full of coffees in a paper carrier. "You guys look like you could use some strong coffee."

Mal stood on her hind legs to greet Gail.

"Sorry pup. No coffee for you." Gail was tall and large-boned and wore her dark brown hair pulled back into a tight ponytail. She handed coffee to the first responders as they stood around a moment to take in the scene. Squatting down by me, she patted Mal on the head with her free hand while handing me a coffee with her other hand. Remnants of black paint covered her cuticles.

"I saw you jump into the lake," she said, her brown eyes filled with concern. "You gave me quite a scare. I had no idea what you were doing. I thought maybe you'd finally had enough of island life and I'd have to come out and get you." She tilted her head. "I wasn't looking forward to jumping into the lake myself, so I called 9-1-1."

"Oh," was all I could say in answer. I sipped the coffee. "That's why Charlene knew it was me when I called."

Gail nodded. "Yeah. I saw you pulling someone out of the water. I would have come out sooner, but I had to wait for Emily to get in to cover the shop."

"You look like you were painting." I pointed at her hands.

"Spray paint," she said and rubbed at the spots. "This is from last night. I've been painting an old dresser. Gotta love the do-it-yourself look. Mine is a bit worse than what you see the pros do on TV." She paused and watched as they zipped the woman up in the black body bag. "It's weird to think you could be painting a dresser one day and dead the next. Just like her." She turned to me. "How did you know she was there?"

"Mal," I replied and pointed at my dog. "She's got a good sniffer."

"She smelled her from the pier?"

"Yes. Crazy, right?"

"Right. Creepy to think some girl was floating dead a few feet from my shop and I didn't know it. Any idea who she is? I couldn't see from the shop."

"Ladies, no details until I get your stories." Rex drew his dark eyebrows together in a look of concern.

"Right." Gail stood. "I've got to get back."

"I'll be in the coffee shop in a few," Rex said. "Thanks for the coffee."

She smiled. "You're welcome. Take care, Allie."

"I will. Thanks."

We watched her walk back to the coffee shop. She was probably ten years older than me—so in her mid to late thirties—and pretty in her black slacks and navy-blue top.

Rex squatted down beside me and absently patted Mal as he looked out over the crowded marina. More people had begun to emerge from the boats to prep for a day of sailing. "Do you know who you pulled out of the lake?"

"No," I said with a shake of my head. "I sort of recognize her, though. Is she a local?"

"Yeah." He looked at me. "Carin Moore. Her family's been on the island for generations. They're members of the yacht club. In fact, see that big yacht—third one down on the more expensive pier?"

I glanced across the boats. "The one that says *Daddy's Girl* on the side?"

"Yes," Rex said with a short nod. "That's her family's boat."

"You said she might have been faceup because she was dead when she hit the water." I chewed on my bottom lip. "Do you think she was killed on the boat and pushed in?"

"I'm not going to speculate," Rex said.

"She had a nice cocktail dress on." I closed my eyes as I pictured the color-blocked silk dress. "I bet it was designer." I paused and looked at Rex. "She wasn't very old, was she?"

"She's around your age," he replied. "She was in Paige Jessop's class in school."

"Oh." I hugged the blanket around me. "I don't know why, but it's worse when someone your age ends up dead."

"Yeah," Rex said, his mouth firm.

"I tried to save her," I said, clinging to the coffee cup as if it would make things right. The EMTs hefted the full body bag onto the stretcher and pulled it toward the ambulance.

"It was too late," he said, his tone low and soothing. "We're going to need your clothes. Shane will be here soon. He'll probably want to take samples from your hair and your nails and such."

"Right." I made a face. "I should be used to this by now. But I'm not." I looked at Rex. "Finding all these bodies, I feel like I have really bad timing. I mean an hour later and someone else would have found her. You know?"

"Maybe you have good timing. Maybe the killers have bad timing."

I sent him a half smile. "Thanks, but I don't think

there's anyone on the island who believes that." Sipping my coffee to try to get warm, I watched them place the stretcher in the ambulance.

George waved as they headed around to the front of the vehicle. I lifted my hand in a short wave.

"You said you left around six AM," Rex said. "Did you go out the back and down the alley or out the front?"

"We walked out the front because Frances had come in already to watch the desk," I said.

"Did you see anyone?"

I drew my eyebrows together. "No, it was too early. Most of the shop owners don't even think about coming in until seven. I think I saw a pair of joggers go by, but I didn't recognize them. They were probably tourists."

"So, only a pair of joggers? Did you walk on the fort side or the harbor side of Main?"

"Mal and I walked down the fort side toward the marina. I crossed at the lawn in front of the fort because I thought it would be nice to see all the boats that have come in for the weekend yacht race." My gaze went to the boats. People were out starting up motors, taxiing out of the marina or raising sails, hopping on the dock to untie the boat, then hopping back on as the boats left the marina and headed out to the lake. "Is it okay that they leave?"

Rex looked at the busy docks. "There's not much I can do without a warrant. They'll be back tonight for tomorrow's race." He turned back to me. "Did you see anyone on the pier? On any boats?"

"I'm sorry," I said with a shake of my head. "I don't remember seeing anyone. I remember thinking the flowers in the flower beds along the walk were lovely when Mal stopped to do her business. I remember listening to the waves lap against the boats and thinking it would be a nice sound to go to sleep to. I wondered if I should save up for a boat. Not a yacht. There's no way I could afford that. Do you have a boat?"

"A fishing boat. I sold my sailing boat."

I blinked at the thought of Rex sailing. I suppose when you grow up on an island, you learn about boats pretty fast. Just another thing I missed by growing up in Detroit.

"You were walking by the boats . . ."

"Right. Like I said, I saw the coffee shop and thought I'd get Frances some scones. We walked up the coffee shop side of the pier and were almost there when Mal tugged me over to the edge. She wouldn't go any farther. Sometimes she can be stubborn. I went over to see what she was sniffing at, looked down, and saw the woman in the water. The rest you know."

Mal barked and raced off. I glanced after her and saw Officer Brown heading our way. He was a nice guy, younger than Rex, less rugged, but still built like a gym rat. Mal greeted him with a happy bark.

"I'm going to have Charles walk you over to the clinic," Rex said. "It'll be easier for Shane to collect evidence without a crowd." He helped me up. "We'll contact Jenn and see if she can bring you clean clothes."

"Okay. It's weird, right?"

"What do you mean?"

"Finding that girl in the marina," I said with a shrug. "Managing to get her on the grass and then having to be looked over like a piece of evidence."

"I'm sorry, Allie. It's a heck of a way to start a day."

"It seems to be the pattern to my summer. What are you going to do?"

"I'm going to go check out the Moores' yacht, then see Gail, and after that try to get more people out here to talk to the boaters. Someone saw something."

"What about Carin's family?"

"When I get a positive ID, I'll go over with the bad news."

"What if they're on the boat? I mean won't they wonder why you're checking out their yacht?"

"Go with Charles," Rex said. "Leave the investigation to me. Okay?"

I nodded. "Okay."

"Good." Rex handed me off to Officer Brown. "See that she's checked out. She's bleeding."

I looked down to see blood dripping down my arm from a long scratch that must have happened when I climbed up on shore.

"I'll take good care of her." Officer Brown's dark green gaze filled with concern as he wrapped his big, warm hand around my elbow. "Come on, Allie. Let's get you to the clinic."

Mal barked her agreement.

Officer Brown had Mal's leash in his hand and it was the first time I realized that I hadn't had Mal's leash since I jumped into the water. Thankfully, she was a good puppy and hadn't left me. I gave Frances a quick call to come get Mal and to have Jenn bring me a bag of clean clothes. Frances had been right when she gave Mal to me. I did need someone to look out for me. Then again, my life wouldn't have been half as exciting without Mal nosing out dead bodies.

It made me wonder what kind of clues she'd find next.

## Coconut Caramel Fudge

### Ingredients

1½ cups granulated sugar
1½ cups packed dark brown sugar
1 cup half and half
3 tablespoons dark corn syrup
1 stick butter plus 1½ teaspoon butter for pan prep
2 teaspoons vanilla extract
1 cup coconut (toasted)
½ cup caramel sauce

### Directions

Prepare an 8- x 2-inch pan by lining it with aluminum foil. Butter the foil with 1½ teaspoon butter.

In a large heavy-bottomed saucepan, combine the sugars, the half and half, and the corn syrup over medium heat. Stir until the sugars dissolve.

Insert a candy thermometer (ensure it does not touch the bottom or sides of the pan) and bring to a boil, stirring occasionally. Allow the mixture to boil, stirring frequently, until it reaches 238 degrees F on a candy thermometer. This takes approximately 10 minutes. (I set the timer to help understand how long it takes for the temperature to reach this point.)

Remove from heat. Take out the thermometer and stir in the butter and vanilla.

Stir the fudge vigorously with a heavy wooden spoon, stirring constantly for 10-15 minutes until the fudge loses its shine and holds its shape.

Pour fudge into the prepared pan and smooth into an even layer. Sprinkle with toasted coconut.

Place caramel sauce in a plastic sandwich bag, clip one corner, and use it as a pastry bag. Ribbon the caramel sauce over the coconut in diagonals.

Refrigerate the fudge for at least 1 hour.

Once set, remove the fudge from the pan using the foil as handles. Cut the fudge into small 1-inch pieces to serve.

Store fudge in an airtight container at room temperature for up to one week.

# Chapter 2

The problem with touching a dead body is that the police liked to take your clothing into evidence. That might have been fine the first time, but with my limited wardrobe and perchance for finding bodies it was getting expensive.

"Bringing you clothes seems to be a big part of my job," Jenn said as she handed me a paper bag.

"You love it. The more clothes I lose to evidence the more you can shop online for me." I dug out fresh underwear, shorts, and a T-shirt and ducked behind the curtain in the clinic room where I'd been checked out and given a couple of stitches on my forearm. "You know how much I hate to clothes shop."

"That's why you have me as your personal shopper." She laughed and followed me in, sitting on the exam couch. "I don't think I've ever met a woman who doesn't like to shop."

"Clothes judge me," I groused. "Food on the other hand never judges. I can grocery shop all day."

"What a weirdo," she teased.

"You have to admit that things are never dull around me." I quickly changed into clean clothes and dropped my wet leggings and shirt into an evidence bag.

"I can't believe you actually jumped into the water and pulled out a dead body." Jenn sat with her hands on her narrow hips. Long legged, tall, and gorgeous, she wore crisp linen slacks and a flowing peasant blouse with embroidered flowers along the drawstring front. Her dark hair was pulled back into a neat chignon and she wore gorgeous sandals. Jenn looked ready for brunch at the country club, mostly because that was what she was doing later in the morning.

"I wasn't sure if she was dead or not when I jumped in," I pointed out as I struggled to put on my wet shoes. My hair was nearly dry and still tangled in bits of lake flotsam. Jenn handed me a comb and I attacked my hair. "I've forgotten how hard it is to swim in regular clothes and drag a non-responsive person to shore."

"Ugh. I remember that training in lifeguard class," Jenn said as her expression went from one of exasperation to one of condolences. "At least she didn't try to drown you. Did they struggle against you when you took your test?"

"Yes." I remembered taking the class. My teacher Mr. Metzger wanted to be sure we were prepared for all situations. He'd told us to be prepared to save him as he struggled like a drowning person. "My instructor was also the football coach so he was 200 pounds of pure muscle. He over did the panic thing, if you ask me. I have no idea how I passed that test, but I did."

"Ha. My instructor refused to get wet. She set up seniors in stations to enact drowning by struggle and dead weight," Jenn said. "I remember my struggle guy was Ryan Wiltz. He had a thing for me so he barely wiggled while I got my arm under his shoulders and swam to the edge of the pool." She sighed. "He was so sexy."

"What happened to him?" I asked.

"Oh, well, it turns out he also had a thing for Jessica Kelley and Amiee Hendricks, and Susy Brown and Ashley Kaufman." She listed four girls then gave up. "Pretty much every girl in my class. He was so cute that he got away with dating two or three at a time."

"But not you," I said, a tad horrified.

"No." She laughed. "Not me. When I found out that Emily Crawford was the only girl he wasn't dating, I moved on to Mike Hancock."

"The senior prom date," I said, recalling a discussion we'd had one late night at our dorm in college.

"Yes." She nodded. "The senior prom date. Huh. Funny how stuff comes back to you. I haven't thought about lifeguard training in years and years."

"Me, neither." I finished making myself somewhat presentable. "Funny what seeing a person in the water will do to you."

There was a knock.

"Have you collected my evidence yet?" Shane called from the other side.

Jenn smiled at the sound of his voice. She hopped down, grabbed the plastic bag filled with my clothing and opened the curtain. "It's right here," she said as she handed it to him. "Do you want me to tag it for you?"

Shane was a tall, skinny guy with dark horn-rimmed glasses. He wore his dark hair slicked back out of his face. He was sexy in a quiet, super-smart kind of way. I could understand why Jenn was so captured. He was wearing a lab coat over a dark green T-shirt with a Think Geek logo and a pair of skinny jeans. His feet were covered in black and white old style high-tops.

"No, thanks. I have my own system." He took the bag from her and gave her an appreciative once over. "Thanks, doll."

"See you later?" she asked and kissed his cheek.

"I'll pick you up tonight as planned."

"I hope this whole dead body thing doesn't put a cramp in your dating style," I said, trying to remain sincere.

"Oh, no, it actually makes it more exciting," Jenn said with a laugh. "It gives us something to talk about."

"Not that I discuss a case with someone outside the system," Shane said with one raised eyebrow. "That wouldn't be appropriate, would it?"

"No," Jenn said with a shake of her head. "It wouldn't be appropriate."

I thought I saw her wink at him.

He pinked slightly, cleared his throat, and turned to head out with the evidence. He worked in the county crime department in St. Ignace where he had what lab equipment the county could muster. Some items were months behind in testing, but he did what he could as a one-man crime scene guy.

"Where do we go now?" Jenn asked me as she took back her comb and shoved it into her purse.

"Rex said I could leave as soon as I gave Shane my clothes. When do you have your meeting at the yacht club?"

Jenn had volunteered us for the yacht race fund-raiser. She, my part-time chocolatier, Sandy Everheart, and I were assigned to put chocolate centerpieces on the tables. Each of the pieces resembled yachts enrolled in this weekend's race. We'd spent two weeks studying pictures of the ships. Sandy then made clay replicas of each ship and cast molds made out of silicon. We'd finished making and pouring the chocolate the night before. All that was left to do with the chocolate was assemble the centerpieces and place them carefully on each table.

Jenn glanced at her wristwatch. "The meeting is in twenty minutes. Not enough time for you to shower and properly dress."

I sighed. "I'll come in late with Sandy to put the pieces on the tables."

"That's probably a good idea. Proper dress and behavior is important to these people. Be sure you're both wearing your best chef coats and hats."

"I've got mine cleaned and pressed," I said dryly. "Please convey to Paige and the rest of the committee my apologies for being late."

"Oh, I'm sure the news of the dead body has

already run through town. They'll expect you to be late."

I shook my head as we left the clinic. "How am I ever going to get rid of this reputation for finding the dead?"

"Don't knock it," Jenn said. "It's great publicity. Everyone knows who you are now. Seriously, the old saying *No press is bad press* is for a reason. You watch. People will be stopping by to purchase fudge all morning."

"Now that makes it all worthwhile," I said with a sarcastic tone. "Doesn't anyone feel for the poor dead girl? I mean she was our age, for goodness sake."

"She was also very mean," Jenn said.

I glanced at her. "How do you know that? Have they officially identified the body?"

"Rex is with the family right now," Jenn said and shrugged. "It's a small island. News this big gets around fast. The Moores are major players in the yacht club set. It's going to be an interesting day setting up for the official race day kickoff."

"Mean or not, no one deserves to die so young."

Jenn nodded. "I can't argue with that." She glanced at her watch. "Okay, I'm heading to the club for the meeting. I'll see you there?"

"Yes, give me half an hour to shower and get dressed."

"See you." Jenn headed down the street to the yacht club, which sat just past the fort and before the Island House Hotel.

I pulled open the door to the historic McMurphy Hotel and Fudge Shop and was hit by the magical scent of chocolate, coffee, and just a hint of age from the building. Frances, my reception manager, sat on the stool behind the reception desk tucked in the far left corner of the room. The McMurphy lobby was large. I had remodeled it just this spring, recreating the original thick pink and white striped walls, refinishing the old wood floors, and adding period replicated area rugs. The back wall housed two sweeping staircases on either side, leading to the second- and then third-floor rooms. The fourth floor was the McMurphy's business office and the owner's apartments that were now my permanent home.

The floors shone from last night's polish. I recently had the area rugs cleaned, which made the entire lobby smell fresh. The reception desk was carefully polished with beeswax. Cubbies for guest mail placement and a locked glass box of unassigned room keys were behind it. The McMurphy held on to the old tradition of metal keys to unlock the rooms. Keys were returned there when people checked out.

Frances had worked as the reception manager for years. She was a retired school teacher and my Grammy Alice's best friend. After Papa Liam died, Frances had stayed on to help me through the current season. I hoped she would continue in her role until she was ready to retire. I prayed that was a long way off, but it was hard to tell. Frances was in her seventies and sometimes talked of traveling.

In the center of the stairs was an old-fashioned elevator, complete with wire-framed gate that pulled closed. You could see through it as you rose from the lobby. The elevator stopped at the third floor offering only a staircase to reach my apartment. The thought was that would help keep guests from going up to my home. So far so good.

In front of the elevator was a grouping of winged-back chairs and a love seat complete with coffee table. To the far right was a coffee bar with carafes full of coffee twenty-four hours a day along with a wide variety of creams, sugars, and bottles of flavoring. To the front right was the fudge shop, which I had closed off with glass walls from floor to ceiling. I'd left the front open initially, but a few weeks ago, I'd adopted a cat we'd named Caramella— Mella for short. Since then, I'd had the entire fudge shop walled off in glass with a wide swinging door so I could demonstrate fudge making without Mella getting into the area. I didn't want her getting hurt from the super-heated sugar that went into candy making.

The front left of the lobby held the fireplace and couches along with reading lamps and a sign announcing free Wi-Fi. The idea was that people would stop in to use the Wi-Fi, get a coffee, and hopefully buy a pound or two of fudge to take home with them.

"Allie, are you okay?" Sandy, my chocolatier and Mackinac native, opened the fudge shop door and came out. The scent of dark chocolate followed her. She'd been putting the finishing touches on the ship centerpieces. Her black hair, pulled back into a long braid down her back was covered by a white chef's cap on her head. Her eyes were so dark brown to be nearly black and her copper colored skin was smooth over high cheekbones. She was shorter than I was—only reaching my shoulder— and slight of build.

"I'm okay," I said with a bit of a smile.

"I heard about the girl in the marina. That is bad luck for the yacht race."

"And for the girl," Frances said from her perch behind the receptionist desk. She still had a full head of brown hair, which she kept cut in a short bob that swung near her shoulders. Unlike me and Sandy with our black slacks and chef's coats, Frances dressed more free-spirited in flowing skirts, sweaters, and blouses. She wore bangles on her wrists and silver hoops in her ears.

I grimaced a little, trying for a smile. "Unfortunately I'm making us late. There is lake water in my hair and I need to shower before I can help you take the centerpieces to the club to set them up."

"You'd better scoot." Frances looked at me over the top of her purple cat-eyed reading glasses. "Jenn told me that the setup is supposed to be done by one o'clock and it's already ten-thirty."

"I'm scooting," I said as I climbed the stairs. "Sandy, you've got everything ready to transport, right?"

"Yes, boss," she called to me. "I'm finishing boxing things up for the move now."

"Great. I'll be down in a jiffy."

When I opened the apartment door, Mal raced over and jumped on me. Her bobbed tail wagging.

"Hello, love," I said and scratched behind her ears. "How are you? Did Frances give you breakfast?" I walked over to see the remains of breakfast in her dishes and freshened her water in her bowl. Then I heard a mewl. I turned to see Mella on the breakfast bar watching me. I gave her a quick pet from head to tail. "Hello there, pretty kitty. How are you getting along?" I glanced over to see that she had some food and water as well. We had separated the dishes. Doggie food was kept on the floor and cat food on the countertop.

I ducked into the bathroom to run a quick shower. My thoughts whirled. Was Carin's death an accident or murder? If an accident, what would cause a girl to slip off a boat and drown? Why didn't anyone see it happen and try to save her?

If it was murder, who would want to kill Carin Moore? I barely knew the girl, but she was my age. How many enemies could she have made only in her twenties? I suppose those answers would have to wait for the coroner's report.

In the meantime, Carin's death would definitely put a damper on the yacht races. I was pretty certain her parents wouldn't be taking their boat out any time soon.

I toweled off and dressed in my chef's gear. Perhaps there would be something to find out at the yacht club. People tended to talk around the help as if we weren't there. Maybe, when we put up the centerpieces, we'd find out what the locals thought of Carin's demise. Then my questions would be answered. I made a mental note to send her parents flowers. Even though I barely knew her, I did pull her from the water. I felt an obligation to extend my condolences, no matter how meager.

# Chapter 3

A heavy quiet filled the yacht club. The building, like most on the island, was over one hundred years old. At one time it was a home that looked out over the marina only a few yards from where I'd pulled Carin's body from the sea. We were in the dining area setting up circular tables of ten. The carpet under my feet was lush and expensive— a far cry from the McMurphy's 1970s green utilitarian carpeted hallways—and the walls were painted a muted tan. Hanging from picture rails over the perfect background were paintings of boats and captains.

Someone had opened the beveled glass windows to let in the soft lake breezes. The china and crystal were set to perfection by the staff. Sandy and I carefully unboxed each chocolate ship sculpture and placed them on mirrored glass rounds in the center of the table.

Jenn was in the den area going over the party details with the committee. The event was to celebrate the kickoff of the yacht races and a fund-raiser to cover updates to the kitchen and other public areas.

I left Sandy to put the finishing touches on the work—thankfully, she was a pro at adhering the thin chocolate strings she had made to represent rigging. In the central hall I ran into Rachel Buckhouse, the event committee chairperson.

"Allie, is it true? Did you find Carin Moore in the marina and pull her on to shore?" Rachel was twenty-eight with golden brown hair and a killer body. Her brown eyes held intelligence and sincerity. Unlike me, she didn't wear a uniform. She had on a pink tweed Chanel skirt and a soft pink sweater set that was most likely cashmere.

"Yes, I pulled a young woman out of the water," I said, my feelings solemn. "I can't say for sure it was Carin as I only met her once or twice. And people look . . . different when they are dead."

Rachel shook her head. "That's terrible. Just terrible. You must be so brave to jump in the water and pull someone out. I'm not at all certain I could do it. It must have been terribly hard."

"It was," I said, remembering the struggle of pulling a hundred and ten pounds of dead weight from the water. I knew that I had bruises in places I didn't usually think about. "I keep thinking about how awful it is to lose a life so young."

"I know," Rachel said with a shudder. "Her family must be devastated, just devastated. I've already been asked to set up a wake for her. The Moores are one of the finest families in the club. People will want to grieve with them."

"So you are certain it's Carin?" I asked.

"Oh, yes. Irene Lombowski is their housekeeper. She told our cook, Mary Smith, that Rex Manning stopped by and asked them to identify the body before they flew it to the coroner in St. Ignace. The Moores came back an hour later devastated. Poor things. I don't imagine they will be attending the opening function tonight. It's going to put a pallor on the entire event. Their table is up near the podium and will be completely empty." Rachel sighed. "I asked if we should discreetly move it to the back of the room, but Amy Hammerstein gave me a firm no. The Moores' table is always in that spot and she isn't going to change that, especially now with this tragedy." Rachel shrugged. "I can see her point. The committee discussed canceling the dinner, but decided to go ahead with it and have the wake instead."

"It's going to be a very quiet party," I said, thinking about how everyone would be affected by the empty table in the front of the room.

Rachel frowned. "I know, but the show must go on." She waved her hand as if she were a stage director. "Now tell me"—she leaned in close—"do you think she was murdered?"

"Who was murdered?" Eleanor Wadsworth had come through the foyer into the hall. "Someone's been murdered?"

"Eleanor, where have you been?" Rachel rushed to the young woman's side. "You missed this morning's emergency meeting."

Eleanor puckered her clear pale brow. "I had a meeting with a client this morning. I told everyone that. What has happened? Did you mention a murder?"

"Oh, dear." Rachel sent me a look. "Come sit down." She steered Eleanor toward the bench in the foyer.

Eleanor was five-foot-six with snow white skin and jet black hair. Her blue eyes gave her the look of the fairy tale character Snow White. She wore a chiffon blouse in a paisley pattern and black slacks. "What's going on?" she asked, confused as she sat on the bench.

I noticed a tremble in her hands as she clutched them together in her lap.

"Carin is dead," Rachel said.

"Who? Carin Moore? There must be some mistake. I just saw her the night before last." Eleanor tilted her head and looked confused.

The door to the den opened and out came some of the younger committee members and Jenn. "What's going on?"

"Eleanor didn't know about Carin," Rachel said, putting her hand on Eleanor's shoulder.

"Amy, tell me this is some sort of bad joke," Eleanor said.

Amy Hammerstein was in her middle thirties and the head of the yacht race subcommittee. She rushed to Eleanor's side. "Oh, honey, this is a terrible way to find out."

"You mean it's true?" Eleanor asked. Her eyes started to tear up.

Jenn leaned toward me and whispered. "Eleanor is Carin's best friend." She crossed her fingers. "They were like this."

"Yes, I'm afraid it's true," Amy said. "Allie pulled Carin out of the marina this morning."

Everyone turned toward me. I couldn't tell if they thought I was a hero or a villain. I swallowed hard. "I saw her floating faceup just off the pier and I jumped in to save her. By the time I got her on shore and tried to pump the water out of her chest . . ." I let the rest trail off.

"No!" Eleanor cried, putting her hand on her mouth in horror. "No," she whispered. "I just talked to her yesterday. She was fine." Eleanor turned toward Amy. "She was happy and laughing. James Jamison was coming in today and she was excited. She was certain he was going to ask her to marry him." She let her words trail off. "Oh, my God, I think I'm going to be sick."

The ladies gathered around and helped Eleanor to her feet, taking her to the restroom. Jenn and I stood in the hallway and looked at each other.

"Wow," I said. "I can't imagine finding out like that."

Jenn put her hand on my shoulder. "It's never going to happen, kiddo. Come on. Let's see if Sandy needs any help."

I glanced at the bathroom door. Poor Eleanor. How many others would be affected by Carin's death?

Later that afternoon, the streets were packed with tourists in for the races or a day on the island. I finished up a fudge-making demonstration and Sandy helped me with the usual flurry of orders that came right after we showed how we made fudge. I had learned how to make fudge—and how to work a crowd—early on by watching my Papa Liam as he demonstrated the McMurphy secret recipe. His dark chocolate English walnut fudge was always a hit and I made it in his honor. When I was upset, it always settled me to step into a familiar routine.

I left Sandy to man the candy counter when the crowd dwindled away. Two demonstrations a day were enough to keep the business going. Outside, the streets were door-to-door people laughing and enjoying the warm sunshine, but I headed toward the stairs.

Frances looked at me over the top of her glasses. "Are you doing okay?"

"I'm going to be fine," I reassured her. "I need a little time alone is all."

"Well, I can certainly understand that. Why don't you make yourself a nice cup of tea."

"I'm actually headed up to pay bills. It might sound strange, but there is something nice about doing something as mundane as bill paying when I am upset."

"Make the tea and then pay the bills," Frances said. "Trust me on this. Oh, and pet that cat."

Mal popped up from her bed behind the reservation counter where she kept Frances company when I was making candy. It was a safe place for her as I couldn't have any animals underfoot when I was pouring boiling sugar. Quickly, she was three steps up the staircase, wagging her stubby tail at me as if to say, *Come on. Let's go.*

"It's not as if Mella is neglected," I said to Frances. "She gets as much attention as Mal. And if she doesn't, she simply walks over the keys of my computer and demands it."

Frances laughed. "Fur babies are necessary to keep you grounded in the world and not stuck so much in your head."

I put my hands on my hips and made a face. "Why would you think I get stuck in my head?"

Frances laughed again. "Honey, you are always creating a new recipe and when you aren't you're puzzling out a murder. If it weren't for your fur babies, you wouldn't even know what time of day it was."

I made a noise as if to protest her words, but it was only halfhearted. She was right. My mind was on Carin and why she died. I headed up the stairs and met my handyman Mr. Devaney on the third floor landing.

"Do you have a moment?" he asked me.

I was startled by the question. Mr. Devaney was a bit of a curmudgeon. He did a great job as my handyman, but he mostly talked only when he was addressed . . . unless he was with Frances. Those two had a thing for each other. It was kind of adorable.

"Sure," I said and stopped on the landing.

He glanced around. "Can we go to your apartment?"

"Sure. Is everything all right?" Mal and I headed up the stairs in front of him. "Are you feeling okay?" I paused on the fourth floor landing. "You aren't retiring on me, are you?"

"Let's just talk in your apartment," he said succinctly. "I'd rather no one have an opportunity to overhear us."

"Okay. You know Jenn stays in my spare bedroom."

"Yes, but she's the only other person who I wouldn't mind talking to about this. That said, she's out at the yacht club. I checked." He walked into my apartment with me and closed the door behind us. "I'd talk in your office, but Frances might pop in. Here, at least she'd knock before entering."

"Okay." I picked up the cat from where she sat on top of the nearest chair.

My apartment was small. It consisted of a combined living and dining area with a galley kitchen along the back wall. Behind the kitchen was the single bathroom and side by side bedrooms. My grandparents had lived above the McMurphy my entire life. When I would visit, I would stay in what was now Jenn's room. When Papa died and I moved in, I didn't want to sleep in his room. It was too filled with memories. It wasn't until after Jenn showed up that I moved my stuff in and his stuff out. I still had to go through it and choose what to keep and what to give away. For now, his stuff was boxed up and stored in the attic above me. An attic I checked every Saturday to ensure that no one was squatting in. I'd once discovered a man living up there. Yeah, creepy, right?

"I'm making tea. Do you want any?" I put the cat down and picked up my teapot and put water in it to boil.

"Yes, thanks," he said to my surprise and sat down on one of the two bar stools that were snugged up against the countertop separating the living area from the kitchen.

Mr. Devaney had a round head and white hair that made a u-shape around his ears. He wore a cotton shirt with corduroy slacks, black athletic shoes, and a navy cardigan with patches on the elbows. He had hazel eyes and a thin mouth set above a strong chin with a dimple in it. He was so smart, I could see why Frances liked him. His gaze held a wealth of wisdom and knowledge.

He used to teach school and once told me that people learned more from making mistakes than being told by someone what they were doing wrong. That's why he didn't say much. He usually waited for me to ask him questions and sometimes he even let me come to my own conclusions.

I grabbed two thick white mugs from the shelf. One had an imprinted picture of a lilac on it from a lilac festival of long ago. The other had a sailboat. I handed him the boat mug and took down a box of assorted teas and offered him his choice. He took a peppermint tea. I took a chocolate tea and tore my package open, laying the pouch of tea in the cup and draping the cord along the side. "So, what's up?"

"I need your help," he said quietly.

That surprised me. Mr. Devaney was more the helping kind than one to ask for help. He seemed restless and a little out of sorts.

"Sure, anything." I controlled the urge to put my hand on his and bit my bottom lip to keep from asking if things were all right. He'd already answered that question.

He glanced up at me. "It's Frances—"

My teapot decided at that moment to start screaming bloody murder.

I sighed, grabbed a pot holder, and pulled the pot from the stove. I turned off the burner and poured the hot water into our mugs, returned the pot, and sent him an encouraging look. "What about Frances?"

"You know she and I have been dating."

"Yes," I replied with a nod. "Everyone suspected as much." I dipped my tea bag. "It's okay, you know. You two make a cute couple."

He cleared his throat and clung to his mug like a lifeline. "Yes, well, at our age there isn't a lot of time to let things go slow." He paused and studied the mug.

I waited patiently, letting him gather his thoughts.

"Anyway, don't be shocked . . ."

"Okay."

"I want to ask Frances to marry me," he mumbled quickly to the countertop.

I wasn't quite sure I'd heard him. "You want to what?" I asked as gently as possible.

He cleared his throat again. "I want to ask Frances to marry me." He finally looked at me. "I'd like you and Jennifer to help me plan something special for her."

"Well"—I leaned my elbows on the counter, my fingers around my warm mug of tea—"before I give my blessing, I want to know how you plan to take care of her. She has been practically family to me my whole life and I won't see her hurt."

"Right." He straightened, undaunted by my reaction. "I have a nice three bedroom cottage not far from her apartment. I own mine outright and want to live there. She would have more room and I have a nice patio with a garden in the back."

"I see." I sipped my drink thoughtfully. "What will you do with her things?"

"I plan on letting her redecorate. The place has been a bit run down since my wife died so it needs a good remodel. I'd let Frances remodel it to her tastes. I trust her instincts and I want her to feel like it's her home, too."

"And finances?" I pressed. "I know Frances has some money stashed. I don't want to find out that you are itching to spend it."

He straightened farther, clearly offended. "I have more than enough to take care of both of us. I would never drain her money. She earned that. Besides"—his shoulders relaxed a bit—"we both have good jobs where our employer would be hard pressed to find replacements."

I let a hint of a smile cross my face. "So you don't have any plans to run off to Europe or travel the world? Not that those are bad things, but—"

"I have enough money that we could do that if that is what will make Frances happy, but she told me just yesterday that she is happiest when she's working at the reception desk of the McMurphy. It makes her feel useful, keeping an eye on you and Jenn and your pets."

As if on cue, Mella jumped up on the counter

and brushed along Mr. Devaney's arm, begging for pets. He absently brushed his hand along her back and down to the tip of her tail. She arched against him, turned, and asked for more.

"So, what you are telling me is that you are going to ask Frances to marry you and you want my help planning something big."

"Yes," he grumbled and put the mug to his lips to taste his tea.

"And that you plan to let Frances remodel your home to her liking," I added.

"Yep."

"Ah, and you can stay in her apartment while the remodel is going on," I surmised.

"That's the plan," he said, his hazel eyes shining.

I leaned in closer and Mella weaved her way over to me. "And you promise to take good care of her and that you will both continue to work at the McMurphy at least through this season."

"That's the plan," he said again.

"Well, then, you have my blessing." I lifted my mug up. "Cheers!"

"I wasn't asking for your blessing," he muttered, and yet he clinked his mug with mine.

"Don't worry," I said after I sipped tea. "Jenn will come up with something fabulous."

He nearly spit his tea out. "Oh, no, no. no, I don't want one of those ridiculous proposals where everyone on the street starts dancing." He waved his hand to emphasize. "I want something very small and intimate, but I want it to be a surprise. I need you girls to help me plan the right date and tell me if I'm dressed right. That sort of thing."

My grin grew.

He scowled at me so I hid my happiness. "Of course. We won't do anything you don't want us to do."

"Good." He stood. "I've got to go work on the closet door in 203. It's sticking."

"Jenn is so going to love this," I said as he walked toward the door.

He stopped just at the door, let out a long exaggerated sigh, and walked out without a word. I grabbed Mal and danced her around my kitchen.

Some things were worth celebrating with dance.

# Chapter 4

"I heard some juicy gossip," Jenn said as she walked into the business office the next afternoon. I looked up from my computer screen, which was filled with inventory and what I needed to order for the next two weeks of fudge making.

The office was quite large, but crammed with file cases. In the center were the two big oak desks that faced each other. Jenn usually occupied one desk and I used the other. If I had things my way, she would start up her own event planning business and use my office. Right now, she worked for me, but was making a lot of connections on the island. She was the best event planner I'd ever known—not that I'd known a lot of them, but still. She had organized me in a matter of weeks and with her event ideas, was bringing in record attendance to the McMurphy.

I hadn't asked her yet, but I hoped that at the end of the season, I'd be able to convince her to stay and make a go of it. The fact that I'd introduced her to her current boyfriend, Shane, was all part of the plan. If they got serious, it would be another reason for her to stay.

Not that I minded running the place alone, but it was nice to have friends about. And what wasn't there to love about Mackinac Island?

"Is your juicy gossip more important than the sixty pounds of cane sugar I need to order before they cut off shipping for today?"

Jenn sat on the corner of my desk and crossed her arms over her spotless chiffon blouse. "Of course it is. It involves the investigation on the girl you pulled out of the lake."

I sat back and drew my brows together. "What do you know? Do they have any idea who did it?"

"It's serious stuff that could potentially rock your world," Jenn hinted. Her poker face was strong. I had no idea what she was going to say next.

"Spill," I demanded. "If only so I can get the supplies ordered under the deadline"—I glanced at the clock—"which happens to be in the next fifteen minutes."

"Fine, don't let me drag out the suspense."

"Tick, tick." I tapped the watch I wasn't wearing.

"Carin was definitely murdered," Jenn said with the matter-of-fact emotion of someone with inside information. "My secret source says that she wasn't breathing when she hit the water."

"Oh, dear. That's terrible. Do they know how she died? I didn't see any gunshot wounds or knife marks."

"She was hit in the back of the head with a blunt instrument and snapped her spinal cord," Jenn said with less enthusiasm. "She died instantly."

"That's horrible," I said. "So whoever killed her dumped her body in the water?"

"Most likely."

I shook my head. "I can't imagine."

"There's more."

"Okay." I leaned toward her. "Do you know the killer?"

"No, but there is talk about a person of interest."

I sighed and glanced at the clock. "Seriously, Jenn, I've got five minutes before they make me wait a day on delivery."

"Oh, right." She stood, making a shooing motion with her hands. "Get the inventory done. I'll go downstairs and get us both some coffee. This might take awhile."

I rolled my eyes as she left the office. Who does that? Who leaves a person in suspense? This was not television. I did not need a commercial break. I worked hard to squash my curiosity and concentrate on the inventory order.

Twenty minutes later, purchase order in place, inventory as done as I was going to get it, I walked into the living room of the apartment to see if Jenn had come upstairs yet. Mella jumped up to greet me and rubbed against my legs. I reached down to run my hands along her thick soft fur. "Hi baby. Where are Mal and Jenn?"

She reacted to my question by jumping up on the countertop and looked at me with soulful kitty eyes.

"Right, they're not here and you are, so why do I need anyone else?" I muttered as I scratched her kitty ears.

My cell phone rang. I reached into my pocket and pulled it out. "Hello?"

"Hey, Allie," came a voice from the other side.

"Jenn? Where are you?"

"I'm downstairs. Rex is here. I told him you were doing inventory and weren't to be disturbed, but he's in his investigation mode."

"I'm done. I'll be right down." I ended the phone call and looked at the cat. "They're downstairs. You could have told me."

She looked at me as if it wasn't her job to keep track of anyone and then she nudged the counter door where the cat treats were kept.

"Fine. You get a treat for letting me pet you. I am your faithful servant." I opened the cupboard and pulled out the bag of cat treats and dumped a handful on the countertop. "We'll keep this between you and me." I kept Mella in the apartment as much as possible during the day when the fudge shop was open to people walking in and out. The last thing I needed was for her to get in the way of hot sugar and get hurt. She didn't mind so much. I'd learned that she wasn't a fan of the crowds that came in during demonstrations.

We settled on her domain of the owner's apartment during the day and the entire McMurphy during the night. Jenn said it was okay that Mella was an indoor/outdoor cat. When the weather was nice, sometimes I'd let her out to hang around the back deck and grab some sunshine. She rarely wandered off, which was odd since she had just shown up at my back door one day. I would have thought she was an alley cat, but she took to being indoors much better than being out.

Since we'd had her spayed, I figured it was okay to let her choose when and where she wanted to be. I'd had the vet put a chip in her for identification and she wore a soft pink collar with her name and my phone number on it in case she got lost.

Downstairs was a madhouse. Sandy was doing the last of the day's demonstrations of fudge making. Tourists were three deep around the fudge shop windows both inside and out. Mal jumped up from her bed beside Frances and the reception desk and greeted me as I came down the staircase. I patted her and picked her up to rub her ears. Jenn and Rex stood beside Frances who sat on her tall stool behind the receptionist desk.

"Hey guys," I said. "What's up?"

"Allie," Rex sad, his blue police uniform perfectly pressed. How he managed to always be so well-groomed after a long day never ceased to amaze me. His hat was in his hand and he wore a gun on his hip. His bald head had that sexy as hell look of an action star.

"Hi Rex. What's going on? Is there news on Carin Moore?"

He frowned. "Can we talk upstairs?"

My gaze went to the filled lobby. Guests were sitting on the couches, enjoying the Wi-Fi. People near the coffee bar were enjoying a five o'clock cup.

"Sure." I gave Frances a look. "What's with all the people?"

"Downtown is hopping due to the yacht races," she said. "People heard that you pulled a girl out of the marina this morning and wanted to be a part of the scene."

"Seriously?" I asked and glanced around. I noticed for the first time that it wasn't the fudge making demonstration that people were looking at. They were here to get a glimpse of me and Rex. I swear they were leaning toward us as if to catch every last word.

"Seriously," Jenn said. "Liz McElroy published an early morning news blog about the incident and people have been coming in off and on all day. Sandy can't keep up with the demand."

"But I've been—"

"At the yacht club." Jenn turned me by the shoulders and pointed me at the staircase. "Then you've been upstairs doing inventory."

"Right," I said.

Mal rested her head against my shoulder as if to sympathize with my lost day.

"Come on, Rex. Let's go up to the office."

He followed me and Jenn up.

"What's going on, Rex?" I asked as we stepped into the office.

He closed the door behind us and leaned against it. "I thought I'd update you on the investigation and ask you a few more questions."

"Sure." I sat on the edge of my desk. "I understand she was positively identified."

"Yes," he said with a nod of his head. "The woman you pulled out of the marina was Carin Moore. Once her parents identified her, we had her body taken to St. Ignace for an autopsy."

"Is that standard?" I asked.

He nodded. "In suspicious cases, it is."

"What was suspicious? I mean she drowned, right? Was she drinking?"

Jenn coughed. I studiously ignored her. I wasn't going to let Rex know that Jenn had already told me the gossip.

"On further investigation, we found damage to the back of her skull so we've flown her over to the ME's office to see if the damage was sustained before or after she was in the water."

"Poor thing," I said. "Was there a party or something last night?"

"There were in fact several parties last night," Rex said. "We're trying to narrow down where she was and when."

"Okay, so what can I do for you?"

"I understand that you and Jenn might have overheard Carin fighting with someone yesterday."

I glanced at Jenn who looked just as surprised by this news as I was. "What do you mean?"

"Were you two at the yacht club yesterday around four PM?"

"Yes." I looked at Jenn and then back at Rex. "We had a consultation on the setup for this evening's affair. Jenn helped plan the event. Sandy and I created chocolate centerpieces. We had a meeting with the manager and a few of the committee members to go over last minute details."

"And do you remember if you overheard an argument at that time?"

I pulled my thoughts to that afternoon. *Jenn and I were in the dining room going over where tables were to be set up. Paige Jessop, my boyfriend Trent's sister, was on*

*the committee and had the idea that we should make small
ships as party favors to match the centerpieces.*

"That's a vague question," I pointed out. "What
are you fishing for?"

"Just asking a simple question," Rex said. "When
you were at the club did you see Carin Moore
there?"

"I don't remember her," I said. My thoughts
went to the dead woman in the silk dress. *Had she
been at the club?* "I was busy putting together what
we would need to create individual chocolate ships.
I thought it was a great idea, but it's more compli-
cated than you think."

"Wait," Jenn said, her eyes lighting up. "I do
remember seeing her. She had golden brown hair
and hazel eyes, right?"

"Yes," Rex said with no inflection.

"There are lots of women who fit that descrip-
tion," I said with a frown. "How do you know it was
Carin?"

"Because Paige got really tense when she walked
into the club," Jenn said. "There was definitely
something going on between them. I was going to
ask you to ask Paige the next time you saw her."

"I haven't seen Paige since that afternoon," I
said. "Trent's been busy prepping his businesses
for the busy weekend. I'm supposed to see him
tonight. He's taking me to the yacht club fund-
raiser."

"So Paige Jessop reacted when Carin Moore
entered the yacht club that afternoon?" Rex took a
notepad out of his breast pocket and made a note.

"Yes," Jenn said. "Paige excused herself and I

asked Rachel Buckhouse who the woman was. She told me it was Carin Moore and that there was some sort of bad feelings between Paige and Carin."

I stared at Jenn. "Paige would never hurt anyone."

"Oh, I'm not saying she did anything." Jenn held up her hand as if to stop my thoughts. "Rex, don't you dare make any notes about that."

"All I'm doing is writing down that you asked Rachel Buckhouse and she said there was something between the two women." He shrugged his broad shoulders. "It's common knowledge that Carin and Paige were not friends. Let's get back to the day at hand. You said that Carin walked into the club and Paige tensed and then left the dining room."

"Yes."

"Where did she go?"

"I'm not sure," Jenn said with a frown. "I got involved with the planning."

"That's right." I snapped my fingers. "I started listing the things we would need to make the ships, estimating the time out loud and you offered to help."

"Yes, I said if I helped with the molds we could assembly line the production and be done in time. We asked Sandy if that were possible. Sandy said that there wasn't enough time to make all ten molds. So we discussed with Rachel and decided on two molds. Rachel said she would go get Paige and ensure that would work for her."

"Did Rachel leave the room?"

"Yes," Jenn and I said at the same time.

"She came back a few minutes later and said

she couldn't talk to Paige but would get back to us within the hour," I said. "So Sandy and Jenn and I left to get started on the mold making. We were actually able to make three molds and stayed up quite late last night putting together the tiny ships. I had some gold and silver edible leaf and we spent the morning wrapping the ships in foil. They turned out quite stunning. I think Paige will be pleased."

"Did you see Paige or Carin again after that?" Rex asked.

"No," I said with a shake of my head. "Sandy and I were deep into the details of making the ships and enough fudge for today's crowd."

"So Paige didn't get back to you about the ships?"

"Rachel called us thirty minutes later and said that Amy Hammerstein, the head of the committee, agreed to three molds and our pricing," Jenn said.

"I see," Rex said. "Did you ask her why she talked to Amy and not Paige?"

Jenn tapped her chin. "I think she said that Paige had left and it was clear she wouldn't be back so she cleared it with Amy instead."

"Did that seem odd to you?"

"No, Amy is the head of the committee. What are you getting at?" I asked him. "Is Paige a suspect?"

"I'm simply trying to piece together what happened to Carin before you found her in the marina."

"Well, that's all we know, right Jenn? We were very busy with the new ships. Sandy had to craft the molds and test them. I created the chocolate. Jenn ran the fudge shop until closing at nine and then she and Sandy and I were in the apartment making ten chocolate ships until midnight when Sandy went home and I went to bed."

"Jenn, did you see Paige or Carin after that afternoon?" Rex asked.

"No. I was invited to a party, but I had to beg off when Allie asked me to help with the ships. Do you think Carin went to that party? It was supposed to be a very big deal."

I frowned, drawing my brows together. "What party are you talking about and why wasn't I invited?"

"The Allisons are on the board at the yacht club. Their son, Brandon, and his friends were hosting the party as a fund-raiser for their mayoral candidate. I was going to go to network and see if they might hire me to help with some of their events. It was going to be very boring," she reassured me. "I'm sure you weren't invited because the Jessops are supporting the current mayor and everyone knows you are dating Trent."

I shook my head. "Trent doesn't tell me who I should or shouldn't vote for."

"It was a fund-raiser, Allie," Jenn said and crossed her arms. "The only reason I was going was because I was drumming up event work for the McMurphy. I figured I could do it and you would remain in the Jessops' good graces."

"I see." I wasn't very politically astute. Frankly, all I cared about was my family, friends, and the success of the McMurphy. I had to trust that Jenn was right on the fact that I shouldn't be involved. Plus it was nice of her to think about drumming up more business for me—even if it was for a candidate that my boyfriend's family didn't support.

"Politics aside," Rex said to Jenn, "you had an invitation to the Allisons' party but didn't go."

"No, I didn't go."

"Do you have anyone who can collaborate that?"

"Well, that's silly." I cocked my head. "I just told you she was here with me until midnight when we went to bed."

He turned his gorgeous blue eyes on me. "Did you see Jenn again after you went to bed? Or are you assuming she went to bed?"

"Well, I—"

"It's okay," Jenn said. "I went to bed at midnight and I didn't get up until Allie woke me at five."

Rex turned to me. "Five? So an hour before you walked Mal and found the body?"

"Yes," I said. "I was up at three and made the morning fudge batches. I woke Jenn because the chocolate ships were ready to be unmolded and then foiled."

Rex slipped and showed a moment of emotion on his face. I swear concern clouded his eyes. "So you are working on three hours of sleep?"

I shrugged. "I planned on napping but finding Carin in the water made that impossible."

"Adrenaline," Rex muttered. "Fine. Thank you for answering my questions. Please let me know if you think of anything else."

"We will," I said and Jenn and I stood.

"No need to walk me out," he said and put the notepad and tiny pencil in his breast pocket. "I know the way." He studied me. "You need to make sure you get more sleep. Lack of sleep sets you up for a lot of health problems." For a moment I thought he was going to touch my cheek, but then he glanced at Jenn and nodded. "Ms. Christensen." He walked out of the office and down the stairs.

"Wow," Jenn said with a sigh. "He is so into you."

"I'm dating Trent," I said. For some reason, I stayed rooted to the spot. "I'm dating Trent."

"For now," Jenn said with a wiggle of her eyebrows.

"Stop it." I smacked her arm. "I think I'm falling in love with Trent."

"Yeah and I'm half in love with Shane. Too bad because Rex is one hot cop."

"There's no denying that," I said with a sigh. "So, now that I lied to Rex about not knowing Carin was murdered, who is the person of interest you were going to tell me about?"

Jen swallowed. "I heard it was Paige Jessop."

"What? Is that why Rex was asking us about Paige and Carin?"

"Yes," Jen said, her mouth in a firm line. "That's what I wanted to tell you, but I'm kind of glad I didn't tell you before Rex questioned us. There's no way you could have kept your emotions out of that interview if you had known."

"Rex thinks that Paige and Carin had a fight at the yacht club that afternoon? That's what he thought we might have seen? A motive for Paige to kill Carin?"

"Yeah," Jen said. Her gaze was filled with concern. "I'm sorry that I added the part about Paige tensing up at the sight of Carin, but it was true."

I rubbed my hands over my face. "It's fine. Tension between two people does not equal motive for murder," I said flatly. "Come on. We've got work to do before I need to dress for tonight's opening event." I turned back to my desk. My thoughts turned to Paige and Carin. *What was between them and why would anyone—especially Rex—think Paige was a suspect?*

I guess those were good questions for Trent when I saw him later. I loved Paige. If anyone were to accuse her, I'd defend her in a heartbeat. No matter what it took. Hopefully this was all just a misunderstanding.

## Fudgie Pudding Cake

This one is warm and yummy.

### Ingredients

1¼ cups sugar, divided into ¾ cup and ½ cup
1 cup flour
3 squares chocolate, melted
2 teaspoons baking powder
½ teaspoon salt
½ cup milk
¼ cup melted butter
1 teaspoon vanilla
½ cup packed brown sugar
¼ cup cocoa
1¼ cups hot water

**Directions**

Heat oven to 350 degrees F.

In a medium bowl mix together ¾ cup sugar, the flour, baking powder, and salt. Add melted chocolate, butter, and vanilla. Stir to make a thick batter.

Pour into an unbuttered 8-inch pan.

In a smaller bowl, stir together ½ cup sugar, the brown sugar, and the cocoa. Sprinkle on top of the batter. Pour the hot water over the top of that.

Bake in the oven 35 minutes until the middle is almost set.

Remove from oven. Let cool for 15 minutes. Serve and enjoy!

# Chapter 5

"You look fantastic," Trent said when I opened the door to my apartment later that night.

I wore a long-sleeved, black, jersey wrap dress, hose, and black designer shoes. My brown hair was twisted into a French twist and sprayed to within an inch of its life to stay in place. I hated hairspray but this was an important society function and I wasn't about to embarrass Trent or the Jessop family. I wanted to show him that I knew how to dress when I needed to. Thankfully, Jenn had helped me with makeup. I wore black-cat eyeliner and just a few false lashes at the corners of my eyes to make it dramatic. The red lipstick on my lips made me feel very much like a Barbie doll. The entire effect had Trent's pupils dilating.

He scooped me up in his arms and kissed me. I wrapped my arms around his neck and clung to his tuxedo clad body. The man was tall, dark, and handsome. His hair was kept short, but styled with elegance and sophistication. His dark eyes sparkled when I took a step back and wiped the lipstick off the edge of his mouth with my thumb.

"I wanted to make you proud," I said.

"Oh, I'm very proud," he said low, giving the skin on my arms goose bumps. He ran his hands along my back. "Maybe we should stay here."

I pushed on his chest. "Can't. I'm responsible for the centerpieces and chocolate favors. I've got to be there to see how well they are received."

"I'm sure everyone will love them." He leaned down and kissed me again. It would be so easy to fall into his arms and forget the rest of the world, but it was a luxury I didn't have time for and our relationship was relatively new. I tried not to push it.

"Hey, you look nice," Jenn said as she came around the corner. She wore a red cap-sleeved body conscious dress that showed off her long legs and a V-neck that showed off her cleavage. She was putting a gold dangle earring in her ear.

I stepped out of Trent's arms. "Is Shane picking you up here?"

"Shane isn't going," she said casually and picked up her clutch.

"What? Wait. Why not?" I asked.

"He has to work on the Moore case tonight." She gave us a bright, yet false smile. "I'm hoping you two will let me be a third leg."

"Oh. Of course," I said.

"It's my honor and pleasure to take two such beautiful women to the club," Trent said, sending us both a charming smile. He held out both arms crooked. "Shall we?"

"Wonderful," I said. We took his arms and left the apartment. I turned and locked the door.

The cat was safely on the stoop outdoors and Mal was with Frances for the night because I didn't know how long I'd be out. Sandy had promised to come in and make the morning fudge. For the first time in a long time I could spend a night out on the town. After the morning's incident I was ready for some fun.

We took the steps down to the third floor center for the elevators. When the elevator opened to take us down to the lobby, Trent ushered us in, closed the door, then punched the button.

"So, Trent, what do you think about Allie being a hero this morning? Jumping into the lake to pull Carin Moore to shore," Jenn asked.

Trent looked at me with love in his gaze. "I wouldn't have expected anything else from Allie."

I flushed that he had pride in his voice. "Mal discovered her. I just pulled her out of the water."

"Terrible thing to find her dead," Jenn said. "Don't you think, Trent?"

"Yes," he agreed as the elevator stopped. He opened the door and held it for us to go out.

The once busy lobby was quiet. Most of the tourists left on the last boats of the evening. Those who stayed on the island overnight were at bars or clubs while the old and the very young were tucked in their rooms with televisions to keep them company.

Unlike most of the hotels on the island, the McMurphy lacked a front or back yard where we could put out chairs and a fire pit for stargazing and marshmallow roasting. What the McMurphy lacked in outdoor space it made up for in its location—smack in the middle of Main Street where most of the shops, restaurants, and fudge shops were located.

"Rex came around asking questions about yesterday at the yacht club," Jenn went on as we walked across the empty lobby.

"Have fun tonight," Megan, my part-time reception desk intern called from Frances's perch behind the registration desk.

"You have my number in case anything goes wrong?" I asked.

"It's all taken care of," she said. "Frances said to call her first. But don't worry. Nothing bad will happen. Go have fun."

Megan was a responsible seventeen-year-old with a neat brown ponytail, a white blouse with frills on the front, and a pink name tag pinned to her left lapel.

It had taken nearly half the summer for me to hire her, but Frances had finally agreed that we needed help at the desk. When Megan's mom came in with her and asked about the posting, Frances interviewed the teen on the spot. She worked four hours a night five nights a week, just enough to give Frances a break.

We stepped into the cool night where a horse-drawn taxi was waiting for us.

I looked at Trent. "We don't live that far from the yacht club."

"I thought it would be a nice treat to ride." He helped Jenn up into the buggy and then me.

It was magical to listen to the horse's hooves on the road as we clipped along Main Street. The thick crowds were gone. A few people strolled hand in hand. Others rode bikes with lights on. Finally, a few horse-drawn taxies carried parties of people from hotels to parties and bars.

"How is Paige doing?" I asked Trent.

"Good," he said and gave me a surprised look. "Why?"

"As Jenn said, Rex came by today with questions about Paige and Carin. I was worried that Paige might need comforting."

Trent threw back his head and laughed. It was charming and unaffected. "Oh, good God, no." He looked at me, his eyes sparkling. "Paige is fine. Don't get me wrong, I'm sure she isn't too broken up about the death. She and Carin have been rivals since elementary school."

"That's a long time," Jenn said.

"It was mostly Carin's doing. That woman was always trying to best Paige. Paige shrugged it off for years. Trust me. My sister thinks enough of herself not to worry about who is intimidated by her. Besides, they had made up recently."

"So that's what was going on? Carin was intimidated by Paige?" I asked.

"If I were to say anything, I think Carin wanted to be Paige. You see, Carin wasn't quite as pretty as my sister so she wasn't as popular with the boys. There was also the healthy grade point competition. Paige hardly ever studied and always beat Carin out on grades. Carin used to crumple up her papers and throw them at Paige."

"Oh, no. Poor Paige," I said.

"Actually, Paige thought it was funny. It did get old though. When they hit high school both ran for homecoming queen. Typically, whoever makes homecoming queen makes the lilac queen the next spring. Carin campaigned hard. At one point, Paige went to her and told her she could have it. Paige pulled her name out of the running because she was worried it was too contentious."

"So Carin won?"

"Yes, Carin won and then began a mean campaign toward my sister. She had two friends, Eleanor Wadsworth and Suzy Olden, who followed her around like she was their queen bee."

"They were mean girls?" I asked. There had been a group of those in my high school, but they had pretty much left me alone. I was never on the radar of the popular girls. The sad part was I wasn't ever invited to any parties, but on the good side, I wasn't bullied.

"Yes," Trent said, his jaw ticking at the memory. "I put Paige's name in for lilac queen and made sure everyone knew that my sister had a better grade point average and service record than Carin. Paige won by a huge margin. Everyone made a big deal about it because no homecoming queen had ever been beaten out of lilac queen the next spring."

"No one but Carin," Jenn said as the carriage pulled up in front of the yacht club.

"Nobody but Carin," Trent said with some satisfaction at the memory. He climbed out of the carriage and helped Jenn out first. "I must admit it was a satisfying success on my part."

"You are a wonderful brother," I said as I slipped my hand in his and he helped me down from the carriage. We headed toward the yacht club.

Jenn followed behind us. "I can see how that might have set up Carin to feel as if Paige were her enemy."

Trent shrugged. "The girl got what she deserved."

"Except in death," I said. "No one deserves to die so young and at the hands of a murderer."

Trent stopped in his tracks. "Wait. What? I thought she had gotten drunk and fallen from her parents' yacht and drowned."

"There is evidence that she was dead when she hit the water," Jenn said. "It's why Shane is working tonight. Carin's body was taken to St. Ignace for an autopsy."

Trent muttered something dark and dangerous under his breath.

"Rex was over this afternoon asking questions about Carin and Paige," I said. "It sounded like he was looking into Paige as a possible suspect."

"That's ridiculous." He stopped at the bottom of the steps to the yacht club.

"That's what I said," I agreed and took a deep breath of the cool night air.

"Do you have any idea if anyone else might have wanted Carin dead?" Jenn asked.

"There are a few people," Trent said.

A party of well-dressed yacht club members pulled up at the gate of the picket fence that surrounded the yacht club.

"Come on, ladies. Let's go in." Once again, Trent held out both his elbows. "Don't worry about Rex Manning's ridiculous imaginings. Concentrate on having fun tonight and networking. There are some big movers and shakers here tonight. It won't hurt for them to get to know you."

I bit my bottom lip to still the worry that welled up in my heart.

The door was opened by a man in a butler's suit. "Welcome, ladies and gentleman," he said stiffly without looking at us. May I have your names and I will announce you."

"Seriously?" I whispered to Trent.

"Trent Jessop, my date Allie McMurphy, and her friend Jenn Christensen," he said smoothly.

"Thank you, sir." The butler turned and called loudly, "Introducing Mr. Trent Jessop, his date Miss Allie McMurphy, and her friend Jenn Christensen," as we stepped into the club foray.

"Trent, welcome." At the front door, Mr. Richard Blake, yacht club president, stood in a reception line with his wife. He shook Trent's hand. "Two lovely ladies on your arms. I always did think of you as a lucky man."

"I am indeed," Trent said smoothly and proceeded to introduce us to everyone in the reception line. The last were two women I knew from working with the committee and their husbands. They remembered Jenn before me, but that was okay. She was charming in the situation.

We made our way to the dining area and the seats with our names on them. Paige sat at our table and stood when she saw us. I gave her a quick hug and she kissed my cheek.

"Are you okay?" I asked and squeezed her hands.

"Yes, of course," she said with a lightness to her voice. She was gorgeous . . . everything I thought of when I thought of high society. She was blond, thin boned with high cheekbones. Her complexion was porcelain. She had long lashes and cornflower blue eyes. Her high-end designer dress most likely cost more than the McMurphy's monthly budget. Not a hair was out of place, her makeup perfect. Her nails were professionally done.

It made me want to hide my polish-free hands.

In addition, she was warm and welcoming. She didn't even notice my hands and soon was hugging Jenn and getting us to sit down. Trent waved the server down and had champagne brought to all of us. Paige's date's chair was empty.

"Where's your Reggie?" I asked carefully.

"He couldn't be here tonight. His family is close to the Moores. His best friend is Carin's brother," Paige said and sipped her champagne. "I told him it was okay. I completely understand. It's good he stayed with Ash Moore. It's tough to lose your sibling." She paused. "Allie, how are you holding up after finding Carin?"

"I'm okay," I said and smiled at the waiter who poured me a white wine. "It feels strange to think it happened just this morning."

"I know," Paige said. "It seems odd to be at a party knowing she died last night."

"Trent was telling us how Carin seemed to feel as

if she was constantly in competition with you," Jenn said. "How do you feel about that?"

"You know, I never really let it get to me. It was crazy. I've heard of brothers and sisters acting out in that way, but Carin and I were merely classmates."

"She must have started out admiring you and that grew into something more," I said. "It's the only reason I can think of for her actions."

"That's a reasonable idea," Paige said. "But things got out of hand after high school. I got accepted into Loyola in Chicago and so Carin had to go to Loyola. It was rumored that she didn't get in until her wealthy father pulled some strings. Loyola got a new tennis court and Carin got in."

"Don't tell me she studied the same thing you studied," I said.

"Oh, no. She studied English lit while I majored in business administration," Paige said.

"Well"—I sat back, relieved—"I guess the strange rivalry stopped then."

"No, it didn't," Paige said. "Carin found out which sorority I pledged and pledged the same. What's worse is her lackey . . . uh, best friend . . . Eleanor Wadsworth also pledged and those two had half the girls in the house against me. I would have dropped the next year but Trent told me to stick with it."

Trent leaned into the conversation. "A Jessop never runs away from a fight. I had some of my frat brothers go to the sorority house and offer to make some much needed improvements to the house. You see, Paige's house was cash strapped due to poor management by the last house mother, so we got donations for paint and materials and then my frat brothers and I went over and spruced things up. Paige was a hero after that. Carin and Eleanor pouted, of course, but they couldn't say anything bad about it."

"The trick was not to have our parents contribute," Paige said. "That way she couldn't say I was flaunting our money."

"That was brilliant," Jenn said. "I bet you got a plaque for sister of the year."

"I did," Paige said with a smile. "It burned Carin every time she passed the honors wall."

"What happened after college?" I asked. "Surely this didn't go on."

"Well, we both have strong ties to Mackinac. So Carin was constantly trying to outdo me on committees and things."

"But Paige got the last laugh," Trent said with a grin.

"What do you mean?" I asked and lifted my wineglass to take a sip.

"Carin brought her boyfriend by the club one night to flaunt him," Paige said. "I had broken up with my college boyfriend a few months before that and hadn't been dating."

"She thought showing off her boyfriend would be a dig at you?" I asked. "That sounds very immature."

"Trust me. It was," Paige said. "Her boyfriend thought so, too. He came to see me the next day to express his disappointment in Carin's behavior."

"How sweet," I said.

"I know. I thought so, too," Paige replied. "We talked all through the night and into the next day. By the end of the visit, Reggie asked me out."

"Oh boy," Jenn said.

"I know," Paige said and sipped her drink. "I told him he had to break up with Carin first. Then wait two weeks to make sure he really meant it before he called me again."

"And did he do what you asked?" I asked.

"He did. He went straight to Carin's house and broke up with her. Then he texted me to let me know that it was done and his two weeks were starting."

"And?" Jenn asked.

"And two weeks later to the hour, he called me and asked me out. I said yes, and the rest is history."

"Wait, you stole Reggie from Carin?"

"No," Paige said with a shake of her head. "Reggie broke up with his girlfriend and two weeks later asked me out." She smiled. "We've been together ever since."

"I bet Carin was livid when she found out," Jenn said as the servers placed the salad plates on the table.

"She was beside herself and tried to corner me about it, but Reggie wouldn't let her. He went straight to her parents and talked to them about his feelings and intentions. He told her family that I had nothing to do with his decision. That it was Carin's own actions that caused the breakup."

"That took a lot of guts," I said.

"Like I said, Reggie has known Carin and her

family since he was seven. His best friend is Carin's brother Ash. It's why he dated Carin in the first place. He was always over at Ash's house and she was there and she was pretty."

"It has to be tough for him," I said.

"Yes," Paige said. "They are his family and he's grieving for Carin as much as they are . . . even if she was mean."

"Can I ask you a question?" I leaned toward Paige.

"Sure."

"Did you and Carin have a run-in yesterday?"

"What do you mean?" Paige asked.

I noticed a nervous tremor in her fingers.

"Rex came to the club meeting and questioned us about yesterday," I said. "Remember when we were talking about the feasibility of creating small party favor ships at the last minute?"

"Yes," Paige said with a smile and held up her gold leafed replica of the ship at the centerpiece of our table. "They turned out amazing."

"Thank you," I said. "Sandy is a craftsman."

"Don't let her give away too much credit," Jenn said. "Both Allie and I stayed up half the night pouring the chocolate into the molds and ensuring they didn't have bubbles. Plus the gold and silver leafing was Allie's idea."

"I thought it would make them easier to handle and take home at the end of the night," I said. "The last thing anyone wants is to stick uncovered chocolate into their bag."

"So, wait. Rex was asking about Paige?" Trent asked.

I nodded. "Yes. Jenn told him she had noticed Carin come into the club and then Paige get tense." I turned to Paige. "Then you walked out."

Paige frowned. "I saw Carin come in and say something to Eleanor. I was afraid they were up to something. Those two can't be trusted. They'll do things just to mess with me. I went to see Amy to ensure that the chocolate party favors would remain on the list of things to have on the table."

"Clearly, she agreed," I said and sipped my wine.

"She did," Paige said. "I went home and left Carin and Eleanor to their devices. After all, what could they do to upset things at that point?"

"I asked Rex if Paige was a suspect, but he wouldn't answer."

"What exactly did he say?" Trent asked.

"He said that he was asking what had happened, that he was putting together Carin's last day."

"I see," Trent said with a frown.

"I wouldn't worry about it." I put my hand on his. "Rex is fair in his assessments. He understands that Carin and Paige were school rivals and nothing more."

A three piece orchestra was playing softly in the background and the room was full of high-society guests. I'd been so busy thinking about Paige and Carin that I hadn't really noticed how far along the event was. I glanced around to see if anyone was noting the centerpieces and it seemed as if a few were being admired.

"Except there is more." Jenn paused while the servers took away our salad plates and put down our dinner plates.

"What?" I was drawn back to Jenn and Paige. "What do you mean *there is more*?"

"You don't think Rex sees that as motive, do you?" I asked Jenn, then turned to Paige. "How long have you and Reggie been dating?"

"Almost two years. He has let me know every step of the way that I'm his one and only."

"There's no reason for Paige to hurt Carin," Trent said. "It's ridiculous to think there is."

"You didn't get into a fight with Carin the day she died?" Jenn asked.

I frowned. "Jenn—"

"What?" Jenn shrugged. "I'm asking because Rex made it sound like they did."

"We might have exchanged words in the hall," Paige said with a nonchalant shrug. "It was nothing."

"What did you talk about?" Jenn asked.

"I think we've spent enough time on Carin," Trent said briskly. "This is supposed to be an enjoyable evening. Let's change subjects."

I noted that couples were swaying slowly on the dance floor as the band played a waltz. I held out my hand. "Come on, Trent. Let's dance."

"My pleasure." He stood, tucked my hand in the crook of his arm, and led me to the parquet dance floor that had been laid down on the far end of the dining area. He took me into his arms and expertly twirled me around the floor.

The rest of the evening was filled with romance

as the orchestra was replaced with a big band. The tables were pushed back and the French doors opened to let in the lake breezes.

It was magical, being in Trent's arms. I let him sweep me away into a world of happiness.

# Chapter 6

"Someone had a good night," Jenn said as I came into my apartment through the fire escape door. It was one in the afternoon and I was wearing the dress I'd worn the night before.

I did a small twirl in the middle of the living area. "It was magical."

"Sweet. I want details," Jenn said from her perch on the couch, her laptop on the coffee table.

"Ladies don't kiss and tell." I headed to the bedroom to strip, shower, and get dressed for the day.

"Oh, you did more than kiss," Jenn said.

"I'm not telling," I called over my shoulder.

"When's the wedding?" she called back at me.

I blew out a long breath, slipped on my bathrobe, and stuck my head out into the hallway. "I'm taking this one day at a time."

"Fine. Promise me I'll be the first to know when it happens."

"I promise you'll be the first to know"—I headed to the bathroom—"but don't tell my mother you were first. She'll have a fit."

"I won't. I promise."

It was good to take a day off every now and then. My day was more of an evening and morning, but hey, time off was time off. Last night with Trent was magical and romantic and I would never forget it. The yacht club raised a record amount of money and Jenn and Sandy and I earned an extra two thousand dollars for our efforts. All in all it was not a bad day.

Luckily, I didn't have any bets on the boats in the race. A squall had picked up and the high winds and waves cut the races short. People had pretty much stayed off the ferries, cutting their days of visiting the island short.

I let Sandy go home at two o'clock and canceled the last fudge demonstration. It was pouring rain outside and only a small group of people had gathered indoors near the fireplace to drink hot coffee and use the Wi-Fi.

I put my raincoat on and headed to Dodd's market to pick up something for dinner. The streets smelled of rain and dust and were mostly bare. A few of the horse-drawn taxis waited out the storm under the trees near the fort. With their heads down, the animals looked miserable. The drivers sat with raincoats pulled around them and their hats dripping wet. The open carriage windows were covered by shades that were rolled down and tied to keep the rain off any customer that might flag them down for a ride.

The bike shop had closed up for the duration of the storm.

I opened the door to the grocery store, the bells jingling on the door. Mary Emry looked up from her trashy celebrity magazine to see who was coming in during the storm.

"Hi Mary." I shook out my umbrella and left it next to the door.

Mary simply nodded her head at my intrusion. I grabbed a basket and made my way to the produce section. I needed things for a salad and figured I'd fry up a chicken to go with it. The choice of fresh meat was nice considering the small size of the store. I grabbed a package of antibiotic free, organic, free-range chicken, a bag of salad along with cucumbers, red and yellow peppers, an onion, olives, carrots, radishes, and zucchini. Finally, I took a loaf of fresh French bread and took them to the register.

"Heard you pulled Carin Moore's dead body out of the marina," Mary said as she rang up my dinner.

I nodded. "Yes, that's right."

"Must have been a terrible sight."

"It was."

She squinted her brown eyes at me. "Are you used to finding the dead yet?"

"What?"

"How many has it been now? Ten?" Her dark head was bent as she rang up my groceries, making it hard to tell what she meant.

*Did she mean to imply it was my fault? Did she mean to imply that she felt sorry for me?* "Four," I corrected her.

"Only four dead bodies and none of them were my fault."

"Didn't say they were," she said as she bagged my groceries. "Just wondered if you were used to finding them."

I realized then that was probably the most talkative Mary Emry had ever been. I leaned against the counter. "Did you know Carin Moore?"

"Everyone on the island knew Carin Moore. That girl had the tongue of a wasp. Could sting anyone with her words and did so frequently and on purpose."

"Do you know who might have wanted her dead?"

She looked up at me. "Paige Jessop."

"Why Paige?"

"Eleanor saw Reggie kissing Carin down by the docks."

"Eleanor is Carin's best friend. Why would she tell anyone what she saw?"

"Because Eleanor would rather be Paige's best friend," Mary said and handed me my bag. "Wouldn't you?"

I took my things and left. Yes, I guess I would rather be Paige's best friend . . . but it had never occurred to me that Eleanor would.


"Shane says there was alcohol in Carin's system," Jenn said as I unpacked the groceries.

"It might have been an accident, then. She could have stumbled overboard and drowned.

"Her lungs were clear of water."

"I tried to push it out," I remembered. "I thought some came out of her mouth."

"Shane said the coroner is certain she didn't breathe any water in. She didn't drown, Allie." Jenn put down her laptop and came over to stand at the bar and talk to me as I started dinner.

"I suppose that's a good thing. Drowning would be terrible. I think." A shiver went down my spine. I put on an apron over my T-shirt and knee length shorts, got out a knife, and began to cut up the chicken.

"You might be right. Hopefully I'll never know. Like I said yesterday, Carin definitely died of the blow to the back of her head. It snapped her brain stem . . . which still could have been an accident . . . but afterward she was clearly dumped in the water. So someone is hiding something."

I put the chicken in the pan with olive oil and onion. "Mary Emry said that Reggie is cheating on Paige with Carin."

"What? First of all, Mary Emry talked to you?"

I smiled. "She did. I know, I was amazed myself."

"Secondly, Reggie would not cheat on Paige. That man is clearly in love with her."

"I guess Eleanor saw them kissing down by the docks and told Paige and anyone else who would listen."

Jenn wrinkled her brow. "Why would Eleanor do that? She worshipped Carin. People call her *the shadow* because she never leaves Carin's side."

"And that's why people believe her when she said she saw Carin and Reggie kissing. Mary implied that Eleanor really wants to be friends with Paige and went to her with the news . . . not to rub Paige's face in it, but to make friends."

"Keep your friends close and your enemies closer," Jenn said and poured herself a glass of iced tea, then hopped up on the bar stool. "So Paige and Eleanor were talking."

"I'm sure Paige shrugged her off. Would you take Eleanor seriously?"

Jenn shook her head. "No." She sipped her drink. "My guess is that Paige laughed it off. I know I would have."

"But it doesn't look good for Paige if you're looking for a motive for murder. I think we should keep digging. I don't want Paige to get hurt. She and Trent are really close. What hurts her, hurts Trent, and I don't want that."

"Of course you don't, sweetie," Jenn said. "I'll keep my ears open and see what the local scuttlebutt is about this. I'm sure the autopsy results will be posted in tomorrow's paper. Let's hope Paige isn't suspect number one."

"I agree." I chopped up salad to have with the chicken. "Oh, I have some other news."

"Trent asked you to marry him?"

"What?! No." I felt the heat of a blush rush up my cheeks. "We've only been dating a couple months. It's Mr. Devaney."

Jenn frowned. "Mr. Devaney asked you to marry him?"

"Stop being silly. Mr. Devaney came to me and asked that you and I put our heads together. He wants to ask Frances to marry him and he wants us to help make it memorable."

Jenn's face lit up. "Oh my gosh. That's fantastic. They are such a cute couple. I have some great ideas already. Did he say if he wanted it to be private and intimate or did he want to go big and public?"

"He said he wanted it to be special, that Frances deserves special. I don't think big and public is their style, do you? He wants us to do what we think Frances would dream of doing."

"Hmmm." Jenn tapped her chin. "They do seem more intimate, and yet how wonderful that they are in love and taking this big step at their age. I think the whole island should celebrate."

"Really?"

"Well, okay. I guess that's not reasonable, but if Shane ever asks you what kind of proposal I want, you tell him I want marching bands and fireworks and planes with banners. I want to make the evening news in five states. I want big and splashy!"

I laughed and shook my head. "You are a nut. That kind of attention would terrify me. Good lord, my mother would get involved and then everything would be her way."

"My mother," Jenn said. "Yes, I want my parents flown in to the island and a festival of Fudgies in my honor." Her eyes sparkled.

I plated dinner and placed one plate in front of her and took the stool beside her. "I think we should do some research, present Mr. Devaney with three options, and let him pick which one he likes best."

"This is so exciting," Jenn said, her dark hair bobbing as she bounced on the bar stool. "We need to kind of hint with Frances and see what kinds of proposal she wants."

I shook my head. "No. I promised we wouldn't let her know anything was going on."

Jenn pulled a face. "Fine"—she stabbed a piece of chicken with her fork and waved it in the air—"but that doesn't mean we can't still find out. I'll tell her I have a couple who want me to plan their engagement. I'll ask her if I could run some ideas by her and see what she has to say."

"Now that sounds better. Just be sure Frances doesn't figure it out. She's very smart. It's tough to put anything passed her."

"I know. She knew I was in love with Shane before I did."

I smiled and forked up my own chicken. "I can't wait to be as smart as she is. She told me that age brings wisdom if you pay attention. I'm paying attention."

"You are good at that," Jenn said.

The door to my apartment opened and Mal came rushing in with Frances behind her.

"Hello girls. I didn't mean to interrupt your dinner. I took Mal for her final walk of the day and thought I'd bring her back to you. We had a great time together, didn't we, Mal?"

I gathered my puppy up near my heart and squeezed her. "Thanks for watching her overnight. I missed my baby."

"Every now and then Mama needs a night off to have a life," Frances said with a twinkle in her eye. "I was young once and remember."

"Thanks, Frances," I said. "Do you want some dinner? I have chicken and salad."

"No, thanks." The twinkle in her wide brown eyes brightened. "I have a date myself."

"Finally she talks about her love life," Jenn teased.

Frances blushed. "We were trying to keep things to ourselves for as long as possible."

"It was pretty evident from the start, but thanks for sharing. Mr. Devaney is a great guy."

"Douglas might just be the love of my life," Frances said and put her hand on her heart. "And here I thought it was too late for a woman of my age."

"Oh, it's never too late," I said, jumping up to hug her. "Come have some tea while we eat. Dish about everything."

"Oh dear. It's tempting, girls"—Frances ran her hand through her hair—"but I really do have a date and must get going." She leaned in to me. "I'm so glad you hired a part-time receptionist this month. It's given me more time for the finer things in life."

"I'm glad, too," I said and gave her another hug. "Promise that we'll talk later?"

"I promise," Frances said and hugged me back. "See you later, girls."

Mal jumped up on me and I picked her up. We said good-bye to Frances and I went over to put kibble in Mal's bowl. Mella the cat was out on the stoop enjoying the cooling evening air.

Jenn looked at me as I returned to my stool and

my dinner plate. "Oh, we have to do something really great for those two. Something romantic."

"Well, if anyone can do romance, it's you."

She smiled a faraway smile. "Do you think she'll wear white at her wedding?"

# Chapter 7

"Paige Jessop has been arrested in the murder of Carin Moore," Frances said when she came in to work the next morning.

"What?" I had just finished cutting and putting pounds of chocolate chunk fudge on trays to be sold when the fudge shop opened. I came out of the shop wiping my hands on a towel. "That's crazy. Where did you hear that?"

"I got a call from Irene Spencer about an hour ago." Frances took off her hat and hung it on the coatrack behind the receptionist desk. "Irene lives next to the Jessops. She heard a commotion outside and saw Rex Manning, Charles Brown, and Officer Kelsey standing in front of the Jessops' porch. The entire Jessop clan was outside in their robes—except Trent. He was dressed for the stables."

"I don't understand. How does she know that Paige was arrested?"

"She went outside to see what was going on," Frances said. "She overheard Rex reading Paige her rights. Officer Kelsey then went into the house with Paige while the others waited outside. It seems Paige's father went in to call his attorney. Trent just stood on the porch with his arms crossed glaring at Rex, who handled everything calmly. After about ten minutes, Paige and Officer Kelsey came outside. Paige was dressed and the three policemen walked her down the street. Paige's mother followed of course. Poor Amanda is beside herself."

"That can't be right," I said and reached for my cell phone. "Paige had no motive."

"They must have something on her or they wouldn't have arrested her." Frances ran her fingers through her chin-length brown hair to fluff it after taking off her hat. Silver dangling earrings jingled from the motion. She had on a white T-shirt with tiny purple flowers, a long dark purple skirt, a beautiful silver belt, and a long dark purple cardigan. She started up the computer on the receptionist desk. "Anyway, the McElroy girl was there so I imagine everything will be up on the newspaper website."

I dialed Trent, but he didn't answer. The call went to his voice mail. "Hi, Trent, It's Allie. I heard about Paige. Please call me. Is she okay? Are you okay? Is there anything I can do?" I hung up and bit my bottom lip. I noticed Frances had taken her mug over to the coffee bar and filled it up with fresh black coffee. "Are you sure Rex arrested Paige?"

"Irene is reliable," Frances said, her big brown gaze filled with concern. She took a sip of her coffee and walked back to the receptionist desk. "She confirmed it with Charlene."

"Why would Irene call Charlene?" I knew the dispatcher was very persnickety about who called the 9-1-1 hotline.

"Charlene starts her shift at 6 AM. Irene figured she would know where the officers were and why, so she called the dispatch line." Frances climbed up onto the tall stool that served as her perch behind the receptionist desk. "Charlene confirmed that Rex had a warrant for Paige Jessop's arrest in the murder of Carin Moore."

I tapped my phone. "I can't believe it. It doesn't make any sense."

Jenn came rushing down the stairs. She wore silk trouser pajamas and her hair was up in a messy bun. "I just read on the *Town Crier* website that Paige Jessop has been arrested in the murder of Carin Moore. Have you heard anything?"

"Irene Spencer saw the whole thing," Frances said. She put on reading glasses as she brought up the *Town Crier* website. "She called me and told me. It looks like Liz McElroy was pretty much on the spot. The headline is 'Jessop Girl Arrested in Connection with the Murder of Carin Moore.'" Frances read, "An arrest warrant was issued this morning for Paige Jessop in connection to the murder of Carin Moore. Moore's body was found floating in the marina earlier this week. Autopsy results are still preliminary, but indicate that Moore was not breathing when she went into the water. Police refused further comment on why Jessop was arrested. There was no early indication that Jessop was even a suspect in the incident. Office Rex Manning states that a press conference will be held at ten AM to give further details as necessary."

"Wow." Jenn went over to the coffee bar and poured herself a cup. "Just wow. How crazy is that? Allie, have you called Trent?"

"Yes. He's not answering."

"I imagine the entire family is not answering their phones right now. The press will be all over this."

"And there is extra press on the island this week to cover the yacht races," Frances pointed out. "That means both Chicago and Detroit press will be interested. It might make the AP newswire."

"That's horrible. I need to go to the police station." I pivoted on my heel and went to close up the fudge shop. It wasn't officially open for another two hours so it wasn't like I would lose business.

"Wait for me to get dressed and I'll go with you. Paige is a good friend." Jenn raced up the stairs.

"Maybe if I call Rex," I said out loud as I pulled the glass doors shut and turned the lock. The lock was a simple key bolt. It wasn't a security measure so much as a way to ensure the cat couldn't open the doors and get into the kitchen.

"Don't," Frances said.

"Why not?"

"First of all, he'll be busy with the investigation." Frances studied me over her reading glasses perched on her nose. Today they were black with white polka dots and were attached to an amethyst chain around her neck. "Second of all, you can't use your friendship with him to help Paige. You know he's a stickler for the rules. All he'll do is tell you he can't say anything."

"Right."

"Third of all, you're on your way down there anyway. I'm sure you'll find out more by being there. Besides, Paige and Trent need your support."

"You're right." I took off my sugar coated chef's jacket and hung it on the coatrack near the receptionist desk. Under the coat I wore a simple pink tee with the McMurphy logo on the top of the left breast pocket and a pair of black slacks. My feet were comfortably ensconced in black athletic shoes.

Jenn came hurrying down the stairs. I don't know how she could change in five minutes and look like she'd spent half an hour getting ready. Her hair flowed softly around her shoulders. She had on mascara and lipstick, which enhanced her golden skin. A blue T-shirt and boyfriend jean shorts completed the outfit. "Ready, let's go."

"Open the fudge shop if I'm not back by ten," I said to Frances. "The trays are full. If we run out we run out."

"Will do. Go be good friends to Paige. Send them my regards."

We left the shop and walked through the cool morning air. The streets were relatively deserted at eight AM. The ferries had just started arriving with a handful of early visitors and most of the yachts and the crews were either out on the water or sleeping in from late nights of partying.

We hurried down the street and around the corner to the white administration building that housed the police and fire department. A small crowd of people stood outside the door. I didn't recognize any. Most looked down at their smartphones and thumbed through them or typed on them.

"What's with the crowd?"

A young woman glanced up from her phone. "They're not letting anyone in the building yet."

"Why?" Jenn asked as I tried the door. The young woman was right. The white doors were locked. It was unusual. Usually you could go right in.

"They said they were scheduling a press conference and until then, only authorized people can go inside."

"Are you press?" Jenn asked.

The girl's blue eyes twinkled. "I'm Kaitlyn Jean. I have a blog that sometimes gets picked up by some of the news agencies. Mostly, my stuff makes the Trending Now info on Internet news sites."

"Huh," I heard Jenn say as I peered into the windows to see if I could see Trent. "Why are you on Mackinac?"

"I was doing a piece on the race. This is even more interesting, though," Kaitlyn said. "I've never covered a murder before. This one is just like the TV shows. Two young beautiful wealthy women competing their entire lives until one is found dead. The other is arrested and two lives are lost forever."

"Do you know why they arrested Paige Jessop?" Jenn asked.

I saw Officer Brown walk by and waved frantically. He glanced my way and then kept going as if not seeing me.

"No," Kaitlyn said to Jenn. "Not officially, but I did a little checking. It seems both women went to the same schools, even the same college. One beat the other out of homecoming queen, then the other beat the one at lilac festival queen. They were both runners up for college homecoming queen. I've been told they even had a boyfriend or two in common. That kind of competition is a setup for murder if there was one."

"That's ridiculous." I searched the windows to see if I could catch someone else's eyes. "People don't murder someone over a homecoming queen position."

"Please, people have been murdered for much less," Kaitlyn said. "I read that a woman was mowed down by a car for two packs of cigarettes. Then there's road rage where strangers shoot each other over being cut off in traffic. It's a mad world."

"I'll say," I said under my breath. It seemed to me that Kaitlyn and the rest of the young faces of the so-called press were a little too eager to convict someone based on a warrant. "Whatever happened to innocent until proven guilty?"

"In the court of public opinion all that matters is that the police arrested you," Kaitlyn said and returned to her phone. "Ask anyone."

I looked at Jenn and she looked at me. That didn't bode well for Paige.

# Chapter 8

"Ladies and gentlemen of the press," Rex Manning said at the top of the stairs, "thank you for your patience."

It had been an hour since Jenn and I had arrived. The throng outside the police station had doubled in size as people heard about the news. Trent had yet to return any of my thirteen calls. I had taken to texting, but he wasn't answering that either. It was frustrating to not be able to help him.

"At this time we are announcing that we have a suspect in custody for the murder of Carin Moore. Exact details will be laid out in court should a not guilty plea be entered."

"What? Of course, she's not guilty. Rex, what is going on?" My voice was drowned out by the questions being shouted by the bloggers and part-time press that circled him. The locals stood on the outside of the ring with their arms crossed, listening carefully but saying nothing.

"That's all I can tell you at this time," he said.

"We'll keep you posted as the judicial process progresses."

"Is it true you found a murder weapon?" someone called out.

I noticed a muscle in Rex's jaw twitched.

"I've got nothing further at this time." He turned and walked back into the building, the door closing behind him.

"Well, that was useless," Kaitlyn said with a sigh. "Just when I thought I had something juicy for my editor."

"I'm headed over to the Jessops' house," one of the young men told Kaitlyn. "I bet the family has plenty to say about this."

"Oh, good idea. I'll come with you," she said.

The crowd seemed to melt away as the small clutch of press headed toward the Jessops' in search of more interesting information. I sighed and leaned against the white clapboard of the building. I dialed Trent one more time as I watched Jenn work the locals, trying to find out something, anything, about what was really going on.

"Hey, Allie," Trent answered. "I can't talk right now."

"Trent, wait," I said before he could hang up on me. "Where are you? What can I do?"

"Nothing. There's nothing for you to do. Go make fudge. I'll talk to you later." He hung up on me.

I stared at the phone, feeling hurt and frustrated. I dialed him again, but it went straight to voice mail. Pushing off the building, I looked through the windows one more time, but there was no one to flag. "Darn it!" I was completely shut out of the situation. "Come on, Jenn. I'm going to the *Crier* to talk to Angus."

Jenn turned from talking to Patricia Evans. "Sure. Talk to you later, Pat." She caught up to me as I strode down the street to the newspaper office. "What do you think Angus will tell you?"

"I don't know, but Trent is shutting me out and I have to do something."

"He's shutting you out? How?"

I lifted my phone. "After thirteen messages, he finally picked up only to tell me he can't talk. Then when I asked where he was and what I could do to help, he told me to go back to fudge making."

"Ouch."

"Right?" I frowned. "I want to help. I should help. I'm not wrong, am I?"

"Oh, no," Jenn reassured me as we walked up to the *Crier*. "You two have been dating for nearly three months. He should expect that, at the very least, you would want to be by his side."

"That's what I thought." I pushed open the door.

Angus sat behind the front counter. He was a big man with bushy white brows and brown eyes. He wore a plaid short-sleeve shirt over a dark T-shirt. "Well, well. Look what the cat dragged in," he said in his deep voice.

"Angus, what is going on with Paige Jessop? Do you know?" I asked as I stormed the counter.

"Did you read the website?" he asked me.

"Of course she did," Jenn said beside me. "It didn't say anything, really."

"It said everything we know," Liz said as she came in from the back room. "What do you know?"

"I don't know anything," I said as frustration slipped into my tone. I ran my hand through my hair. "Trent isn't talking to me and neither is Rex."

"The Jessops are all hunkered down, waiting for their high-powered attorney to fly in from Chicago," Liz said. "I talked to Sophie. They've chartered the Grand Hotel's plane to bring him onto the island. She left an hour ago to go get him."

"Well, that's something," I said and crossed my arms.

"I sort of figured you'd be with the Jessops right now," Liz said, "or I would have called you."

"They're shutting her out," Jenn said.

"Seriously?" Liz looked at me with concern in her hazel gaze. She was a tall, pretty woman our age. She had dark curly hair that was currently brushed back into a no nonsense ponytail. She wore a light blue camp shirt and a pair of jeans.

"Yes," I said with disgust. "Trent told me to go make fudge."

"Ouch," Liz said.

"They're circling the wagons," Angus said. "I don't think it's personal."

"But I thought I was part of his family," I said. "At this point, I should be there with him."

"You found the body," Angus said. "Their attorney might have told them to keep you out of things."

"I don't like it," I said with a pout.

"Of course you don't." Jenn patted my back. "But attorneys think of things we don't."

"But clearly Paige is innocent," I pointed out. "There is no reason for her to have killed Carin— no motive and no evidence."

"There's enough for them to get a warrant and arrest her," Angus said. He raised one of his bushy brows. "Or it wouldn't have happened."

"Why weren't you at the press conference?" I asked Liz.

"I have insider info. I knew Rex wasn't going to say anything that I haven't already published."

I frowned. "Really? What else do you know?"

"I can't say," she said, her face suddenly serious.

"What do you mean *you can't say*?" Jenn pushed her. "This is important to us. Spill!"

"I can't say," Liz said again and looked me square in the eyes. "Or I'll lose my exclusive."

"You dug up something, didn't you?" I asked, wanting to pull my hair out. "What?"

"She can't say"—Angus crossed his arms, looking downright chipper—"but if you are nice to me, I might be able to point you in the right direction."

"Oh for goodness sakes." I wanted to leap over the counter and shake him, but I restrained myself. These were my friends, after all.

"Spill!" Jenn was the one to step in and push him.

"There may have been a witness to an incident the evening Carin was killed," he said obliquely.

"Someone saw Carin and Paige fighting?" I jumped to a conclusion I hoped was wrong.

"Maybe," Angus said.

Liz had hitched her hip on the edge of the desk behind the counter, picked up a pen, and started doodling.

"Maybe," I said with a sigh. My thoughts tumbled. "So there has to be a strong motive and there has to be evidence for them to arrest Paige. That means that this witness most likely has provided something the police think is strong motive."

"Who's the witness?" Jenn asked, cutting to the chase.

"Can't say," Angus said.

"Well, what did they see happen?" I asked.

"Can't say."

"Fine. Blink once for yes and twice for no," I said, putting my hands on my hips. "Did the witness see Paige push Carin into the water?"

He blinked twice and chuckled.

"Well, that's a relief," I said.

"Did they see Paige on the pier or the yachts with Carin?" Jenn asked.

He blinked twice.

"Well, then what could they have seen that would be a strong motive?" I mused.

"That's not a yes or no question," Angus said.

"Wait. Liz, you told Angus, but you can't tell us?" I pointed my finger at her grandfather.

She stopped doodling and looked up. "He's the adviser for the paper."

"I thought he was the editor," I said.

"And adviser and publisher," Angus said with a smile, his arms still crossed. "I'm also a lawyer so I know a bit about the law. She came to me for advice."

"If you're a lawyer," I said with a sigh, "you aren't going to tell us anything. Are you?"

He blinked once.

I tossed up my hands. "This is all ridiculous. How can I help if no one will let me?"

"Maybe you really do need to go make fudge,"

Liz said and walked over to me. She handed me a folded piece of paper. "Here's my order. I hope you deliver."

"We don't deliver," Jenn said defensively.

"Maybe you should start," Liz said. "Listen. It's been fun talking, but I've got to run. There's news to deliver and Grandpa needs lunch. See ya."

"You can't just dismiss us like this," Jenn protested.

The weight of the paper Liz handed me was interesting. I suspected there was more than a fudge order on it. I put my arm through Jenn's and pulled her toward the door. "Bye, guys. I'll send Frances over with your order."

Once we were outside in the sunlight, Jenn pulled away from me. "What was that all about?"

I opened up the paper. "This is more than an order for fudge." I glanced at the top of the paper. It did indeed list three fudges and the desired quantities. But under that was the message I was looking for—*deliver the fudge to Eleanor Wadsworth*. I glanced up at Jenn. "I think I know who we need to talk to next."

# Fudgie Cheesecake Brownie

## Ingredients

  ½ cup butter, melted
  1¼ cup sugar
  ⅓ cup cocoa
  ¼ teaspoon salt
  2 eggs

½ teaspoon of vanilla
½ cup flour
1 8-ounce package cream cheese
1 cup powdered sugar
½ cup heavy whipping cream
2 cups dark chocolate chips
2 tablespoons butter

**Directions**

Preheat oven to 325 degrees F. Butter an 8-inch round pan.

In a medium bowl, stir together the butter, sugar, cocoa, and salt.

Stir the eggs into the butter, sugar, cocoa mixture. Do not overbeat the eggs.

Gently add the flour and stir until all lumps are gone. Pour into pan and bake for 20 minutes until center is set.

Remove and cool.

In a medium bowl, mix the cream cheese and powdered sugar.

Pour the heavy whipping cream into a clean cold bowl and whip until stiff peaks form. Fold the whipping cream into the cream cheese mixture and spread over cooled cake. Refrigerate for over an hour.

In a microwaveable bowl, add the chocolate chips and butter. Microwave on 50 percent power for one minute. Stir until smooth. Pour over the cooled cheesecake-covered brownies and spread. Refrigerate for 2 hours.

Slice and serve. Enjoy!

# Chapter 9

Eleanor Wadsworth's family home was modest compared to most of the Victorian summer cottages on the island. But then again it was occupied year round.

With a package of three fudges carefully boxed, I knocked on the door. I imagined that Eleanor would have a housekeeper guarding the door and ran a few scenarios through my head about how I was going to get through the housekeeper to Eleanor. I didn't expect her to answer the door.

"Yes?" she asked as she opened the door.

I saw recognition in her eyes. "Hi, Eleanor." I sent her a sympathetic smile. "I was thinking that everyone was worried about the Moores and the Jessops and no one was thinking about how you just lost your best friend. So I brought you some fudge." I lifted the package. "May I come in?"

"Oh," she said, her eyebrows lifting in surprise. "Thank you. Yes, please come inside." She took the fudge from me as I stepped into the foyer of the older home.

It had that quiet feel of solid wood that you didn't get in new homes. Perhaps it was the plaster walls or the thicker wood floors. The wide foyer led into a central hallway and narrowed as stairs took up one side.

She ushered me into a powder blue parlor in the left front. "Please sit. I'll take this to the kitchen and bring us some tea."

"Do you want me to help?" I asked.

"No, no, it's fine." She waved toward the hump-backed couch with needlepoint pillows. "Please make yourself at home. It won't take me but a minute. I was making tea when you rang the doorbell. All I need to do is add a second cup." She left the room.

I looked around. The wallpaper was blue and white striped silk. A delicate brick fireplace had been painted white. Above it was a seascape that looked as if it belonged in a museum. The heavy silk curtains were white on white striped and old-fashioned sheer curtains spanned the big picture window.

The couch faced two winged-back chairs with toile print in blue and white. A glass-topped coffee table with white wood trim stood on a thick, expensive area rug on top of the plush pale blue, wall-to-wall carpet. The air smelled of fresh flowers from the bouquet in the center of the coffee table. Visible under the glass top were coffee table books of ships and seascapes.

I took a seat on the couch when I heard her coming down the hall.

She came in with a tray in her hands and set it down on the coffee table. "I plated some cookies. I figured you get enough fudge at work."

"Thanks," I said and took the teacup of hot water she handed me. The china cup and saucer were lightweight, expensive porcelain.

"I have several kinds of tea." She opened a small wooden box. "Please pick out what you want. There's also cream and sugar if you need that."

"Earl Grey is good for me. Thanks." I snagged the tea packet and put the cup and saucer on my lap. Opening the pouch, I removed the bag and dipped it in my water. Then I looked her in the eyes. "How are you? Are you okay?"

She looked away and fussed with her tea. "I'm okay."

"I doubt that." I sat back.

She glanced at me with surprise in her gaze.

"You just lost your best friend. You must be devastated. I know if I lost Jenn, I'd be a mess."

Her eyes teared up. "You're right. I am devastated. I simply don't know what to do with myself. It's all so unexpected and so terrible. I don't know how anyone could have hurt Carin, let alone murder her." She put a sugar cube in her tea and stirred it with a delicate silver spoon.

I noted that her fingernails were freshly manicured in a subdued French tip. She wore a cream chiffon blouse and black linen slacks. Her toenails were painted a shell pink and she wore black sandals. Eleanor was not a pretty woman, but she was so well groomed that she pulled off a sort of patrician look that made me feel as if I came from a totally different social class.

"I heard that the police suspect Carin was murdered," I said and sipped my tea. "When I found her, I thought she had hit her head and fallen into the lake."

"It's much worse than that, I fear," Eleanor said. "I understand she was bashed in the base of the skull with the side of an oar and then dumped into the marina."

"What?" I leaned forward. "How do you know that? I mean, that's horrible. Are you sure that's how she died?"

"Yes," Eleanor said with a short nod of her head. "I got the information from the Moores themselves. Carin's parents are like my own. I would be with them now except they asked for a day of privacy to wrap their hearts around their loss."

"They must really be grieving," I said, thinking of my own parents and how devastated they would be. "I bet your presence reminds them of Carin. It might be a while before they can see you again."

"Yes, perhaps you are right," she said with a sigh. "I hadn't thought of that. I miss them and wish I could be with them right now during this tragic time."

I reached over and patted her hand. "Give them some time. Maybe after the funeral they'll be more open to grieving with you."

"I hope so. I lost my parents when I was in junior high. The Moores are the closest thing I have to relatives. They even took me in during the summers when I was growing up."

"I'm sorry to hear about your parents," I said. "It must have been terribly difficult."

"It was," she assured me. "It still is during times like this." Her eyes welled up with tears.

I snagged a tissue out of the box on the end table and handed it to her.

"Thank you," she said.

I looked around at the opulent home. "Did your parents leave you this house? It's quite beautiful."

"Thank you. It belongs to my grandparents. They let me stay here to look after the place. I manage their gift shop employees during the summers. The Lilac Gift Shop is only one of several retail stores my family owns. I come here in the summers to be with Carin." She took a deep breath. "I don't know what I'll do now. She was like a sister to me."

"Terrible, just terrible that someone would murder anyone, let alone a girl our age," I said. "Do they have any idea who would do such a thing and why?"

"I'm certain it was Paige Jessop," Carin said with a sudden hard glint in her eye. "That girl never liked Carin."

I sat back, instinctively recoiling from the wave of hate. "Dislike . . . even hatred . . . is not enough motive for murder. Is it?"

"Perhaps not." She gave a shrill laugh. "I suppose if it were, there would be a lot more murders." She shook her head. "I suspect it was a crime of passion."

"A crime of passion?"

"Oh yes." She leaned in with a glint in her eye. "You see, I happen to know that Paige's boyfriend Reggie was hitting on Carin."

"Oh, no. Really?" I said, trying to draw out more information. Inside, I was skeptical. I happened to know that Paige and Reggie were deeply in love.

"Yes, really." She sipped her tea. "Janet Biggs told me she came around the corner at the yacht club the other night to find Carin and Reggie in each other's arms."

"Janet," I said. "Janet from the committee?"

"Yes, I believe you know her. Her family runs the marina."

"Yes, I did meet her. Wow. Did Carin tell you anything about the encounter? I mean, she was your best friend."

"Well, you know that Carin and Reggie were engaged at one point."

"No, I didn't know," I said truthfully. "He seems so in love with Paige."

"Yes, well, when Reggie broke off the engagement, he broke Carin's heart. I held her hand through her grief. It was a full year before she started dating again. Meanwhile, he went straight into dating Paige Jessop." The contempt was clear on Eleanor's face as her upper lip curled. "I told her she was better off without him. Carin was far too beautiful and smart for the likes of Reginald Owens."

"You must have been shocked to hear from Janet that Reggie was hitting on Carin," I pointed out. "I know my best friend Jenn tells me everything. I'd be so hurt if I found out from someone else that she was seeing her old beau."

"I was hurt," she said, her eyebrows drawing together as if she hadn't realized it until that moment. "I didn't believe Janet, of course."

"Of course," I said.

"I went straight to Carin."

"What did Carin say about it?"

"She said that he cornered her in the hallway and said he wanted her back. When she asked him about Paige, he said he was done with her, that Paige wasn't nearly the woman Carin was."

"Oh," I said, trying to process that Reggie might have actually done this. He seemed like such a great guy. My heart hurt for Paige. "Don't tell me Carin was thinking about taking him back."

"No, no," Eleanor said. "She reassured me that she had learned her lesson. She didn't want nor need Paige Jessop's leftovers. Carin told me that she stopped the embrace and told Reggie to take a hike."

"Ouch. Did Reggie do it?"

"Carin said that he tried to plead with her, but she wasn't having any of it. Besides, she had started dating James Jamison—a far better catch than Reggie. In fact, I think Carin told James what Reggie did."

"That had to have gotten back to Paige."

"It did," Eleanor said. "Paige confronted Carin about it at the yacht club in front of me and Janet. She said that Carin needed to keep her hands off her boyfriend. Carin told her that it was Reggie who needed to keep his hands off her."

"Oh dear. Then what happened?"

"Well, Paige got all red in the face and I was worried she would do something terrible."

"Like what?" I asked.

"Like hit her," Eleanor said. "Paige's fists were balled up and she'd stepped forward, so I got in between them and told Paige she needed to go outside and cool off. Ask Janet. She was there to witness it."

"Wow," I said again. "You must have been so scared for Carin."

"I was. Paige didn't back off until Janet took her by the arm and walked her away."

"It sounds intense," I said. "But not something that would lead to murder."

"That's what Officer Manning said when I mentioned it," Eleanor said. "I was disappointed at first, but now I understand they have Paige in custody. So he wised up."

"You went to the police about the fight?"

"Yes." Eleanor sat back, full of pride. "Of course, as soon as Carin was discovered, I knew it was Paige Jessop who killed her. I went straight to the police about her. There has been no love lost between them from the time they were kids."

"When did you go? Before or after the news about the autopsy?"

"Before. I knew that Carin wouldn't fall into the marina and drown. We all grew up on the island and on boats. It's second nature to be careful around the water. I told Rex that and he agreed. I'm sure that's why they called for the autopsy." She put down her teacup and glanced at her watch.

"Dear me. I have to make some phone calls. Thank you for the visit."

I put down my half-finished tea and stood. "Of course." I dug out my business card. "Please feel free to call me if you need anything. I hope you don't mind if I check in on you."

She took my card. "How sweet of you. Thanks. Let me show you out."

I stepped out of the house, gave her a quick hug, and walked away. So Eleanor saw Paige in a fight with Carin the afternoon Carin was murdered. Surely that wasn't enough motive for Rex to arrest Paige. Maybe Janet knew more. I checked my watch. It had been an hour since I'd called Trent. I sent him a quick text asking if he needed anything. He answered with a simple but definitive no.

I sighed. I hated that he'd shut me out, but that wouldn't stop me from helping. It was time to take Mal for a walk. It wouldn't hurt to go by Janet Biggs' place and see what she had to say about the fight. It was clear Liz thought Eleanor knew something. Maybe Janet would know more.

# Chapter 10

I could always count on Mal to help me get on someone's good side. It helped that Janet Biggs was an older woman who lived in a small cottage on the middle class side of the island. It meant she didn't have a gardener and was outside pruning her flowers when we walked by. She also had a small dog, a terrier mix who jumped up at the sight of us and started barking.

I saw Janet turn toward the sound and I waved. She waved back and walked over as the dogs went nose to nose through the three foot white picket fence that surrounded her property.

"Hi. It's Janet, right?"

"Yes." She smiled at me. In her late fifties, she had let her hair go gray and had the slightly weathered look of a person who loved to spend time in her garden. The plants around the cottage showed she had a green thumb.

I held out my hand to shake hers. "Allie Mc-Murphy. We met at the yacht club. I was hired to do the centerpieces for the fund-raiser."

"Hi, Allie. I remember." She took off her garden glove and shook my hand. Janet wore a wide-brimmed hat, long sleeved denim shirt, and a pair of old jeans. On her feet were garden clogs.

"Your garden is gorgeous," I said as way of introduction. It was gorgeous. Curving beds of flowering plants went from a few inches tall to over the top of the fence. "Are you a professional?"

She blushed. "I wanted to be when I was younger, but life got in the way as it has a habit of doing." She glanced at Mal. "Who's this?"

"This is Marshmallow," I said. "Everyone calls her Mal."

Mal stood up on her hind legs, her front paws on the fence and her stubby tail wagging.

"Well, hello, Mal." Janet reached down and patted her head. "Would you like to come in and play with Jeffery for a bit?"

"Oh, I don't mean to interrupt your day," I said. "We were out for a walk."

"Nonsense." She opened her gate.

Mal rushed in to sniff Jeffery. The little white terrier sniffed back and then did a play bow. Just like that, the two dogs were friends, running around the thick perfectly groomed grass.

"Come in. Let me get you some iced tea. I need a break and it'd be nice to get to know you a little bit better. You do have the time for a visit, don't you?"

I made a pretense of looking at my watch. "Sure, I have time." It was three PM and I knew Sandy had the fudge shop covered. Frances would be busy checking in guests, which gave me time to see if

Janet knew anything about why Paige had been arrested.

"Please, have a seat." Janet pointed to the pair of white cast iron French bistro chairs that butted up to a matching table. It looked like a white doily and fit perfectly on the stone patio outside the front door of her little cottage. "I'll bring out the tea."

The dogs were playing on the lawn. The gentle lake breezes blew the flowers just enough that they danced. The sky was true blue. I took a deep breath. It was a gorgeous moment in a troubling day.

Janet stepped out with a tray of iced tea and frosted cookies.

"Oh, that looks lovely," I said as she set it down and took the chair next to mine. "So many people here have been so kind."

"But not everyone, I bet." Her gaze filled with the experience of her years. "You have been quite busy since the season started."

"You've been keeping track of me?" I asked as I took a sip of my tea.

She smiled. "You are quite famous on the island."

I frowned. "Not on purpose."

"Ha! Of course not. But as in any small town, you have your friends and your not so friendlies." She lifted her glass in a toast. "I, for one, happen to be a fan."

"Oh, thank you." I clinked her glass with mine. "I'm a fan of you as well." We sipped our tea. "I'm sorry, what exactly do you do at the yacht club? I didn't get the feeling you were part of the committee."

"Caught that, did you?" She shook her head. "All

those RBs and their silly clubs." She sighed. "I cater for some of the lunches."

I figured it out. "Oh, you're a chef."

"Classically trained. My late husband Bill was head chef at the Grand for twenty-five years."

"No wonder you have such a lovely garden. I can imagine all the fresh things you cook."

"And I imagine you didn't just wander over to my little part of the island to walk your sweet puppy." She patted Mal on the head.

I felt a blush creep over my cheeks. "Oh boy." I blew out a long breath.

"This has something to do with that girl you pulled out of the marina, doesn't it?"

"Mostly"—I looked her in the eye—"but not entirely. I did need to walk Mal. And I was talking to Eleanor Wadsworth today and she mentioned your name. I realized that I didn't really know you and should rectify that."

"And," she said with more curiosity than anger.

"And I did want to get your take on the fight between Carin and Paige Jessop that Eleanor said took place at the yacht club."

"It was a minor dust up," Janet said. "Really."

"Eleanor said that she had to step between them. That Paige had her fists balled up and was ready to strike Carin. She also said you pulled Paige away and talked her down. Paige is a friend of mine. I would like to hear your version of what happened."

"So did Rex," Janet said. "It seems Eleanor is pointing fingers and Paige got the brunt of it."

"I think Eleanor is hurting. She lost her best friend and is looking for someone to blame."

"You give her a lot of credit. It's clear you haven't known her very long."

I shifted in my chair. "Have you?"

"Yes, I've known them all since they were kids. I've watched them grow up over the years." She shook her head. "The rivalry between Carin and Paige was intense when they were in junior high and high school, but things settled down in college. I was surprised to learn they went to the same college and they ran against each other for homecoming queen there, as well."

"Who won?"

Janet sipped her tea, put down the glass, and snagged a star shaped cookie. "Neither. They were both beat out by Amelia Hanson who went on to be first runner up in the Miss Michigan contest that year."

"Ha," I said. "That should have given them a common thread."

"It did." Janet bit into the cookie and chewed thoughtfully. "There was a sort of truce between them until Carin's brother brought Reggie home. He took one look at Paige and fell head over heels. The very first day it was obvious to everyone—even Carin."

"Ouch." I took a cookie. Mine was tulip-shaped and clearly homemade. It tasted of sugar cookie and bright lemon with a sweet tart crumble. "Wow, these are really good."

"I was a pastry chef after a while. Bill preferred

to prepare the meat portion of the meals so I took the desserts."

"You should sell them online. You'd make a fortune."

"I don't need a fortune," Janet said with a shrug. "I have everything I need here." She waved at her gorgeous garden and the perfect view of the lake.

"I feel the same way. I love the McMurphy and all I need is enough money to keep it going until my children and grandchildren can inherit it."

"Speaking of children, are you married? I thought I heard you were dating the Jessop boy."

"Yes, I'm dating Trent. No, I'm not married, was never married, and I have no children, yet. I have a few years before I'm going to worry about that."

"Good girl," she said and lifted her glass to me. The ice cubes in the tea clinked against the side. "Children are a blessing that should be planned for and appreciated."

"Do you have children?"

"I had a boy," she said and looked at the horizon. "He died suddenly when he was five."

"I'm so sorry."

"It's all right." She seemed to shake herself out of it. "These things happen."

"May I ask how he died?"

"It was a fever." She took a swig of her tea, put the glass down, and fiddled with her cloth napkin. "I took him to the doctor. They said he had the flu. I picked up some over the counter medicine and brought him home. He passed in the middle of the night. It happens sometimes. You don't think so in today's day and age, but it does. They did an autopsy. Natural causes. He just left and went to heaven."

I reached out and touched her hand. "I'm sorry."

She lifted one side of her mouth in a half smile. "We tried to have more, but it didn't work out. So I have my dog Jeffery and my garden."

"And your talent to make fantastic cookies," I said and took another bite.

"You didn't come to hear about old wounds. You came to know about the fight between Carin and Paige that day." Janet sat back farther in her seat, once more aware of her surroundings. "As I said, it was more of a dustup than a fight. Paige came in apparently looking for Carin. She found her in the hallway in front of the kitchen doorway. The door was open so I saw the encounter. Paige was clearly upset. She said something to Carin. Carin shrugged and made an indifferent face. Paige's voice raised. I heard her tell Carin to stay out of her and Reggie's business."

"Eleanor said that Carin told her Reggie made a pass at her. That you saw it happen."

"What I saw was Carin crying and Reggie comforting her," Janet said. "I wouldn't call it a pass. Doubt it was even romantic. Seemed more like a friend holding another friend who was having a bad day."

"Eleanor told Paige that Reggie made a pass at Carin," I said. "Is that what they were fighting about that day?"

"Like I told Rex, I didn't hear exactly what they were talking about until Paige raised her voice. Then Eleanor stepped in between them. She pushed Paige so I left the kitchen to make sure the girls were okay."

"And were they?"

"I could tell Paige was upset, but I don't know if it was because of Eleanor or Carin or both," Janet said. "I took her by the arm and walked her away from them."

"That was kind."

"I like Paige. She is a good girl even if she is a little privileged. I offered her some lemonade. She took me up on the offer."

"Did you two talk?"

"A little," Janet said.

As Mal and Jeffery chased each other around the lawn like kids playing tag, I waited for Janet to expound.

She blew out a long breath. "In essence, Paige had had a rough day. Her mother was upset over the guest list for the yacht club event. They had forgotten an important donor . . . but they had run out of room."

"Ouch. What did they do?"

"Paige offered to give up her and Reggie's seats, but her mother said that wouldn't do. So Paige had to choose another person to uninvite. She had just called April Schmidt to tell her she had been put on the waiting list, which hadn't gone well. Then I guess Carin had made a remark at lunch about Paige and Reggie getting special treatment. Paige came to speak to her about it. That's what I saw." Janet shrugged. "None of that is motive for murder."

"I agree. So why has Rex arrested Paige for Carin's murder?"

"I don't know," Janet said with a shake of her head. "I tried to find out the answer to that question, but no one knows. He's playing this one very close to his vest." She looked at me hard. "I would think the Jessops would have told you. You do have a reputation for helping to solve crimes."

I made a disgusted face. "Yes, well, it seems when a Jessop is arrested, they close ranks."

"They shut you out, didn't they, dear?" It was Janet's turn to pat my hand.

"Yes," I said with a sigh. "Whatever Rex has on Paige must be wrong. I don't see how she could have hurt anyone. No matter how mad they made her."

"It seems to me to arrest someone of Paige Jessop's formidable character you'd better have some pretty damning evidence."

"Means, motive, and murder weapon." I ticked off the three *m*'s on my fingertips. "I haven't figured out what they have."

"I'm sorry I wasn't much help."

"Oh, you were a big help. You gave me a more realistic view of what happened that day."

"Maybe you should speak to Reggie," Janet said. "If the Jessops have pushed you out, they may have pushed him out as well."

"Great idea," I said and stood. "I've really taken up way too much of your time."

"It was my pleasure." She got up and hugged me. "Stop by with Mal anytime. Jeffery is tired but certainly looks happy for the visit." We both looked down to see the little terrier lying in the grass, panting hard, his pink tongue hanging out but what looked like a smile in his eyes. Mal wagged her tail and gave a little bark.

"I think we all will be great friends," I said. "Stop by the McMurphy anytime. We have free coffee and I'd love to continue our friendship. And since you do still cater, I'll let my friend Jenn know. She's been coordinating events for the McMurphy and is always looking for a good caterer."

"Thanks. I'd like that."

I leashed Mal and we walked out. I waved at Janet and Jeffery as we hurried down the hill toward the McMurphy. It was certainly interesting that Janet had such a different perspective from Eleanor. Maybe Janet was right. Maybe Reggie could shine a better light on what was happening.

I glanced at my cell phone. It was pretty clear Trent wasn't talking. It made me sad to be so shut out. It didn't seem right. But then again, we'd only been dating for three months. Still, I was falling in love with the man and I wanted to be a part of his family. That meant taking on the family troubles.

All I needed to do was show him that I could and would help. No matter what. Even if it meant proving Rex wrong. More important, especially if it meant proving Paige's innocence.

# Chapter 11

"What's the scoop?" Jenn asked as she came into the apartment after a date with Shane. She threw herself down on the sofa and Mella jumped up on her chest for long, slow pets. Mella was in heaven as Jenn stroked her from ear to tail.

It was after dinner and I was doing the dishes. "The scoop is that Paige has been arrested and is out on fast tracked bail. Trent hasn't had time to do anything more than text me that he's okay and I'm to let their lawyers handle it."

"Well, that stinks," Jenn said with a frown.

"Did Shane tell you anything?" I wiped the last pot and put it away.

"He wouldn't tell me," she said with a sigh. "It's super hush-hush because the Jessops have high-powered attorneys. We are not allowed to blow the case."

"But the case is wrong," I said with certainty.

Mal followed me from the kitchen to the open living area and jumped up to get Jenn's attention.

Mella swatted her away as if to say Jenn was her human at the moment.

"There is no way Paige killed anyone."

"I agree. Shane isn't telling me if he agrees or not." Jenn frowned. "It's not like him. Usually he shares tidbits with me."

"Yes, it seems everyone is keeping us from investigating." I crossed my arms. "It isn't right."

"Frances says the yacht races are huge again this year. In fact, Carin's murder has made the businesses all the more busy with day-trippers. Every room on the island has been booked for almost a year so newshounds have had to take the ferries over every day or sleep on the streets."

"The mayor won't let people sleep on the streets, so the ferry guys must be happy. The first crews from Chicago came in today. We sold out of fudge by noon. Sandy made some late batches, but we aren't even trying to do demonstrations. The streets are too crowded. I'm not complaining." I sat down.

Mal jumped up in my lap and I petted her as she and the cat played silent glaring war.

"It's the biggest race weekend ever and our cash registers are showing it. But I'm not happy that Trent hasn't called me. He's supposed to lean on me during bad times, isn't he?"

"I'd certainly think so," Jenn said. "Did you learn anything from Eleanor today?"

"Only that she exaggerates things." I shook my head. "I went to see Janet Biggs at her cottage afterwards."

"You did? How is she?"

"She's actually very nice. And a great pastry chef. Did you know she is the yacht club's caterer?"

"Yes, silly," Jenn said. "I'm surprised you didn't. She's quite well-known on the island for her pastries . . . especially her cookies."

"I had one this afternoon and she does have a magic touch. I asked her if she would be willing to cater some of your events and she said yes if it didn't conflict with her existing gigs."

"That's wonderful." Jenn sat up straight, accidently pushing the cat to the floor.

Mal took the opportunity and leapt from me to Jenn.

"She's a known name. It will help make our events legitimate with the island crowd."

"She also told me that Paige had to kick April Schmidt and her date to a waiting list for the yacht club fund-raiser because an important donor was left off the list."

"Ouch," Jenn said.

"Yes. I guess April was livid. Frances told me it takes two to three years or more to get from the waiting list to the actual event. April had been on the list for the last five years."

"Is that motive enough to frame Paige?" Jenn asked.

"What? No, of course not," I said. "At least I don't think so. Janet suggested I talk to Paige's boyfriend Reggie Owens."

"Oh, that's a good idea," Jenn said as she petted Mal.

Mella jumped up on the kitchen bar and licked her paw as if the last thing she wanted was for Jenn to be petting her like she petted Mal. I loved my fur babies, but they were still getting used to each other and their little games were entertainingly human.

"Janet suggested that if the Jessops were shutting me out of the investigation, maybe they were shutting Reggie out as well."

"That makes him all the more likely to talk to you about what he may or may not know." Jenn's gaze lit up. "Did you call him?"

"Yes. He didn't answer so I left a message."

"Good. He has to at least be able to alibi Paige. I mean, wasn't he with her the night of the murder?"

"I'm hoping so," I said. "And yet if he was, how could Rex arrest her?"

"True." Jenn tapped her finger on her chin. "This is harder than I thought. Let's say for some reason Reggie wasn't with Paige. How would the killer know that? And why would they frame Paige?"

"Paige must have some idea, but the Jessops aren't answering any of my calls. I hate that they don't see that I can help."

"You are great at helping." Jenn got up and patted my shoulder. "Until you hear from Reggie, I think we should concentrate on other things. Things that are less frustrating, like planning Mr. Devaney's proposal to Frances. Did he say when he wanted to propose?"

"He said as soon as possible, since they weren't getting any younger."

"Now that sounds like Mr. Devaney." Jenn pulled two sodas out of the fridge, grabbed two glasses, and brought me a glass and soda. "What are you thinking we should do for this? He wants private, right?"

"Yes," I said. "Private, romantic, and super special. Frances deserves super special."

"Yes, she does," Jenn agreed. She went into the end table drawer and pulled out a paper and a pen. "Okay, let's brainstorm. What would be private yet special?"

"Well, remember how he has a private beach area for viewing the fireworks? Maybe we could do something there."

Jenn wrote down *beach*, but frowned. "Do you think he would show it to us so we could decorate it?"

"Most likely not." I drew my eyebrows together. "What about decorating the roof of the McMurphy? It's flat. It's private and has a view of Main Street and the lighthouse, as well as the fort. Would be romantic at night."

"That's a great idea," Jenn said. "I've been up there a couple times looking at it as an event space. You were going to reinforce it for crowds, remember?"

"That's right." I pursed my lips. "I guess that idea sort of got lost in all the other events we've had this season, but I did have Mr. Devaney look into it. Although it is flat, it does not meet code for parties over ten persons. In order for that to happen, we have to have the roof reinforced from underneath. It would require pulling up the roofing, adding new joists and underpinnings to ensure the foundation can hold the extra weight. Then replace the roofing and the safety rail." I opened my soda and poured it into my glass slowly. It bubbled and fizzed, tickling me with carbonation. The sweet smell of cola filled the air as I ran the financial numbers through my brain. "I think I remember the quote on the work was five to eight thousand dollars. That's a lot of money. Plus stairs to the roof would have to be added inside and out, which is another thousand."

"Yes," Jenn agreed. "But you could make that up in one season of events like rehearsal dinners, birthday parties, and fireworks viewing. It would be so totally worth it."

"Yes, but I just spent all of Papa's money on remodeling of the McMurphy lobby and an extra five grand on putting in the glass doors to keep Caramella out when we're making candy."

"Again, cats add value to a hotel. People love pets and so those were both good investments."

"I'd rather talk romantic engagements than investments," I said, bringing her back to the task at hand.

"Fine. Does he have a theme?"

"Mr. Devaney with a theme? Can you imagine that?"

We laughed.

She was quick to reply. "That's why he asked us to help him do this. Okay, so back to rooftops. What if we did a romantic rooftop theme? You know, soft music, catered Italian dinner, flowers, bistro-like setup."

"Do you think that's too cliché?"

Jenn frowned. "You want original romantic rooftop theme. Hmmm."

"What about something personal to them?"

"The only thing I know about them as a couple is they are both dedicated to you and the Mc-Murphy," Jenn said. "But that is a point. We could find something they've done together and create a more personal setting with mementos and such."

"We'll have to do some snooping," I said. "I think we're pretty good at that."

Jenn laughed again. "Yes, yes we are." She lifted her glass of cola and toasted me. "Here's to our investigations. May they always result in positive outcomes."

"I agree." I clinked glasses with her and sipped my cola. *Had I really been so busy this summer that I didn't know more about Frances? Who did she hang out with besides Jenn and me and Mr. Devaney? Didn't she have older friends?*

Maybe a trip to the senior center would help me find out more. I put it on my to-do list—right along with talking to Reggie and trying to figure out what evidence the police had. What did they have against Paige that they could issue a warrant for her arrest? All this and yacht racing madness was making my head spin. At least the yacht club fund-raiser had been a hit. Jenn and Sandy had gotten a few more inquiries to plan events and to make chocolate sculptures.

I thought of the money in the bank. I had enough reserve to make any repairs winter would bring and to get me started into the next season. Fall would be a great time to make the additions on the roof, but could I spend that much of my reserve? Jenn hadn't said she was coming back next season and I wasn't paying her what she could make elsewhere.

I glanced at my cell phone and noted that Trent hadn't called me today.

I hated when my life was in chaos. It seemed that nothing about it was on track. I remember Papa Liam telling me the only certain things in life were death and taxes . . . which reminded me that the accountant I outsourced was working on second quarter taxes. I'd wait for that bill before I committed the funds to reinforcing the roof. One thing I'd learned since Papa Liam died. Life was uncertain and it was good to be prepared for whatever happened next.

"I heard they found the murder weapon," Mrs. O'Malley said when I walked into the senior center with two pounds of fresh fudge. Ninety years old, she sat at the first crafting table beside her seventy-year-old daughter, Mrs. Helmsworth.

It was craft day—painting teacups that would be auctioned off at the fall sale to raise money for more craft supplies. Craft day was held twice a week. They played cards three times a week and often held tournaments for cards and chess.

There were more women at the center for craft day. A bird watching lecture was scheduled for after lunch. I had brought the fudge in hopes of learning more about Frances. I remembered most of the seniors—they were the older set now—from my summers staying with Grammy Alice and Papa Liam. When I was young, they were the middle-aged people bringing their parents to the center.

"Excuse me," I said. "Mrs. O'Malley, Mrs. Helmsworth, would you like a piece of fudge?"

"What kind is it, dear?" Mrs. Helmsworth asked.

"Dark chocolate with Traverse City Cherries, English toffee, and walnuts."

"Well, the nuts and toffee will crack my dentures," Mrs. Helmsworth said.

"You can suck on it," her mother advised. "That's what I do. I love toffee and walnuts." The elder woman took two pieces of the ill-advised fudge and winked at me.

"Frances said it was a favorite here at the center." I frowned. "I didn't realize it could crack your teeth."

"Of course it's a favorite," Mrs. Helmsworth said. "Anything that is bad for you is favored here. We're old. We like to tempt fate." She took a piece of each kind of fudge. "Are you here to investigate the murder?"

"Well, actually, no," I said and stepped over to Mrs. Albert and Mrs. Tunisian. "But you were saying you heard they found the murder weapon? The one that killed Carin Moore?"

"Yes," Mrs. O'Malley said, her mouth full of fudge.

"I heard the police got a warrant for the Jessops' yacht—the *Scoundrel*," Mrs. Albert said. "That's where they found the murder weapon. Right in plain sight."

"That doesn't seem right to me," I said.

"It was an oar with the Jessops' ship name printed right on it," Mrs. Helmsworth said as she bit into the fudge. "It matched the mark at the base of Carin's skull. They ran some tests and found Carin's blood on it."

"That's horrible." I tried to remain calm. "I didn't know the Jessops had a yacht. I mean, I imagine they did because they are so active on the island. I don't remember seeing a boat with that name on it the morning I fished Carin out of the water."

"You date that Jessop boy, don't you?" Mrs. O'Malley asked and reached for a third piece of fudge.

"Yes," I answered.

"I'm surprised you didn't know they had a yacht. In my day, a young man would take his girl sailing pretty early on in the courtship. He had to see if she had sea legs," Mrs. Albert said with a cackle.

"Trent is busy with the stables." I frowned as I was tapped on the back. I turned and Mrs. Finch was there with a small plate.

"Can I take some fudge to my table?"

"Certainly." I put eight pieces on her plate, figuring two for each person at the table.

"You shouldn't have done that," Mrs. O'Malley said. "She had the sugars, you know. She'll go into a coma and never come out."

"That was for her table," I said.

"She doesn't have a table," Mrs. Tunisian informed me.

I glanced around to see that Mrs. Finch had

indeed taken the plate of fudge to the corner and was currently stuffing it in her purse. I frowned.

"It does seem reckless," Mrs. O'Malley said.

"Giving her that much fudge?" I asked.

"No, leaving the murder weapon out in plain view." Mrs. O'Malley picked up her paintbrush and dipped it in a small bowl of blue paint. "Anyone with any sense would have gotten rid of the thing. I would have tossed it right along with the body."

"I would have broken it up and burned it," Mrs. Albert said. "You can't find blood in ashes."

"It does seem suspicious," Mrs. Helmsworth said. "But if there's any funny business, you'll figure that out, won't you, dear?" She patted my rear.

I blinked. "What?"

"I bet you already knew about the oar, didn't you?" Mrs. Tunisian said. "You are a bright girl with connections to the Jessops. You most likely already have the real killer fingered. Isn't that right, dear?"

"Um . . ."

"You can't ask her that," Mrs. Helmsworth said. "You'll ruin the investigation."

Mrs. Tunisian pouted. "I don't see how my knowing who she thinks did it will ruin the investigation. Unlike some people I know, I don't tell people things."

"Well, I never!"

"You most certainly do," Mrs. O'Malley said with a grin. "I'm your mother. I would know. Now, Allie, dear, everyone here knows you didn't just decide to bring us fudge for no reason. Please tell us what is on your mind."

"Well"—I pulled up a chair and sat down—"I really wanted to know more about Frances."

"Seriously?" Mrs. Albert asked, her expression one of disappointment. "She works with you. What do you need us for?"

"Well, you see"—I looked at their expressions, wondered how much I could really trust them not to say anything, and dialed back my line of questioning—"I want to do something special for her birthday and I wondered, you know, who her best friends are. What types of hobbies she has. What things does she find silly or romantic . . . or funny or well, weird . . . you know."

"You don't want to hire a clown if she's afraid of clowns," Mrs. Helmsworth deduced.

"Exactly," I said and sat back. "What can you tell me about her?"

"Wouldn't you rather speculate about the murder?" Mrs. O'Malley asked hopefully. "I mean we have the means, but what was the motive and what do the police know that they were able to build a case around Paige Jessop of all people?"

"I heard they have an eyewitness," Mrs. Tunisian said.

"No way," Mrs. Albert said.

"Oh, yes, way," Mrs. Tunisian replied. "My daughter Katy said that Paige's boyfriend Ronald saw the whole thing."

"Ronald? Who's Ronald?" I asked.

"His name is Reggie," Mrs. Albert said.

"No, I'm certain she said it was Ronald who saw the whole thing," Mrs. Tunisian said. "It was quite the catfight. leading Paige to grab the oar and smack Carin at the back of the skull. She hit her so hard the girl went flying into the water. Paige dropped the oar and ran away in tears."

"None of that makes sense," Mrs. Albert said. "Who runs away and leaves a murder weapon on the deck? Paige Jessop is a smart girl. She would have called the Coast Guard or done something to save Carin."

"Why is there an oar on a yacht?" I had to ask. "Don't they have motors or sails or something?"

"Oh, dear girl," Mrs. Helmsworth said and patted my hand. "You might know fudge, but you don't know anything about sailing, do you?"

"Well . . ."

"Of course she doesn't. She's from Chicago." Mrs. Albert turned to me as if I were a small child. "The yachts all have lifeboats for emergencies. The oar belonged to a lifeboat, dear."

"So the yachts all have oars hanging around on the decks at easy reach?" I asked. It seemed a simple question.

The ladies all reacted with a gasp.

"What?"

"You're right," Mrs. Tunisian said. "The oars aren't stored on the deck. They are usually tucked away either in or near the lifeboats. Which means—"

"It was premeditated," Mrs. O'Malley said and pursed her lips. "I can't buy that. Someone would have seen Paige take an oar out. They would have noticed it sitting on the deck. Wouldn't they wonder why?"

"None of it makes sense, now that you mention

it," Mrs. Albert said. "Who is this Ronald person? Can we trust him as a witness?"

"Well, it seems the police trust him," Mrs. Tunisian said. "They arrested Paige, didn't they?"

"I don't like it," Mrs. O'Malley said. "What are your theories, Allie?"

They all turned and looked at me.

"What can you tell me about Frances?" I asked lamely.

"Stop trying to change the subject," Mrs. Albert said. "We know you are investigating this murder."

"She probably can't tell us anything yet. Can you, dear." Mrs. O'Malley winked at me. "How about we guess and you blink once for yes and twice for no?"

"What? No, I'm sorry I can't. I really need to get some private information on Frances." I put my head in my hands.

"Why?" Mrs. Albert asked.

"Do you think she needs a background check?" Mrs. O'Malley said. "I hear all employers do a background check on their employees on a regular basis these days."

"My background hasn't been checked in years," Mrs. Tunisian said with a throaty chuckle.

"Oh please. Your husband hasn't been dead that long," Mrs. Albert said.

"I know," Mrs. Tunisian said, her eyes flashing. All the old ladies laughed.

I tried not to join in because I didn't know how appropriate it was. I felt the lightest tug on my shirt sleeve and uncovered my eyes to see Mrs. Finch standing beside me. Even though I was sitting and she was standing, she was so tiny we still looked at each other eye to eye.

"If you want to know about Frances, you should ask Margaret Vanderbilt. They've been best friends for decades."

"They have?" I asked.

Mrs. Finch nodded. Her big gray eyes looked very sincere.

"Who's Margaret Vanderbilt?" I asked the group.

"She's running this craft class." Mrs. O'Malley pointed to a woman wearing a colorful smock.

I could have kissed Mrs. Finch. Instead, I snuck her an extra piece of fudge with a wink. "Thanks." I got up.

"Wait!" Mrs. O'Malley said. "You are coming back with an update on the case, right?"

"Um, sure. I'll be by with more fudge next craft day." I touched Mrs. Helmsworth's shoulder. "I'll be sure to bring some plain. No teeth damage will be done on my watch."

"Make it super dark chocolate," she said and went back to her teacup and paints. "The more percent cacao, the better."

"Got it." I picked up my nearly empty platter, keeping my gaze on the teacher in the front of the class while I handed out the few pieces of remaining fudge.

Margaret Vanderbilt was five-foot-five with long, curly, gray hair that was pulled back into a low ponytail. She wore delicate but well-done makeup that accented her dewy skin and wide blue eyes. She wore cat-eyed glasses with purple sparkly frames, the colorful smock, and long flowing slacks that ended in sturdy black shoes. She had silver and gold rings on each finger and large hoop earrings made of gold and silver intertwined. As she helped people, she talked as much with her hands as her mouth, delicately using tiny paint brushes to accent a piece here and there or to show the painter how to do something.

"Hi," I said when she paused for a moment and saw me with my nearly empty platter. "Would you like some fudge?"

"You're the McMurphy girl, aren't you?" Her smile widened with pleasure.

"Yes," I said with a short nod. I juggled the tray to hold out my hand. "I'm Allie and I've been told your name is Margaret."

"Yes, but you can call me Maggs. Why we're practically family. I've been hearing about you since you were knee high to a grasshopper."

"Do you have time to get a coffee?" I asked.

She glanced at the big clock on the wall. "It is about lunchtime and I think their attention spans are done. Give me ten minutes to wrap things up here, okay?"

"Sounds great," I said.

She clapped her hands and gave them instructions on how to store their teacups to dry until the next craft class. By the time they had put the supplies away, the two assistants and five volunteers were washing the tables and setting up the lunch.

"Well," Maggs said. "Allie McMurphy in the flesh."

"I'm so sorry we haven't met sooner."

"Oh, we've met, dear," she said and took off her smock, revealing a V-necked T-shirt underneath.

Margaret was slender and firm for a woman in her seventies. Between her and Frances aging so well, I had great role models for growing old.

"We did?"

Maggs smiled. "Yes. Once when you were six. Then again that summer you were eight and had the pigtails. Then when you were thirteen and had braces."

I frowned. "Why don't I remember you? I should remember you."

"Most likely because you were usually with your Grammy Alice running errands," she said with a casual wave of her hand. "I used to have red hair but about five years ago, I decided to stop coloring it and now it's all gray."

I did have a vague memory of one of Grammy Alice's friends with gorgeous red curls and chandelier earrings. "Oh, you were the one who had the diamond and pearl earrings that shimmered in the sunlight."

"Yes," she said, her gaze lighting up. "You do remember."

"I remember how pretty you were, like Ariel from *The Little Mermaid*."

"Oh, how sweet."

"Well, please let me take you out to lunch." I held the door for her. "To make up for not remembering you sooner and then stealing you away from the obvious feast they are serving here today."

"It's ham and cheese day. I think I'll survive not eating their lunch."

"Perfect. Shall we go to the Portage Café? I hear they have some great salads and pasta."

"Sounds good."

The café was three blocks from the senior center and off Main Street. With it being yacht race weekend, the place was hopping.

"Hi Allie, Hi Maggs," Patty Dens said. "Table for two?"

"Yes, please," I said. "Do you have anything out in the garden seating?"

"Actually I do," she said and picked up two menus. "Follow me."

We did and were soon seated at a glass table with a shady umbrella in the back corner of the lot. I didn't mind as we were out of the way and could hear each other talk. I ordered salad and Maggs ordered a pasta bowl with meatballs.

"Well, this is nice," she said.

"I agree."

"Were you at the senior center looking for clues to Carin Moore's murder?"

"What? No." I shook my head. "Why does everyone think that?"

She shrugged. "Maybe because we all know that the senior center is the best place to get the scoop an anything that is going on on the island."

"Huh," I said. "That's good to know. So when Frances tells me things—"

"She usually hears it at the center. I'm surprised she hasn't taken you there before. In fact, I'm surprised she wasn't with you today."

"She wasn't with me because I didn't want her with me."

"Why not?" Maggs drew her eyebrows together in a worried frown.

"Because I've been tasked by Douglas Devaney to help plan a romantic, private, proposal for Frances that is memorable and as remarkable as she is."

"Well, I'll be," Maggs said and sat back. "He's going to propose marriage?"

"Yes."

"When?"

"As soon as Jenn and I come up with something nice and memorable that shows he has taken care and wants to make her happy."

"Wow." Maggs grinned. "That is the happiest thing I've heard in a long time."

"Yes, well, Jenn and I were discussing some ideas when I realized that I have no idea what Frances thinks is romantic or memorable or anything like that. We realized we don't even know Frances's friends outside of the McMurphy."

"So you decided to come to the senior center and find out."

"Yes," I said with a nod. "But when I got there, all anyone wanted to do was talk about Carin Moore and the investigation—which I don't know anything about, by the way. Finally, Mrs. Finch mentioned that you were Frances's best friend."

"And here we are," Maggs finished my story.

"Yes." I sent her a pathetic look. "Here we are. Me buying you lunch because I never asked Frances about her life. I've been quite selfish, thinking I know all about her when I actually don't. I know about her from my summers here and from what Grammy Alice used to say. I know what she does for me at the McMurphy and I'm pretty sure she is in love with Mr. Devaney."

"Douglas," Maggs said. "Yes, she is quite over the moon about him. They are like two teenagers together. It's adorable."

"See." I waved my hand at her. "They've been sneaking around us at the hotel and making us guess they were dating."

"Oh, it's pretty clear they've been head over heels since he started working there."

"Yes," I said with a firm nod. "But they didn't come out and say they were dating. When I called Frances on it after six weeks, she admitted to it and said they wanted to keep it to themselves for a while."

"Frances didn't want you to worry that Douglas would quit if things didn't work out for them. She told me how invaluable he is to you right now. Especially since the original handyman turned out to be a dud."

"You know she is like family to me," I said. "It's why I'm kind of upset I didn't look into her life or pay attention to what she does outside of the McMurphy. I mean, she let me stay with her for a few days when I was first on the island and remodeling and such, but we mostly talked about my Grammy Alice and Papa Liam. Nowadays, we mostly talk about our day and what we plan next. It's terrible. Mr. Devaney came to me thinking I knew her well enough to put together the perfect proposal and I didn't even know you were her best friend."

"Well, you do now, honey," Maggs said, patting

my hand. "Ah, here's lunch." The waitress set down my giant plate of chopped salad and Maggs' pasta, checked our drinks, and left.

"We were thinking perhaps a candlelight dinner on top of the McMurphy with views of Main Street, the fort, and the marina, but then that didn't seem really special."

"But it is special," Maggs said as she twirled pasta with a fork and pasta spoon. "The McMurphy is where they met, where they work, and where they feel their family is, which is you, by the way."

"Oh, so you think the rooftop would be a good idea?"

"Certainly," she said.

"I need a couple ideas to run past Mr. Devaney," I admitted as I forked up salad. "I thought of his secret beach spot, but then it wouldn't be secret anymore if we decorate it."

"I see." She bit into a meatball.

"There are the obvious places with great views. The Grand, the fort, and all the other places people come for romantic weddings and parties, but we wanted this to be more personal. Do you know of any other places?"

"He could take her for a moonlight carriage ride around the island," Maggs suggested. "They did that on their first date."

"Oh, wonderful. I could have Trent help set it up with his best carriage and driver. They could stop at Lover's Point and we could have a picnic set up for them there."

"Very nice," Maggs said.

"Great. So we have two outdoor ideas. We should

probably consider one indoor in case the weather is bad."

"You could rent the sunporch at the Grand. I know it's cliché, but it is quite lovely. You could have a three piece orchestra play the entire night. There is enough room for two people to dance and watch the lights out on the lake."

"It all sounds so lovely," I said with a sigh. "I really want this to be special for Frances. She deserves it."

"Her husband has been gone for nearly ten years," Maggs said. "I wasn't sure she'd ever find another man like him. I'm so glad you introduced her to Douglas."

"I'm surprised they didn't meet before. Mr. Devaney had been teaching on the island for years. Frances is a retired teacher. They could have met at the library or the school or church . . . even the senior center."

"But they didn't," Maggs said. "It took you and the McMurphy to bring them together. So, no, that wouldn't be a corny place for him to propose."

"What other things do they like to do together? Are there pictures of special trips I should know about? Any memory that we could maybe project on the dance floor?"

"Oh, that's a romantic idea," Maggs said. "I have some pictures of them out walking his dogs on the beach."

"Mr. Devaney has dogs?"

"Two Newfoundlands," Maggs said with a smile. "They are gorgeous animals and they love the water and the snow."

"I didn't know." I paused. "Did she give them to him as a gift?"

"Yes, she did. How did you know?"

"Because she brought Mal to me. What are their names?"

"Winston and Minnie," Maggs said. "Cute, right?"

"So cute. He could have them groomed and they could be there to witness. I know that Frances's cat recently passed away. She told me she would take her time to find a new shelter kitty. In fact, she didn't even take Caramella home."

"It's because the dogs are growing pups and she wants them to be more mature before she brings a cat onto the scene."

"Smart," I said. "Maybe we can get her a cat when she comes home from her honeymoon."

"Oh my. We will have a wedding to plan!" Maggs clapped and people stopped to look at us. "Oops," she said, her tone light. "I don't want to draw too much attention and spill the beans."

"Mr. Devaney is a private man. I can't imagine they will want a big wedding."

"Oh, I quite agree. When Frances married Joe, they had the entire island community invited, plus some. It was held at the chapel at the fort and the cannons saluted. I'm betting this time we'll be lucky to witness."

"Oh, I hope to attend. They mean that much to me."

"I'll let her know," Maggs said and patted my hand again. "Later . . . after the proposal when she starts planning the wedding. I'll make sure she doesn't run off without you."

"Oh, thank you. You are wonderful." I hugged her.

She hugged me back. "I'm so glad you stopped by the senior center today."

"So am I, Maggs, so am I. More than you will ever know."

Not only did I learn more about Frances, but I learned that the senior center was the best place for gossip. I'd somehow doubled my duty. Not bad for a few hours away from fudge making.

# Chapter 12

"Reggie Owens stopped by to see you," Frances said when I entered the McMurphy. "What did you learn at the senior center?"

I'd told Frances I was going to see what gossip I could turn up. I was lucky to have some to report. "The murder weapon was an oar with the name of the Jessops' boat, the *Scoundrel*, printed right on it."

"That's weirdly obvious," Frances said.

"I agree and so do the ladies at the senior center." I grabbed my chef's coat and pulled it on. "I've got a demonstration in ten minutes. Did Reggie leave a message?"

"Yes. He said he'll meet you at three PM at the Boar's Head if you can make it."

I glanced at my watch. There was just enough time for the fudge demonstration and a change of clothes. "Great, how late are you working?"

"I'll be here until seven, then Megan takes over."

"Perfect. Thanks, Frances." I paused and added, "Oh, I ran into Margaret Vanderbilt. We had lunch together. She's great."

Frances nodded. "Maggs is one of a kind."

"So are you," I said and went into the fudge shop.

Outside, the streets were wall-to-wall tourists. We locals affectionately called them Fudgies as they came for the fudge as well as the sites. Main Street heralded a fudge shop on every block. That meant the competition was fierce. Every fudge maker had to be good at catching people's attention.

The yacht races had been going on for over one hundred years and each year they drew more and more people. Each boat had a crew of ten to twenty. As they came in, they would hit the bars and parties. The horse-drawn taxis were in direct competition for space. People outside the Mc-Murphy windows moved in a fluid stream.

Only half a block off the dock where the ferries loaded and unloaded passengers, the McMurphy was in a prime spot. Porters on bikes would pick up luggage and deliver it to the various hotels around. The bigger hotels used horse-drawn trailers to move the luggage.

I hooked a microphone up to my chef's coat and started talking as I poured ingredients into the giant copper fudge pot. Demonstrations were between ten and twenty minutes long. People would come and go at first but near the end they would gather to watch the fudge solidify and grab a taste of the fresh batch.

That was when we would entice them into buying. Making just enough fudge to sell out each day was our goal. The McMurphy was known for small batches and specialty fudges. We rarely had leftovers.

The crowd gathered as I buttered the marble

fudge table. "The marble is cooled with ice water that runs underneath the table top," I explained. "We use marble because it absorbs the heat from the fudge slowly and consistently. That way, we can control the fudge's cooling and add air to give it a light texture."

Jenn stepped into the kitchen area to help me lift the pot and pour the hot fudge onto the table.

"Pouring the fudge is always a two-man job—for safety reasons and because the pot is so large," I explained. "It allows me to scrape all the goodness out onto the table. Thanks, Jenn." She nodded and took the empty pot over to the sink.

"You'll notice the stainless steel edges I've added to the table. This keeps the liquid from dripping off onto the floor as I stir it with a long-handled scraper." I picked up the stirrer and began the lifting and twisting motion that was so familiar to me I swear I did it in my sleep. "This lifting and stirring adds air to the fudge and helps it cool at a consistent rate. As a candy maker becomes skilled, we learn to tell by feel how long to use this method before the fudge needs to be formed and the extra ingredients added."

I switched to the short-handed scraper and continued on with the demonstration. More crowd gathered as I added a premixed bucket of nuts and cranberries to the fudge and folded it into a long loaf. When it had set, I cut the loaf into one-pound sections. Jenn put taster pieces on a platter and opened the door, handing the tasters out to the crowd. As their eyes grew wide, little kids held out their hands to get a taste of fudge. Adults, as well, were eager to taste and compare my fudge to the others that were available just blocks away.

"Hey," someone in the crowd said. "Are you that fudge maker on the candy cook off show?"

Surprised, I turned to them. "Yes, but I didn't think it was showing yet."

"I saw the previews," the man went on.

"Do you win?" one of the women asked as she tasted my fudge. "Because this is really good fudge."

"Thanks," I said. "But you'll have to watch the show to find out what happens."

"Aw, spoiler," the man said and then grinned.

"It starts airing next month," I said. "I hope you enjoy watching."

Jenn and I were busy measuring out boxes and selling fudge as the crowd flowed out of the Mc-Murphy and back into the streets. A glance at the time told me it was already 4:30.

I turned to her. "Can you handle the rest of this? I've got a meeting with Paige's boyfriend Reggie at five."

"Sure thing," Jenn said. "How'd it go at the senior center?"

"Great." I stepped closer. "I found Frances's best friend. Her name is Margaret Vanderbilt."

"Oh, Maggs?" Jenn said.

"Yes." I shook my head. "How do you know her?"

"She does these great craft events. I looked into using her for a birthday party. She's a real artist and a sweetheart."

"I need to get out of the McMurphy more often," I muttered.

Jenn grinned at me. "Yes, you do."

"Maggs gave me some great ideas for you know what," I said.

"Perfect. We'll talk later. Have you heard from Trent or Paige today?"

"No." I tried not to let the disappointment show in my voice. "I called and left a message and I texted twice, but he's completely shut me out at this point."

"I wouldn't take it personal," Jenn said. "Powerful families are known to do that when threatened."

"Well, it only makes me more wanting to prove that I can help them. I'm going to find out what Reggie knows. Then I'm going to go see if I can't get Rex to talk to me."

"Good luck." Jenn waved me off. "I'll see you after dinner."

"Do you have a date with Shane tonight?"

"Yes . . . and yes, I'll see if I can't convince him to tell me more. We'll see what a little wine and nookie can do."

"You are a woman after my own heart," I teased. "Together we'll get this thing figured out."


Reggie was tall and sun-kissed handsome in that preppy sort of manner that rich boys had. His light brown hair was styled perfectly. He wore a white polo, khaki shorts, and deck shoes. His nose was long and thin, his jaw square and his brown eyes charming. "Allie," he called when I walked into the busy bar.

I moved to him as he snagged two craft beers off the bar and handed me one. "I'm thinking you need this as much as I do. Let's go out on the deck and see if we can't get a seat."

The deck overlooked the marina and was filled with people. Throbbing music poured out of speakers attached to the building. A portico gave off just enough shade that we didn't need a hat.

"I guess this really isn't the best place to talk," he shouted over the top of the music.

"Let's grab a bench by the marina."

He nodded his agreement. We went out the gate and down the crowded sidewalk to the soft grass and benches that faced the boats. At least there we could hear each other, even if it wasn't very private.

I sat on the bench and took a swig of the cold beer. It was bright and fizzy.

"How are you holding up?" he asked.

"I'm okay. I'm missing Trent. The Jessops have completely shut me out. He's not even returning my texts. How about you? Have you heard from Paige?"

"Only through her lawyer." He scowled and took a long draught of his beer. "It's as if I've done something wrong."

"I know what you mean." I studied the waterfront. "I feel like they should let me in. I could help them figure this out. Paige is innocent. Right? Why are they shutting us out?"

"It's a Jessop thing," he said, his tone flat. "Blood is thicker than water. If you plan on being part of the clan, then expect this kind of treatment." He glanced my way. "Once you have kids, you're in— at least your kids are in. I'm not sure non-blood relatives are ever truly let into the Jessop family."

"That doesn't make any sense," I said. "I'm Paige's friend. I love Trent. Should we get married, I would be family."

"It's a different way of looking at things. Trust me. If you ever marry Trent, there will be a prenup and you won't get squat."

"I'm okay with that. I'm not dating him for his family's money."

"Yeah, I told Paige that, as well. My family has its own issues and its own money." Reggie shrugged.

"Do you have any idea why they arrested Paige? I heard they discovered a murder weapon. Do you know anything about that?"

"I heard a rumor. Nothing official. I wish I knew how Paige is. She must be going through hell right now."

"Have you called her?"

"Called and texted. Like you, they shut me out."

"I'm certain she's innocent."

"Yeah, there's no way she would have done it. I'm pissed off at Rex Manning for even going so far as to arrest her."

"Did you go to the bail hearing? Do you know what the charges are?"

"The bail hearing was closed." He glanced at me. "I figured you knew that."

"No, I've been busy with the shop and didn't get a chance to go. Besides, Rex has shut me out of this one."

"Well, that stinks." Reggie swigged his beer. "I was hoping you could clue me in on things. You are the one who seems to have the in with the cops and the locals."

"Don't get me wrong. I'm working on the investigation. Were you with Paige that night?" I wasn't about to tell him what the senior rumors were where he was concerned.

"Yeah, we had a date. Paige wanted to take a bunch of us out on the yacht for dinner and drinks and dancing. A party, really. I got to the boat at seven. Some of her friends were already there."

"Who was invited? Do you know?"

"The usual crew," he said with a shrug. "Paige and her best friend Beatrice. Ashley Warner, Meghan Bush, and their boyfriends Matt and Christen. Beatrice's boyfriend Jacob was on one of the yachts racing up from Chicago so he wasn't there. "Reggie raised his hands and ticked off people as he named them. "Ryan and Amy, Brian and Sue, and me. You and Trent didn't come."

"I wasn't invited."

He shrugged. "Paige said it was just her gang. Even the old folks weren't there."

"You mean Paige's mom and dad?"

"Yeah. Mostly it was Paige's crew. We took the boat out into the straits . . . just on the other side of the bridge and watched the sunset. There was an open bar and a lot of drinking and goofing around."

"How late did you stay out?" I didn't want to tell him I hadn't seen the *Scoundrel* at the marina the morning I found Carin. I wondered if I had just missed the boat or if in fact it hadn't been there.

"We didn't get back to the marina until around noon the next day. It's why I don't understand them pinning this murder on Paige. We were all out on the boat when Carin went into the water."

"I heard Paige and Carin fought over you." I sipped my drink and watched his reaction out of the corner of my eye.

He seemed taken aback by my suggestion. "What? No. I haven't seen Carin since I broke it off with her and started dating Paige."

"There's an eyewitness who said she saw you and Carin in a compromising position at the yacht club two days before the murder."

"Yeah, well, your eyewitness has the wrong guy. Two days before the party, I was in Chicago at a conference. I've got 300 witnesses." He glanced at me. "I did a seminar that took up the entire day."

"You could have flown back to the island that night," I said.

"Yeah, well, I didn't," he said, his mouth set in a grim line. "I was tired. I went to my room and went to bed. You can check the flight manifests."

"I'm sure the police already did." I frowned. "If it wasn't you with Carin, who was it?"

"Got me." He shrugged. "Look, her brother and I are good friends, but that girl was grade A nutso. I was lucky to get away from her."

"If it wasn't you Carin and Paige fought over, who was it?" I muttered. "Were you with Paige all night the night Carin died? I mean, aren't you her alibi?"

"Yeah, well, I sort of got drunk and passed out

early. Paige was pissed at me. We had a fight about it the next morning."

"Do you know what they think the murder weapon is?"

"No." He turned toward me. "Do you?"

"I heard a rumor that Carin was hit in the back of the skull with an oar from the *Scoundrel*."

"An oar? Off the yacht? Do they even have oars?"

I shook my head. "That's what I said. I guess they are part of the lifeboats. Anyway, the oar had the *Scoundrel*'s name printed on it and Carin's blood on the edge of the blade."

"Well, shoot," he said and took another swig of his drink. "Anyone could have taken that oar off the boat. No one uses them. They have to have some evidence that traces it to Paige."

"Yes," I agreed. "I was hoping you could help me with that."

"I don't know how."

"I heard you were an eyewitness to the fight on the dock."

"What? That's ridiculous." He scowled. "First off, I was on the boat in the middle of the straits at the time. Second, I was passed out. There's no way I saw anything." He shook his head. "What a day to choose to drink. If I had been sober that night, I could be Paige's alibi and she wouldn't be in this mess."

"Why did you get drunk?"

"I don't know." He shook his head. "I was just having a beer or two when it hit me like a ton of bricks. I heard I simply lay down on the cabin floor and passed out."

"You could have been drugged." I tapped my chin. "You should get checked. There may still be some drugs in your system."

"Huh. I wouldn't have thought of that. Drugged, like in date rape?"

"Maybe. If Carin's murder was premeditated, someone on the *Scoundrel* could have taken the oar earlier and then drugged you, knowing you would be unable to alibi Paige."

"What about the others on the boat?" he asked. "Can't Beatrice or any of the others alibi Paige?"

"Someone is clearly framing Paige. I don't know why and I don't know who, but I'm going to find out. I wish I knew what evidence Rex has that condemns her. Right now, I can only guess that he has someone who witnessed an argument between Paige and Carin. Then there's the oar with the *Scoundrel*'s name and Carin's blood. But what puts the oar in Paige's hands?"

"I suppose they could have fingerprints or DNA from Paige," Reggie said with a shrug.

"That only means Paige handled the oar, not that she swung it."

"Reasonable doubt. All they have to do is convince a jury that the evidence proves Paige did it beyond a reasonable doubt."

"Things aren't adding up. I have Eleanor who told me that she and Janet Biggs saw you and Carin in a compromising position in the hall at the yacht club."

"It wasn't me."

I raised my hand. "Hold on a minute. Let me continue. Here's what I've learned. Eleanor then told Paige that you and Carin have been fooling around and Paige confronted Carin at the yacht club. Janet and Eleanor stepped between them and cooled things off.

"The next morning, I found Carin floating in the marina. She was dead when she hit the water from a blow to the base of the skull. The island rumor mill tells me the murder weapon is a lifeboat oar emblazoned with the name of the Jessops' yacht—the *Scoundrel*. It has Carin's blood on it. We assume it has Paige's fingerprints and DNA. No one has come forward to alibi Paige."

"And we're locked out of the Jessops' family circle left to guess at what else the cops may have that points to Paige in this terrible thing."

"Exactly." I nodded. "Someone is lying."

"Someone has framed Paige. Who would do that and why? Paige isn't exactly a saint, but she never hurt anyone on purpose."

"Someone said they thought it was a crime of passion," I said. "It had to be premeditated in order for them to have the oar and to ensure no one was able to alibi Paige."

"Maybe it was a crime of revenge rather than passion," Reggie said. "Carin was no saint either, if you get my drift."

"That's it!" I stood. "I've been spending my time looking into Paige's activities. Perhaps what I should have been doing was looking into Carin's."

"Someone killed Carin for a reason," Reggie said with a nod. "Paige might simply have been the easiest person to frame."

"I agree. Most likely the real killer is a woman.

Even though Carin was hit with an oar, I can't imagine a man premeditating this kind of frame up with Paige at the center."

"Somehow that makes sense to me," Reggie said. "A dude would frame another dude . . . unless he really hated the chick. I tell you what. I'll poke around and see if any other guys hit on Paige lately. But even if she turned them down, they wouldn't want to frame her by killing Carin. It's too indirect for a dude, you know?"

"Yes, I know." I held out my hand to shake his. "Thanks for the beer, Reggie. Keep me posted if you learn anything or if you get into the Jessops'. Okay?"

"Deal." He shook my hand and then snagged the glass bottle. "Thanks for the talk, Allie. Trent doesn't know it, but he has a real catch in you."

"Thanks." I felt the heat of a blush rush over my cheeks. "Oh . . . go see your doctor. You might still have a tiny amount of drug in you to prove you were slipped something."

"It's a long shot, but I'll go." He walked back toward the bar and I headed into the crowd on Main Street.

I pulled out my phone and texted Trent. I miss you. At least let me know you and Paige are okay. ~Allie

All my sleuthing hadn't gotten me very far. Maybe I should go see Liz and find out what the press knew about Carin's last day on earth. I was missing something.

I was stubborn enough to keep looking until I found it. I don't know if that was considered a good trait or not, but it was all I had.

# Chocolate Chip Pecan Bread Pudding

## Ingredients

- 8 cups cubed bread (Choose French bread or premium white bread.)
- 6 eggs
- 1 14-ounce can of sweetened condensed milk
- ¾ cup dark corn syrup
- ½ cup brown sugar, packed
- ½ cup butter, melted
- 2 teaspoons vanilla
- 1 cup coarsely chopped pecans
- 1 cup chocolate chips

## Directions

In a large bowl, beat eggs until fluffy. Blend in the sweetened condensed milk, corn syrup, brown sugar, butter, and vanilla until well combined.

Fold in bread cubes, pecans, and chocolate chips. Pour into a greased 13- x 9-inch baking pan and allow to sit for 30 minutes so that the bread absorbs the egg mixture.

Preheat oven to 350 degrees F.

Bake 40-45 minutes until golden brown. Remove from oven. Cool for 5 minutes.

You can serve this warm or refrigerate and serve cold. Enjoy!

# Chapter 13

"Bringing me fudge as a bribe does not mean I'm going to tell you anything important," Angus McElroy said as he dove into the sampler box I brought by the *Town Crier* office.

"I didn't expect you to spill any beans," I said casually. "I'm just glad you haven't gotten out the rabbit's foot." He had a habit of taking out a lucky rabbit's foot whenever I was nearby. He claimed I had a penchant for finding old men dead. Since he wanted to stay alive for a while longer, he kept the rabbit's foot to counter my bad juju.

"Oh, I don't need the foot anymore. I've got a rope of garlic around my neck." He pulled out a necklace made of tiny garlic bulbs.

"Well, that will come in handy should we run across any vampires," I said.

"It works for bad juju, too. I read it on the Internet. We all know that anything on the Internet is gospel."

I rolled my eyes and he chuckled. Angus reminded me of my Papa Liam—all bluster and teasing. I liked him and I swear he liked me even if he did pretend to be superstitious about the bodies I found.

"Carin Moore was neither old nor a man," I said. "So you can just put away your theory that I am responsible for the deaths of men your age."

"That poor girl had a viper's tongue and not a lot of friends, but that didn't mean she should have ended up dead."

"I know," I said, leaning against the counter. "I think we all think it would be cool if mean girls got bumped off, but when it happens in real life it's not so great."

"She was only twenty-eight"—he took another piece of fudge—"way too young to lose her life."

"I don't really know that much about her. I thought I'd see what, if anything, the newspaper had on her. I mean, I hear she was homecoming queen her senior year of high school. There must be more such write-ups in the newspaper archives."

"Oh, probably a thing or two," he said with a shrug of his shoulders. He wore a white dress shirt with red suspenders holding up black slacks. His short sleeves were rolled up revealing large forearms and big hands. "Most of the information will be in the obituary that comes out in tonight's paper."

"Who wrote the obit?"

"We ask the family to do that. It's really personal."

"Oh, that's right. My father wrote Papa Liam's obituary." I frowned. "Who in Carin's family wrote hers?"

"Her mother passed, you know, so the job went to her oldest sister."

"Wait. Carin had siblings?"

"Sure, an older sister and a younger brother." Angus shook his head. "Those three were trouble, but Carin was the worst of them. That girl was always too big for her britches."

"Do they live on the island?"

"No, her sister lives in Detroit and her brother in Flint. He gave me a sideways look. "You really need to Google the girl." He pointed to the computer in the corner. "We scanned in our archives in the 1990s. Everything is available on the Internet. We like to think we have some control of our data if we keep it in-house. Don't know if that's true or not, but that's our story and we're sticking to it."

I went over to the computer monitor and keyboard and pulled up a chair. A wiggle of the mouse brought up the screen search bar. I typed in CARIN MOORE. There wasn't a whole lot—two pages at best of links that started with her birth announcement to a first grade play to fifth grade Girl Scouts to high school and homecoming and college. In between was a debutant ball, but nothing criminal. It ended of course with the report of me pulling her body from the water and her obituary. All in all, a sad thought that someone so young left so quickly.

I felt a tap on my shoulder and turned to see Liz standing beside me. Her curly, dark hair was pulled back into a low ponytail. She wore a striped camp shirt, navy Bermuda shorts, and black Keds. "We're getting ready to close."

"Okay." I closed out of the computer. "There wasn't that much to read anyway."

"Who are you researching? Paige or Carin?"

"Carin. I did everything I could think of for Paige so I thought maybe if I tried to figure out who would hurt Carin, I could do a better job."

Liz frowned. "What makes you want to solve this puzzle?"

"You mean besides trying to prove to Trent and his family that I'm one of them?" I asked as I stood. "I suppose I feel compelled to know who would do this to Carin."

"I could name a dozen people who would have liked to," Liz said with a shrug. "Carin wasn't nice to anyone. I swear she had to feel really bad to put so many people down. It didn't matter who it was, she had to be better than them every time."

"Usually a middle child is the one to calm the waters and be a good negotiator . . . if you believe in birth order theory. So why was Carin such an exception to the norm?"

"Probably because her older sister was prettier and was the honor student, the homecoming queen, the lilac queen, valedictorian of her class, went to Harvard, and married into a very wealthy family. Her younger brother was the son of the house. He got all the joy of being the boy, the heir, and the baby of the family."

"So Carin never got enough self-esteem at home," I surmised as we stepped out of the newspaper office and Liz locked the front door. "That had to be tough."

"Carin made up for it by being demanding and petty and downright mean. I hated her in school, but then again, so did many others."

"Did you hate her enough to kill her?" I asked.

Liz laughed out loud at the idea. "Ha! Sometimes I wanted to punch her in the face and knock her teeth out, but no, I never really wanted her *dead*. I tried very hard to understand her. She was pathetically lonely."

"Until Eleanor showed up," I pointed out. "From what I understand, they were inseparable."

"Eleanor." Liz shook her head. "That poor creature. I don't know why she put up with Carin's abuse, but she did. She let Carin push her around all through high school and then followed her to college. It's crazy. I swear she got the job as manager of yacht club operations to be close to Carin."

"What did Carin have that Eleanor wanted? I mean why else would she be so loyal?"

"Maybe Carin blackmailed Eleanor," Liz said with a tad too much glee in her voice. "Like that movie, *I Know What You Did Last Summer*."

"Oh, stop." I shook my head. "Just because a relationship doesn't make sense to you doesn't mean it is blackmail or murder."

"I know. I was just joking," Liz said as she walked with me toward Main Street. "Did you go see Eleanor?"

"I did, but I didn't get why you sent me to her. She really didn't have anything to offer me."

"What did she tell you?"

"She said that she thought Paige was guilty, that Paige and Carin got into a fight at the yacht club, and that Janet Biggs could corroborate the story."

"Yes," Liz said. "She told me that, too, but I didn't see enough motive in that for Rex to arrest

Paige. What have the Jessops told you? Why was Paige charged for the murder?"

"I don't know," I said with a disgusted shrug. "Trent hasn't talked to me since Paige was arrested."

"Ouch. I'm sorry."

"I know. I feel as if they are blaming me so I got ahold of Paige's boyfriend Reggie Owens."

"What does he say about it?"

"They shut him out, too." I shoved my hands into the pockets of my black slacks. "It seems it's not personal."

"I bet it feels personal," Liz said.

I nodded my agreement. "Yes, it feels very personal. I would have hoped that Trent would come to me for support and comfort. Instead, all I get are messages that say, 'Stay out of it.'"

"Ouch."

"Yes, I know. It only makes me want to help more."

"What if Paige did it?" Liz asked.

I stopped in my tracks and stared at her. "What? Of course Paige didn't do it. Not even accidently. I'm certain this wasn't an accident. I'm certain that Paige is being framed."

"What makes you so certain?"

"I know Paige. She's no more capable of hurting someone than I am."

"That's saying a lot since you have been known to defend yourself," Liz said.

"I've never killed anyone," I protested. "Nor would I."

Liz shrugged. "If it were me against someone, I'd certainly ensure it wasn't me."

I shook my head. "Someone pinched that oar from the *Scoundrel*, ensured that Paige's prints were on it, and then snuck up behind Carin and clocked her on the base of the skull. That is premeditated if you ask me and means it wasn't self-defense. There is no way Paige would do that. Besides, who puts the oar back in the boat right on the top deck to be easily found by the police? No, this was not a crime of passion."

"Someone had to have a lot of hate for Carin to go to all that trouble," Liz said thoughtfully.

"That's what I thought."

We headed toward the McMurphy. The streets were clearing a bit as families were headed off the island and boaters were headed toward their parties.

"That's why you were looking up information on Carin," Liz said. "There wasn't much published."

"Yeah." I frowned. "Nothing that would cause someone to plan and execute her murder. I'm really stuck on the motive. I don't understand what Rex has decided is motive. When I was looking into Paige's actions that last day I didn't see anything that would suggest she wanted or needed to kill Carin."

"Eleanor suggested that Paige and Carin fought over Reggie," Liz said.

I looked at Liz. "You know better than that."

"Yes." She sighed. "My research didn't turn up anything on that end but rumor and conjecture. In fact, Reggie denied the entire thing."

"So if it wasn't Reggie, who was it?"

"What do you mean?"

"Sometimes it's easier to tell a lie if you stick close to the truth," I said. "Someone wants us all to think Carin was killed over a dispute about a man. If it wasn't Reggie, who was it?"

"Well, that's a good question." Liz gave me a long look. "You are very good at this. You should be a reporter."

"I'm a fudge maker. I'm not as good a writer as you are."

"But you are a good investigator. You have skills, girl." She pushed me and we both laughed.

I stopped short as I came face-to-face with Rex. He was in full uniform and a formidable figure of a man.

"Allie. Liz."

"Hi Rex." I swallowed hard. "I haven't seen you in a few days. How's the murder investigation going?"

He tilted his head and raised an eyebrow. "Why don't you tell me?"

For some reason the look in his blue, blue eyes made me feel a flash of guilt.

"She thinks you arrested the wrong person," Liz said, crossing her arms in front of her.

"Oh, she does, does she?" Rex looked from her to me. "Why would you think that, Allie?"

"Because Paige doesn't have a motive. Whoever did this thought it through enough to have hit Carin from behind with an oar that had Paige's fingerprints on it. An oar that should not have been on the pier that night because the *Scoundrel* was out on the lake."

"How do you know Paige doesn't have a motive?" He crossed his arms and spread his legs wide, intimidating me a little.

I lifted my chin in response. "Because Reggie wasn't messing around with Carin. He told me so himself."

"Maybe he lied," Rex said softly.

"Why would he lie to me?" I asked and drew my eyebrows together.

"To save Paige," Rex continued. "You'd be surprised what people will say to protect the woman they love."

Why did I blush at that statement? I was dating Trent for goodness sakes. Still, there was something about Rex that could turn a girl's head if she wasn't careful.

"What if Reggie wasn't lying?" Liz asked. "What does that do to Paige's motive?"

"Motive or not, how can Paige be guilty if she was out on the lake with her friends at the time Carin was killed? We both know the *Scoundrel* wasn't docked when I found Carin. That means they either left very early or didn't come back until late."

"I can't talk about the case," Rex said. "All I can do is advise you not to get involved."

"How can I not get involved?" I asked. "Paige is a good friend."

"She's practically Allie's sister," Liz added. "Isn't that right, Allie?"

"Sure," I said, although it sounded lame. I didn't look at Rex. I didn't want to see if he'd flinched.

"I'm going to advise you both to leave this to the proper authorities." His gaze was on Liz.

She didn't seem as easily flustered as I was. "The public has a right to know what is going on with this case."

"That's what press conferences are for. And Allie, if you want details of the case, you should ask the Jessops."

"They won't tell me anything," I blurted.

"They might have a good reason why," Rex said, his tone suddenly soft. "Have a good day, ladies." With that, he walked between us and down the street.

We both stared for a moment at his toned back-side.

"Well, that wasn't helpful," Liz said.

"I agree. If he knows Paige was out on the lake, how can he say she is a suspect in Carin's murder?"

"Maybe he thinks that she got into the lifeboat and rowed to the pier where she confronted Carin, hit her with the oar, then got back in the boat and rowed back to the *Scoundrel.*" Liz hypothesized.

"That's ridiculous. Wouldn't using the oar destroy the blood evidence?"

"Maybe that's what the killer hoped, but if there were any cracks or splinters from the blow, blood or even hair could have gotten caught. Maybe that's what they found in the lab."

I frowned. "I'm going to see what Shane will tell me."

"I already tried, but he won't talk to me," Liz said.

"Yes, well, I have an insider who might be able to get some information out of him."

"Oh, can I use her as a source?"

"I'm not sure," I said. "Isn't secondhand information not useful?"

"Only in a court of law," Liz said with a grin. "Come on. Let's buy Jenn a cup of coffee and see if she's learned anything new."

# Chapter 14

Early the next morning when the first batches of fudge were done, I took Mal out for her walk . . . away from the marina. Most of the yachts had arrived and the marina was filled with people coming and going at all hours. It was good for the coffee shop, but not so good for me.

The sun was slowly rising in the east and the sky was deep blue in the west as we walked down Main Street. Jenn hadn't been able to help us any further. It seemed that Shane was tight-lipped on the evidence in the case. So far, my biggest leads had come from the senior center. Perhaps I'd go back with more fudge and see what new rumors might have popped up.

I remembered that one woman had said *Ronald*, not Reggie as Paige's boyfriend, and everyone had corrected her. What if the man involved in Carin's murder was Ronald and not Paige's Reggie? If so, who was Ronald? And why would he kill Carin . . . or worse, cause someone else to kill her?

We turned the corner and I saw Mrs. Tunisian

and Mrs. Albert power walking toward us. They wore pastel jogging suits with white stripes that looked as if they had been purchased in the eighties, but the shoes they wore were bright white and brand new walkers. Both women walked with purpose and huffed and puffed in the early morning air.

"Allie, good to see you," Mrs. Tunisian said. "Is this your little dog?"

"Yes, this is Mal—short for Marshmallow."

Mal stood up and did a little pirouette for them as a means of introduction.

"Oh so cute," Mrs. Albert said. "What a smart little girl you are, too." The older woman reached down and patted Mal's head.

"So, Allie, how goes the investigation?" Mrs. Tunisian asked. "Do you know who did it yet?"

"Not quite yet. I must admit I'm stumped."

"Well, we believe in you, my dear." Mrs. Albert patted my arm. "You'll figure it out."

"You know, the other day you said that Ronald was an eyewitness," I said to Mrs. Tunisian. "I thought you meant it was Reggie, Paige's boyfriend. Remember? We corrected you."

"Yes," Mrs. Tunisian said.

"Were we wrong? Did you really mean Ronald?"

"Yes, I did mean Ronald, not Reggie." She looked at Mrs. Albert. "I am certain that I heard it was Ronald Lorrie who witnessed the crime."

"You know Ronald, don't you?" Mrs. Albert asked me. "He is a young man about your age. Very handsome, too. I think he's relatively new to the island."

I shook my head. "No, I don't know him. At least, I don't think so."

"Oh, you would remember if you did meet him," she said with a twinkle in her eye. "He's an adorable young man with coal black hair and light blue eyes."

"And a rear that is really high and tight," Mrs. Tunisian added with a grin.

I struggled not to shake my head at her.

"He works as the manager for the Island House Hotel," Mrs. Albert said. "It's next door to the yacht club."

"I think he's related to the Andersons. They have a large cottage on the island and two yachts in the race," Mrs. Tunisian added. "They've been an island family for nearly my whole life—around eighty years."

"That's right," Mrs. Albert said. "I think he is Jeannine Anderson's nephew. He lives in their cottage and is managing the hotel. I'm surprised you haven't met him."

"Well, I'm still getting to know everyone on the island. I'm not the kind to go out to the bars much as I'm up early to make fudge."

"And I bet that handsome boyfriend of yours would prefer you didn't get to know a boy as good looking as Ronald." Mrs. Albert kept the twinkle in her eye.

I smiled. "Trent has nothing to worry about."

"Of course, he doesn't, dear." She patted my arm. "Everyone knows you are of good character. Unlike some other girls your age."

"Like who?" I asked, drawing my eyebrows together.

Mal was busy jumping on Mrs. Tunisian, who patted her on the head and rewarded her for being bad.

"Well, that Eleanor Wadsworth for one and the unfortunate Miss Carin Moore for another," Mrs. Albert said. "Two bad seeds if you ask me—no disrespect to the dead."

"Why do you think they are bad?" I asked.

"Everyone knows those two had to be the center of attention. If anyone got something, they had to get twice as much." Mrs. Tunisian shook her head. "It must make for a miserable life if you are always worried about what others have."

"Well, dear"—Mrs. Albert looked at her oversized watch—"we have to get going. We have another mile to walk and we're supposed to meet the crochet club for coffee and bagels at seven. Tootles." She waggled her fingers at us and they took off, their elbows bent and their strides long and filled with purpose.

I glanced at Mal who tugged me down the street toward a patch of grass. "That was certainly an interesting meeting."

Mal seemed unimpressed. There was a walk to be had and pets to be won. Thankfully, she hadn't turned up any more dead bodies.

"Trent, please call me," I said into my cell phone. "It's been days. I need to know how you are. I want to know how Paige is. I miss you. Please, don't shut me out. Call me, today, okay? I'm worried." I hung up with a sigh and knew I sounded needy and whiny. But sheesh, I was his girlfriend and his sister was being charged with murder. I think I should be there for him and I wasn't understanding why he'd shut me out.

Her hair pulled into a high ponytail, Jenn bounced into the office and stopped in front of our desks. "Well, hello, Miss Sad Face. What is up? Or should I guess? Trent still hasn't talked to you? It's been nearly four days."

"He hasn't even texted," I said and dropped my phone on my desktop. "It's ridiculous. I just left a needy, whiny message." I put my head in my hands. "I've become that girl."

Jenn patted me on the back. "You are not that needy girlfriend. You care for him and he's shut you out. It seems to me he is in the wrong here, not you."

I looked up at her. "Thanks for the reassurance."

"Any time." She sat down at her desk opposite me. "Now, what's up? Any new ideas on who killed Carin and why?"

"Yes. What do you know about Ronald Lorrie?"

"Oh, the hunky guy who manages the Island House Hotel?"

"Yes." I tried not to sigh. "How is it you know so many people?"

"I get out. You are McMurphy bound, my dear. I'm free to move about the island. Besides, if I'm planning events, I need to know the competition."

"Right."

"Why do you want to know about Ronald?"

"It's something Mrs. Tunisian said when I was at the senior center the other day. She said that Ronald was the eyewitness and I thought she was mistaken. I thought she meant Reggie—Paige's boyfriend."

"Huh." Jenn leaned on her elbows. "Now you think she really meant Ronald?"

"Yes. You see, Reggie isn't part of the investigation. He was drunk and passed out. Can't even alibi Paige. Rex has to have more than an oar to tie Paige to the crime. It makes sense he has an eyewitness. I ran into Mrs. Tunisian this morning and she confirmed she really did mean Ronald not Reggie."

"So you think she's right? Ronald Lorrie is the eyewitness?"

"She's certain she heard it was Ronald. She's guessing it was Ronald Lorrie."

"It's a small island." Jenn drummed her fingers. "There could be another Ronald, but I haven't met one. Are you going to go see Ronald Lorrie and ask him if he knows anything?"

"The problem is we haven't met. I can't just go up to him and say are you Ronald Lorrie? Are you the witness who is framing Paige Jessop?"

Jenn laughed. "No, I don't suppose you can." She paused thoughtfully.

"What?"

"Well, the Island House runs specials. Included in the weekend package are dinners at their restaurant and a certificate for two pounds of fudge at one of the local shops."

"So?"

"So, why don't you set up an appointment with Ronald for a business meeting?"

"But he's a competitor," I argued. "The McMurphy is a hotel, not just a fudge shop."

"A competitor in a different market place. They have a restaurant, you don't. You offer fudge, they don't. You could approach him to see if he would be willing to send his overflow your way. In exchange, you would give your customers certificates to his restaurant and he could give his people certificates for two pounds of free McMurphy fudge. It's win-win. The people will taste your fudge and get to see how quaint the McMurphy is. We are right down the street from the Island House and they can feel comfortable coming to stay with us when the Island House is full."

"Hmmm. It does sound good if I can afford gift certificates to his restaurant."

"See if he'll give you dinner certificates at cost. You could offer him free fudge for the entire season."

"And after we meet, I could ask him about Carin," I said.

"Yes," Jenn said with a grin. "I mean, you will know him better then. You might even offer to take him out for a drink."

I thought about Trent shutting me out. "Yes, I may." I reached for my phone. "Thanks! You are always the best at problem solving."

"I aim to please," Jenn said. "Now, I'm off to an island charity club meeting. We'll see if I can't drum up another event."

"Good luck."

# Chapter 15

The Island House Hotel was a large white capital *I*-shaped hotel whose lobby faced the marina. The hotel had a wide front lawn with a fire pit for roasting marshmallows, a smattering of lawn chairs for people to relax in, and a wide front porch that overlooked the marina and the yachts coming and going. It evoked a feeling of service and old money that the McMurphy didn't quite have. We were more like staying with family situated in the middle of Main Street's hustle and bustle.

I walked into the cool spacious lobby. The restaurant was to my right, the reception desk in front, and stairs to the rooms to the left.

"Good afternoon. How can I help you?" A lovely young woman in a black and white uniform stood up from behind the desk when I entered.

"Hi, yes. I have an appointment to see Mr. Lorrie," I said.

"Can I have your name, please?"

"I'm Allie McMurphy."

"Perfect. Yes, I see a note to send you on up. If you wait a moment, I'll let him know you are here and then walk you up."

"Great. Thanks." I was dressed in clean black slacks and a pink and white polo with the Mc-Murphy logo. I held a leather bound notebook in my hand with two copies of my proposal in it. I looked around at the slightly faded elegance of the Island House. There was a sign on a pole at the entrance to the restaurant saying it was closed until five PM. I could hear the waitstaff and kitchen people at work. A glance at my watch told me I was right on time.

"Right this way please, Ms. McMurphy." The girl's gold name tag said ANGIE.

I followed her up a short flight of stairs and to the right in the hallway. I estimated we were directly above the reception desk when she stopped and knocked on a door marked OFFICE.

"Come in."

She opened the door. "Mr. Lorrie, Ms. McMurphy to see you."

"Thanks, Angie."

She waved for me to step inside and closed the door behind me. The office was a nice size—about the size of one suite of rooms. The walls were a yellow cream color and the carpet a muted green. A closet door was to my left and an open bathroom door to my right. In front of me were a couch and wingback chair arranged with a view of the pool house behind the hotel. To the right of that was a massive oak desk with two wooden chairs in front of it.

Sitting at the desk was Ronald Lorrie, who was just as handsome as the ladies told me he would be. He rose and offered his hand. "Hello, Ms. McMurphy, Ronald Lorrie. It's nice to finally meet you."

I shook his hand and tried not to stare at his pale blue eyes and dark black hair. He wore a crisp, long sleeved dress shirt the color of a summer sky. It was reflected in those eyes that were ringed with black lashes. He also had on a blue and black striped tie and black dress slacks. He could have stepped right out of *GQ* magazine.

"Please, call me Allie." I pulled my gaze away. "May I sit?"

"Certainly." He waved toward the seats in front of his desk.

I sat down quickly and placed the notebook on his desk. He sat back down and put his hands on his desk and smiled at me. I had to swallow hard not to drool.

"How can I help you, Allie?"

"My event planner, Jenn Christensen, told me that you offer weekend packages that include coupons for two pounds of free fudge."

"Yes, it's sort of a tradition here at the Island House Hotel."

"Well, I would like the McMurphy fudge to be a part of that offer." I pushed the notebook toward him. "I know you can sort of see us as a competitor, but let's be honest, we have a very different vibe at the McMurphy."

He opened up my notebook and thumbed

through the proposal. "Yes, you do," he said with certainty.

It felt as if he was implying that his hotel was the *Queen Mary* and mine was a tugboat. I tried not to take it personally . . . to let it roll off of me. "I thought perhaps we could exchange coupons. I would offer your people two pounds of free fudge and you could offer my people a fifteen percent discount on meals at your restaurant. Reservations only, of course."

"Of course." He looked at the proposal a little closer. Then he looked up at me. "Our restaurant is filled almost every day. I really don't need to run a special to get butts in my seats."

"Well, that may be true, but I'm willing to offer your customers two pounds of free McMurphy fudge at no cost to you."

"I see. Why would I encourage my customers to go into your hotel so they can draw comparisons?" Not only was he handsome, he was shrewd.

I tried not to wiggle. "As I said, we offer two completely different hotel experiences. I truly doubt your customers would change their room reservations at the sight of my lobby. That said, I would like to drum up more business for my fudge shop. If they get two pounds free, they are more likely to buy a pound or two on top of that."

"We already have an understanding with one of the other fudge shops."

"Yes, but can they do chocolate sculptures?"

He sat back and tilted his head as if considering. "No, they make fudge."

"Sandy Everheart is my chocolatier. She could make small chocolate replicas of the Island House hotel. We could offer them to your customers at cost instead of free fudge."

"And what would be the advantage for you?" He drew his dark black brows together.

I smiled. "They would come into the shop and may be more likely to purchase fudge or to order a sculpture for their own special occasion."

"I see. This sounds very interesting. Can I take a few days to look it over?" He tapped the notebook.

"Yes, I can have Sandy send you pricing for the replicas. We use dark chocolate, milk chocolate, and white chocolate. Your customers would have their choice."

"I certainly like the idea. It would be a great souvenir for them to take home and remind them of their stay on the island."

"That's the plan. If we're successful, the island is successful and that is good, right?"

"All boats rise in a lifting tide." He sat back. "Now that business is done, why don't you tell me a little about yourself? I've heard so much about Allie McMurphy and her little white dog. It's an honor to finally meet you in person."

I grinned. "Funny. I was hoping you'd do the same."

A hint of a smile crossed his face. "You didn't have to bring me a business proposal to meet with me."

"I'm sincere about the proposal," I said, feeling the hint of a blush rush over my cheeks. "It's good business to partner with other hotels."

He leaned in toward me, his elbows on the top

of his desk. "I heard that your grandfather died this spring. I'm so sorry for your loss."

"Thank you. I wasn't expecting to take on the family business all at once. I had hoped to have a season or two with Papa Liam's guidance, but . . ." I shrugged.

"You are brave for doing all that you are doing on your own. This is my first season on the island also," he said. "I've managed hotels in Traverse City and in Mackinaw City, but this is my first big gig on the island. It's a bit different to say the least."

A feeling of comradery washed over me. "I agree. Who knew that it would be so hard to get extra help during the festival weekends?"

"And the horses create so much dust. I cringe every time I hear a customer tell how they opened a window to let in the lake breezes."

I understood. "You have a restaurant, too. I have trouble getting supplies for the fudge shop. How do you manage to keep things going with a full kitchen?"

"I'm lucky. The staff has its routine down. My head chef has been working here for fifteen years. He knows exactly who to call when he needs something special shipped in."

"How are you doing with the locals?" I had to ask. "I don't remember seeing you at any of the festival committees."

"The owners are more involved with those things. I'm lucky in that most see me as a manager and think I live with the rest of the staff in the cheaper apartments. Only a few know I'm staying at my aunt's."

"Aren't those summer cottages huge?" I asked. "Does your aunt own one of the Painted Lady Victorians? Do you have six or eight bedrooms and three baths? Or have they converted them all to en suite rooms?"

"Oh, the old place is quite original, so one bath upstairs and a half bath in a converted closet space on the first floor. But I'm not staying there. I'm renting the apartment above the carriage house."

"Wow, you live above the horses?"

"No," he said with a laugh. "They haven't had horses on the property for over fifty years. They keep them at the Jessops' stables. Three carriages are stored beneath the apartment, no animals."

"Whew. I would have worried about the smell." I sat back. "So who do you know on the island besides your family? When I got here, I knew mostly people my grandfather's age. Since then, I've been slowly making my way into the layer of society closer to my age."

"I'm lucky in that the Island House is right next door to the yacht club. I get to meet quite a few of the island's elite." He paused. "It's where I met Carin Moore and Eleanor Wadsworth."

"You knew Carin?"

"Yes." His voice wavered and his eyes grew red. He rubbed them to cover up the emotion. "I was in love with her."

"Oh, dear. I'm so sorry for your loss." I got up and reached over to pat his shoulder. It was an awkward gesture. "I didn't know. I thought she was dating James Jamison."

"Yeah, we were keeping things secret," Ronald

said. "The Jamison thing was political. Her family pushed her into it. At first, she liked all the politics and such, but then she got tired of it always being about him. We hooked up last month. My aunt didn't approve of Carin. She said she was one of 'those' kinds of girls. But she didn't seem that way to me. All I ever knew was a warm, happy, loving woman. It boggles my mind to think that she's dead. That some monster killed her and left her to float away in the lake." He looked up at me with pain in his gaze. "You found her, didn't you?"

"Yes." I stepped back, hugging my waist. "I thought she was merely floating in the water at first. Then I thought she might have hit her head and was unconscious so I jumped in and took her to the grass. I tried CPR."

"That's what I heard. I wanted to thank you for finding her and trying to save her."

"I was far too late," I said.

"I'm glad they have the killer—even if she did get released after putting up bail. At least they have her. Carin will get her day in court."

I frowned. "Were you with her the night she was killed?"

"Sadly no. She had a party to go to. It was just more politics. I wasn't invited, of course, plus I had to work until eleven. When I got off, she met me just outside the Island House. She was tipsy and had a bottle of wine in her hand. She said she missed me." His voice broke into a half sob. "She had on this beautiful watercolor dress. It looked so great against her skin."

"I can imagine. So she left the party to meet you?"

"Yes," he said with a nod of his head. "I told her I missed her, too, but that she needed to get back. It was important that she be there. She protested, but I knew everyone still thought she was seeing James. I kissed her and sent her away."

"Nice."

"I know that now," he said, his tone bleak. "If only I had stayed with her, it might not have happened."

"What time was that?"

"Eleven fifteen or so. I pulled away finally and turned her around to face the pier. I told her to go back to her party. I was going to go home and change and I'd meet her afterwards. She was supposed to text me when it was over. I would have never let her go had I known I would never see her alive again." He shivered.

"Then what happened?"

"I went home and showered and grabbed a dress shirt and slacks. I sat down on my bed for a minute and apparently fell asleep."

"You had to have been exhausted."

"It was a fourteen-hour day. There had been a problem in the kitchen and then we had yacht race guests arriving for hours. The porters needed extra staffing to help move all the luggage from the pier to here and then sort it into people's rooms."

"I know how hectic it can get," I reassured him. "There have been times when I've been asleep on my feet, as well."

"Yes, well, I woke up about three AM and she hadn't texted me yet. I decided to go out and see if the party was still hopping. Carin could keep things going until dawn."

"Really." I sat and leaned toward him. "Did you see anything?"

"The music was still going, although more muted than usual. I heard later that they had had a complaint from people docked nearby. It was pretty dark and a bit foggy. I boarded the yacht and talked to a few people. Mostly I asked if anyone had seen Carin."

"And did they?"

"Yes, people who were sober enough to answer pointed me in one direction or the other. I checked below deck but didn't find her. I had almost given up when I thought I saw her talking with someone on the dock."

"Did you go to her?"

"No." He shook his head. "I wish to God I had, but I just thought she was having a private conversation. You know?"

"Do you have any idea who she was talking to?"

"It looked like another woman," Ronald said. "That's what I told Rex. But there's no way I could swear to who it was exactly. I remember something about Paige Jessop and Carin fighting that afternoon. It could have been Paige with her." He slammed his fist on the desk top. "I should have gone to her. She might still be alive if I had. Instead, I grabbed a beer and waited by the gangplank. I figured I'd catch her when she came back. After all, she was talking to a woman. How long could they stand out there? It was getting chilly."

"Oh, it could have been hours. I've been known

to stand in the hot sun chatting with a friend for hours without even noticing the time going by. Plus, Carin had been drinking so her perception of time had to be all off. Did she go back to the boat?"

"No," Ronald said. "I went looking for her, but couldn't find her. So I texted her. When she didn't answer, I got angry and went home."

"Do you remember what time you got home?"

"No." He ran his hands through his gorgeous thick hair. "I kick myself every day. I could have walked right passed her in the water."

"There's nothing you could have done even if you'd found her. They tell me she was dead when she hit the water."

"Somehow that doesn't make me feel any better," he said grimly. "What if I was the last person to see her?"

"You weren't. Whoever she was talking to may have been the last person."

"I'm surprised no one saw anything. We weren't the only boat with a party on it that night. The pier was hopping."

"Was it still hopping when you saw Carin was talking to the woman?"

"No, things had quieted down a bit. Like I said it was after three AM. Some of the boaters were closing up to get rest for the morning's race."

"You didn't see who the woman was?"

"No, they were in shadow, just outside the lights from the nearest rig."

"Did they look like they were fighting?"

"You are full of questions," he said suddenly.

"I'm trying to find out what happened," I said.

"The police seem to know as they have arrested a suspect already."

"Yes, well, I'm wondering if they have the wrong person."

"Why would you wonder that?" Ronald asked, his expression sincere. "Is it because Paige Jessop is your boyfriend's sister?"

I sat up straight. "Did you tell Rex it was Paige you saw with Carin?"

Things in the room were tense as he looked at me as if sizing me up. Finally he broke the tension. "I told him what I told you. No more, no less."

"I see." I shook my head. "What I don't understand is why the police can build a case around that. It could have been any woman on the island."

"No. She was young."

"Wait. If they were in the shadows, how do you know that?"

"Her figure, her hair. She was wearing pants and a jacket and had long hair. She might have been in shadow, but there was no hiding her figure. I could also tell her height. She was face-to-face with Carin, so they had to be the same height."

"That means it could have been any woman on the island her height, including me."

He tilted his head and narrowed his eyes. "Were you on the dock that night?"

"No. I was at home in bed. I had fudge to make the next morning. I usually get up at four and make fudge from four-thirty to six or seven o'clock, depending on the way the fudge sets up. Some days are more humid and it takes longer for the fudge to set."

"So you had no one to substantiate your alibi."

I shrugged. "I guess, but I'm not a suspect."

"Not too many people have alibis that late at night, Ms. McMurphy—especially women who live alone. The police only found one person with motive strong enough to suspect of killing Carin and they arrested her." He stood, clearly signaling the end of our meeting. "It was nice to meet you, Allie. I wanted to know who pulled Carin from the water."

"It was nice to meet you as well, Ronald. I'm sorry for your loss. Please look over the business proposal. It was a serious one."

He nodded. "I will."

"Thanks." I headed toward the door then stopped and pivoted on my heel. "One last thing . . ."

"Yes?"

"Did you identify Paige in a line up?"

"No," he said with a shake of his head. "I told the police I didn't see the woman's face. I'm not a monster out to get your friend. I'm simply hoping to convict the person responsible for this heinous crime."

"I understand. I want the same thing."

"Even if it means your friend Paige is guilty?"

I studied him for a moment. "Yes, even if it means Paige is guilty."

"Thanks, Allie. For being open to the truth."

"I want you to know that I intend to find that truth. Whatever that truth might be."

"Good luck," he said sincerely.

I left his office and hurried out of the hotel. The last person to talk to Carin may have been a woman, but that didn't mean a woman killed her. I needed to talk to Shane. I needed to know if the killing blow came from above or below. When Ronald mentioned the women were face-to-face, it made me realize that the angle of the blow to the back of the head could tell me the height of the killer. It might just be a way to save Paige.

# Chapter 16

"Allie." Eleanor Wadsworth stopped me as Mal and I walked down Main Street toward the yacht club. It was early evening and Mal and I were out for her before-dinner walk.

"Oh, hi, Eleanor," I said and stopped as she approached. "How are you?"

She wore a plain black dress and black flats. "I'm holding up," she said with an exaggerated sigh. "The visitation was today. You weren't there."

"I was afraid I'd just be a reminder of how I found her in the water." I sent flowers. I really didn't know Carin at all besides seeing her once or twice at the yacht club committee meetings."

"Oh, yes. I suppose that's wise," Eleanor said. "I understand you are investigating Carin's murder."

"I'm just asking some questions," I said.

"I told you that the police have the right suspect." She pushed her point. "You really shouldn't be going around talking to people like Reggie. All you're doing is pouring salt into an open wound."

"I'm sorry. I didn't mean to cause anyone distress," I said, studying her.

Her expression was one of sorrow and anxiety. "Reggie means the world to me. He's pretty torn up about Carin's death. I really think you should stay away from him. Besides, don't you have Trent to think about?"

"Yes, I do have Trent to think about. And his sister Paige, who I don't believe killed Carin. Did you know that Carin was having an affair with Ronald Lorrie? That she led everyone to believe she was in love with James Jamison?"

Eleanor's mouth pinched up as if she tasted something bad. "Ronald Lorrie is making that up. Carin never looked sideways at him. The nerve of the man to say she did. As for James, well, Carin was going to leave him for Reggie the moment Reggie said the word. If anyone was having an affair with Carin it was Reggie. Paige found out about it and killed Carin in a fit of rage."

"I don't believe you. I talked to Reggie. Paige didn't have any reason to be angry."

"Well, the police believe she did and that's good enough for me," Eleanor said. "And it should be good enough for you. Really, Allie, I thought you were on my side with this."

"I am on your side. I'm looking for justice for Carin. That justice won't happen if the wrong person goes to trial. All that will happen then is that the police will stop looking for the real killer."

"I know they have the real killer," Eleanor said. "You should know that, too."

"I just want to be certain," I said.

"Well, the only way to be certain is to let the police do their job." She bristled. "And leave Reggie out of your gossip. He is a kind and upstanding man and I won't see him further abused."

"Okay," I said.

"Okay. Well, then good." Eleanor glanced down at Mal and patted her head. "The funeral is tomorrow. I don't expect that you'll come."

I shook my head. "No."

"Good," she replied again and lifted her nose in the air. "As you said, you'll only remind them that you pulled Carin out of the marina. Terrible, just terrible." She walked away toward the Moores' home.

I looked down at Mal, who wagged her stubbed tail at me. "That was awkward." My cell phone rang and I fished it out of my pocket. "Hello?"

"Allie."

"Trent," I said with relief. "How are you? Are you okay? Is Paige okay? Is there anything I can do? Why haven't you called me? I miss you."

"Allie, we've been advised by our lawyer not to talk to anyone outside the family."

"Well, I consider myself family, Trent. You know I care about you and Paige. I talked to Reggie. He misses Paige, too. We need to know what's going on."

"Allie, I called because I heard you were asking questions around town."

"You shut me out. I need to know what Rex has on Paige. It's clear she was set up. Let me help."

"Allie, I called because I need you to stop investigating."

"What? Why?"

"You're causing more harm than good," he said sternly.

"Trent, I'm just asking questions."

"Don't."

"But—"

"Allie, stay out of it. We don't want you asking questions. We don't need your help. Is that clear?"

"Crystal," I said.

"Good. I've got to go."

"Trent—" He had already hung up on me. I sighed, frustrated by the lack of communication on his part. Why weren't they letting me in? Did I really mean so little to him that he could ditch me when the going got tough?

Mal tugged on the leash as if to say Let's go. There are interesting smells and neighborhood gossip to learn.

"All right, Mal," I muttered. "It seems no one wants us to help."

She looked up at me with her puppy smile and then buried her nose in the grass and pulled me toward the yacht club.

"Fine," I muttered. "Just don't find any more body parts, okay? I don't need grief from any more people."

Our walk took us around the corner and down the alley between the McMurphy and the pool house of the hotel behind us. My friend and neighbor, Mr. Beecher, was walking down the alley when we got to the back of the McMurphy.

"Hello, Allie, how are you? And Mal, my little friend, how are you?" Mr. Beecher was an old man, round in stature. He always wore a waistcoat and jacket, slacks and held a walking cane. He walked every day and often took a shortcut down the alley behind the McMurphy. Lately, he'd started to carry little dog treats in his pocket. Mal was wise to this and when she spotted him, she would stand on her back legs and turn circles.

"Hi Mr. Beecher," I said. "I think you have Mal convinced you are made of dog treats."

He chuckled and took one out of his pocket. "Sit and give us a shake."

Mal sat and held out her paw.

Mr. Beecher shook her paw and then gave her the treat and patted her on the head. "She's a good girl and deserves all the treats she wants."

"That's easy for you to say," I said. "You don't have to worry she'll get fat. Then I'll have to buy diet food and limit her meals."

He chuckled. "That dog is not likely to get fat any time soon. Are you girl? You look out for your girlie figure, don't you?" He patted her on the head again and sneaked her a second treat.

I rolled my eyes. "Well, one thing's for certain. Mal will never go hungry."

"That's a good thing in my book," Mr. Beecher said. "You have a nice evening, now."

"Good night," I said and turned to the McMurphy. After my first month living at the hotel,

I'd replaced the metal fire escape ladder that had serviced the back door to my apartment. We climbed the real stairway, my mind on Trent and the serious tone of his voice. He meant business when it came to my asking questions. It sort of got my back up. Just because we were dating and I was half in love with him didn't mean he could tell me what to do and expect me to follow like a dog or a small child. I'd have to have a talk with him next time we were alone together.

I hit the top of the stairs and came to a screeching halt. I grabbed Mal a second before she stepped into an open bear trap. The metal was rusted, but the teeth looked sharp and ready. The springs were loaded, ready for some unsuspecting soul to step inside. It was baited with a piece of raw meat.

My heart raced as I held Mal to my chest and stared at the trap. A note was taped to the back door of my apartment. *Watch where you're stepping. You or someone you love just might get hurt.*

I pulled my phone out of my pocket and dialed Rex.

"Rex Manning," he barked into the phone.

"Rex, it's Allie."

"Allie, I'm not going to talk about the investigation," he warned.

"I know. It's not that. I need you to come around to the back of the McMurphy. Someone has placed an open bear trap near my door. A threatening note is taped to the door."

"Don't touch anything. I'll be right there."

I hung up the phone and to my horror saw Caramella jump up on the deck rail between me and the bear trap. "Oh, lord," I whispered, trying not to scare the cat into jumping down. "Stay right there, Mella, Mella. Good kitty."

Terrified, I watched as she noticed the raw meat in the center of the trap. "Mella," I said with a warning tone in my voice.

Mal started to whimper at my distress. The cat eyed me as if I was of little interest to her. Her tail twitched behind her. It was a sure sign that she was thinking about how juicy that piece of meat looked and how annoying I was to call her away from it.

I held my breath and took a careful step toward her. She arched her back as if to leap. I stopped in my tracks. "No, Mella," I said soft and low. "Don't do it."

The razor sharp prongs on the bear trap seemed to glisten ominously. I wasn't sure what to do next. I tried to keep one eye on Mella as I dialed Jenn's phone.

"Hey, Allie. What's up?"

I felt a bit of relief at the sound of her voice. "Jenn, where are you? Are you at the McMurphy?"

"Sure. I'm in the office. Why?" Jenn said. "You sound worried."

"How fast can you get around the building and up to the deck?"

"I can go out your door in less than two minutes."

I heard her get up and shouted, "No!" I flinched when I saw Mella startle.

She froze, but her tail was twitching.

I wasn't sure what she would do. I said into the phone to Jenn, "I need you to go around the building and up the steps as quickly as you can. Don't come out the apartment door."

"Okay," Jenn said. "Okay, I'm headed down. I'll be there in a few. Do you need me to stay on the phone?"

"I've got a situation where I may need to drop Mal to get Mella out of danger," I said.

"Let Mal go," Jenn said. "I'm outside. Tell Mal to find me."

That was smart. "Got it." Keeping my gaze on Mella, who looked like she might jump into the trap at any second, I put Mal down facing the steps. "Mal, go get Jenn. Go, Mal. Get Jenn."

Mal seemed to understand and rushed down the stairs. I stood slowly and inched around the trap toward Mella. All I could do was hope that Mal went straight to Jenn. She was smart. I was counting on it.

"Here, kitty, kitty," I said, drumming my fingers on the top of the deck rail. My hope was to distract Mella from the raw meat in the center of the trap. Mella turned her gaze to my fingers and stayed put. "Mella, want a kitty treat?"

She began to wash her front paw. I breathed a bit. If she was acting indifferent, at least she wasn't staring into the jaws of death with interest.

"Holy crap, what is that?" Jenn's voice came from behind me.

I kept my gaze on Mella. "It's a bear trap."

"Right," Jenn said.

"Mella keeps eyeing the meat in the center. How do I get her and keep her safe?" I asked Jenn because she had more experience with cats than I did.

"Here," she said and handed me Mal. "Take Mal and let me get Mella."

I took Mal. "Okay."

"Mella, no!" Jenn rushed forward.

I held Mal close to my chest and closed my eyes waiting for the nasty sound of the trap going off.

Silence.

Then Jenn patted me on the shoulder.

I opened my eyes to see that she had Mella safely in her arms. I let out a long breath. "Oh, thank goodness. How did you get her?"

Jenn seemed out of breath. "She jumped and I caught her. What the heck? Who put that there?"

"I don't know. I called Rex. He's on his way."

"He's here," Jenn said as she looked over the railing. "Let me take the pets."

I put Mal down because she was still wearing her leash. Jenn went down the steps holding Mella in her arms and Mal's leash in her hand. Rex came up and the two met at the first floor landing.

They said something to each other, but I couldn't tell what. I'd try to remember to ask Jenn later. Rex wore his neat police uniform and hat. He came up the rest of the way and studied my face. "Jenn said you almost lost your cat."

"Hi Rex." I moved aside. "Someone left this at my door." I pointed toward the open bear trap.

He blew out a breath when he spotted it. "Is that the note?" He nodded toward the door.

"Yes. My first thought was getting Mal before

she could step into the trap. She tends to run up the stairs before me. Then I saw Mella hop up on the railing and I nearly had a heart attack when she spotted the meat in the center."

"I see." He laid down a pencil to give the trap size comparisons, then pulled out his cell phone and began to take pictures from all angles. The trap was quite large—large enough to hurt a human very badly. Large enough to kill a cat or a small dog.

"Whoever did this should be shot," I said.

"When we find who did this—he glanced at me from where he squatted beside the trap—they will be prosecuted to the fullest extent of the law."

"Thank you," I said and hugged my waist.

He pulled his bully stick out of his waistband and stood. "Stand back!"

I went down two steps off the deck.

He gave the lever a good hard smack and the trap snapped closed with a solid crunching sound of metal against metal. He pulled a plastic evidence bag out of the pocket on his gun belt. Then he took a cloth handkerchief out and carefully picked up the bear trap and slid it into the evidence bag. He read the note, snapped photos of it attached to my back door, then carefully pulled it off and placed it in a second evidence bag. "All right. It's words cut from magazines and pasted on. I'm sure the uneven typeface was meant to scare you."

I grimaced. "I think the bear trap teeth did that."

"Which way did you come up?"

"We came up from Market Street."

"Did you see anyone in the alleyway?"

"Mr. Beecher, but I highly doubt he did something this cruel. He loves Mal. He even carries treats every day . . . . in case he runs into her."

Rex nodded and wrote down what I said. "I'm sure he's not the culprit, but he might have seen something." He stopped and looked me dead in the eye. "What have you been investigating, Allie?"

"What do you mean?" I put my hands on my hips. "You think this is my fault?"

"I think someone isn't happy with the questions you've been asking."

"Maybe because I'm close to proving Paige Jessop's innocence and the real killer is not happy about it."

"Or one of the Jessops wants us to think that." He pushed his hat up with the end of his pencil.

"They would not harm me or my pets," I said with indignation. "I am appalled you would even suggest such a thing."

"You need to stop investigating, Allie," he said with soft authority. "You have to trust me to do my job."

"But there is no way Paige killed Carin. I simply won't believe it. Besides, I can't find a single motive for her to do it or a single person who can put her at the crime scene. Any evidence you have is purely circumstantial."

"Oh, so you think you know what evidence I have?"

"Everyone knows what evidence you have," I retorted. "This is a small island. All you have to do is ask the senior citizens and they'll tell you every time the wind changes direction. They are great sleuths."

"You don't know what my evidence is, Allie, and it's driving you nuts." He lifted an eyebrow at me.

Challenged, I put my hands on my hips. "Carin was murdered. She was dead before she hit the water, which is why I couldn't pump any water from her lungs. She was killed by a blow to the back of her skull with a blunt object. An oar from a lifeboat is the murder weapon. The lab found traces of blood and Carin's hair on it. That oar came from the Jessops' yacht, the *Scoundrel*. You arrested Paige because of a rumored confrontation she had with Carin that morning. But you see, Paige was out in the straits with a party of twenty all night. That's why the *Scoundrel* wasn't docked the morning I pulled Carin from the marina."

"That's a lot of information for a woman who isn't investigating," he said quietly. "You don't think perhaps all that digging is what caused someone to try to harm you or your pets?" He raised the evidence bag.

"If it is, then it's because I'm closing in on the real killer," I said.

"And who is that killer, Allie?" he asked quietly.

I wanted to stomp my foot, but held myself back. "I don't know. I haven't found a motive for anyone to kill Carin."

"Someone thinks you have. Maybe I should take you down to the station and debrief you."

"There's nothing to debrief. I'm the one threatened here. Don't you think you need to figure out who wants to harm me?"

Rex nodded, "I do. I can do that by finding out who you've talked to and what they've said. Come on. Let's go to my office."

"Do I need a lawyer?" I asked.

"I don't know," he replied grimly. "Do you?"

"I don't know what you'd charge me for," I said stubbornly.

"How about obstruction of justice? I can start there. We'll see what else pops up."

"Now you're just being mean," I said and started down the stairs.

"I warned you not to get involved, Allie."

"I was involved from the moment Mal spotted Carin floating in the marina," I said. "You should have let me help."

"It wasn't my call," he said grimly and guided me down the alley toward the police station.

"Then whose was it?"

"Trent Jessop."

## Hot Fudge Banana Split Trifle

### Ingredients

Brownie mix including eggs, oil, and water amounts on the box.

1 large package instant vanilla pudding and milk per the pudding box.

Whipped topping, split into 2 cups and 1 cup

Hot fudge topping

Pineapple topping

Caramel sauce

Four bananas, split then quartered.

Cherry pie filling

**Directions**

Make brownies and instant pudding per the instructions on the boxes. Once the pudding is set fold in 2 cups of whipped topping until light and smooth.

In a large glass trifle bowl or large glass bowl, crumble half of the brownies.

Over the crumbled brownies, pour half of the caramel sauce and half of the pudding mixture. Add half of the bananas in layers. Layer on hot fudge ¼-inch thick, pineapple topping, and half of the cherry filling.

Crumble the rest of the brownies into the bowl and repeat all layers. Use remaining cup of whipped topping on top.

Garnish with 2 tablespoons cherry filling and a drizzle of hot fudge sauce.

Chill 6 hours or overnight. Enjoy!

# Chapter 17

"Trent, you have to talk to me now," I said into the cell phone, letting his voice message record me. "If you don't call me back tonight, I'm going to consider that you are breaking up with me. Is that what you want?" I paused to see if he was listening, but he didn't pick up. "Fine. It's nine PM. You have two hours to call me or come to my door and talk to me." I paused again and knew I couldn't remain tough. "Trent, seriously, I don't want to break up with you. I'm falling in love with you, but I can't love a man who doesn't trust me. The least you can do is break up to my face. It's what a real man would do." I hit END before I stooped to begging and threw my cell phone across the room. It skidded on the floor and bumped up against the wall. Mella thought it was great fun and pounced on it, batting it around like a toy.

I turned my back on the phone and the living room. Tears sprang to my eyes. I had spent three hours at the police station telling Rex exactly who I'd talked to and what they'd said. In exchange, I learned nothing more about his case against Paige. It was infuriating. He claimed he needed to know everything so he could figure out who set the trap. I wasn't sure that was even related to my investigation.

For all I knew, it could have been some neighbor out to get me. There were a few who weren't all that happy to see me thrive during my first season. The innkeeper behind me was the perfect example. I told Rex that. He made a note and told me to let the police do their job.

I hated being patted on the head and told to go make fudge. Not that that wasn't what I was best at, but still. I wasn't half bad at figuring out who the heck killed someone. How could I let whoever had set that bear trap bully me into stopping?

Unfortunately, Rex threatened me with jail time for obstruction if I continued to ask questions about Carin. That didn't mean I couldn't ask about who might have left that trap on my doorstep. Yes, Mr. Beecher would be the first person I talked to about it. Someone had to know something. Like who owned bear traps? Who sold bear traps? And who bought hamburger to bait the trap?

"What was that noise?" Jenn came out of the bathroom with her hair in a towel and her pajamas on.

"I threw my phone," I said with a childish pout. "I left a message for Trent."

"Again? How long has it been since he talked to you?"

"He called today, but all he did was tell me to butt out. Then he hung up on me. I left him a voice message that said if he didn't talk to me in the next two hours, I would have to consider that a breakup."

"Ouch," Jenn said. "Isn't that a little harsh?"

"He doesn't even know about the bear trap that threatened me and my babies," I said. "What kind of boyfriend misses that kind of information?"

"A bad one," Jenn said with a sigh. "I guess you were right. He does need to talk to you. Do you think he's breaking up with you?"

"I hope not." I plopped down on my living room chair. "I think I'm falling in love with him."

"What if he's off the island or doing something else and won't get the message in time?" Jenn asked. "Will you really break up with him?"

"How can I date someone who doesn't trust me when important things are going on in his life? I'm going to have to break up with him. It's the only right thing to do."

Jenn shook her head. "I don't know how you can let all that gorgeous man go. You're my friend so if you break up with him, I'll support you."

"I'd certainly hope so," I said.

The phone rang.

I raced across the room and snagged it out from under the sofa where the cat had batted it. "Hello? Trent?"

"Allie, it's Frances."

"Oh, hi Frances. I'm sorry I missed you tonight. Rex kept me a long time at the station. Did everything go well today?"

"Everything is fine. I was calling to see how you were. I heard from Jenn that someone left a baited bear trap at your doorstep. Are you locking your doors? I want you to be safe."

"The doors are locked," I said, glancing over to

see that I did indeed turn the deadbolt on the back door. "I can't believe anyone would do that. Have you heard any rumors about it?"

"There is some speculation," Frances said, "but nothing definitive. Bear traps aren't sold on the island. Whoever had it brought it in."

"Or they might have found one brought in years and years ago," I said. "It looked kind of old, but the teeth on it were shiny like they were recently filed."

"I still can't believe anyone would put you and your pets in danger like that," Frances said. "They have to be mad."

"I think I'm closing in on Carin's true killer or someone is worried that I am. The note on the door said to be careful where I was stepping. I don't think they meant where I put my feet. Rex thinks it wasn't meant to hurt my pets. He said a bear trap is overkill if you want to get rid of a cat or dog."

"I agree," Frances said. "It was a statement. Do we need to huddle as a group and go over the clues you've uncovered?"

"That might be a good idea," I said thoughtfully. "How about tomorrow night?"

"Sounds good. I'll let Douglas know."

"Please be careful, as well," I said. "A threat to me is a threat to all my friends."

"We'll be careful," Frances said. "Try to sleep tonight."

"I will. Thanks!" I hit OFF on the phone.

"Not Trent?" Jenn said when I put the phone down on the counter.

"No, it was Frances."

"What are you going to do if he doesn't call?"

My heart skipped a beat. "I don't know. I hate to give ultimatums for that reason. I don't want to break up with him, but if he can't include me in his life, especially during hard times, then why am I dating him?"

"You do have to be strong," Jenn said. "You have a lot going for you, Allie. You deserve a guy who is there for you and lets you be there for him."

"I know." I sat down on my couch and put my head in my hands. "Why can't things be easy?"

Jenn chuckled. "You know the old saying. *Nothing worth having is ever easy.*"

I stuck my tongue out at her. "Just because it's true does not mean I want to hear it." The phone rang and I jumped up and grabbed it. A glance at the number told me it was Trent. I headed toward my bedroom. "Hello?"

"Allie, it's Trent."

"Really? I thought maybe you were dead. What other reason would you have for not doing anything more than bark orders at me?"

"I don't bark orders."

"I think I'll just agree to disagree on that point," I said and closed my bedroom door. I climbed up on my bed and sat cross-legged. "More importantly, why have you shut me out? It hurts me to think you can't share the hard part of your life with me."

"Allie."

I could picture him running his hand through his hair like he does whenever he is finding me difficult. Let's face it: relationships were difficult. "Trent."

"We were advised by our lawyers to not talk to anyone about what's going on," he said.

"That's a sorry excuse. You could have called me to tell me how you were feeling. You could have called to see how I was feeling."

"I've been a little overwhelmed."

I was at once frustrated, sad, and oddly understanding. "I know you are a busy man."

"Allie, stop. You are right. You are important to me and I should be sharing my day with you no matter what has happened. I'm sorry."

I chewed on my bottom lip. Apologies were tricky. Was he saying it just to get me off his back or did he really mean it?

"Allie," he spoke into the silence. "I really mean it. I don't blame you if you are mad at me and want to break up. I've been out of line not including you."

"I don't want to break up. I need to know that you won't shut me out of your life."

"I won't. I mean it, Allie. I know you won't endanger the investigation or put Paige at risk. It was stupid of me to allow my mother and the lawyers to pressure me into excluding you."

"Yes, it was," I said. "And I accept your apology. How's Paige doing?"

"She's taking this hard. It's difficult for her to believe anyone would think her capable of murder."

"Can you tell me anything about the case they have against her?"

"What do you know?"

"I know bits and pieces," I said. "Although someone seems to think I know enough to be a danger."

"Why? What happened?" His voice turned stern.

"So, now you want to know what's going on with me."

"Allie . . ."

"Fine. Someone left a baited bear trap open at my back door."

"What?"

"A steel metal trap that grabs a bear's paw and doesn't let go."

"I know what a bear trap is. I thought they were illegal."

"They aren't sold on the island," I said. "We think it was an old one out of someone's home."

"Who is we?"

"Jenn and me. I called Rex and he came and took it away. He took me to the office and questioned me for hours. Then he wrote up a report and said he'd find whoever put the trap there. Trent, it could have killed Mal or Mella. It could have seriously hurt me or anyone who might have stepped out of my apartment without looking first."

"That's outrageous."

"I know. I agree."

"When did it happen?"

"Late this afternoon. Rex seems to think it's linked to my questioning people about Carin and her death."

"Allie," Trent said grimly, "you have to let this investigation go. I can't lose both you and Paige."

"I'm not going anywhere. I'm trying to help Paige. I want to help you, Trent. It's clear your sister is being framed. I want to know who would do that and why."

"Listen, Allie. I know you love me. Paige knows you are a good friend, but you shouldn't risk your life or the lives of the ones you love to help us. We have a lot of resources, Allie. A lot of people are helping us."

I frowned. "You shut me out. What else was I supposed to do? Not help? Go about my day as if I wasn't involved in this? *I* found Carin. *I* dragged her from the water. I feel some responsibility. Besides, I don't want to be the one who got your sister into this mess."

"You aren't the one," Trent said. "We know it. My entire family knows you aren't behind this frame up. Please, Allie, stop what you're doing. I need you to take care of yourself. Can you do that for me?"

"But I might know something that can help Paige."

"I tell you what," he said. "I'll send our investigator over to talk with you and get the details you know. That way you've helped, but you have to promise me you'll stop investigating. I need to know you're safe."

"Fine," I said, saddened. "I'll stop."

"Thank you." The relief was clear in his voice. "Other than that, how are you? I miss you. I miss our dinners together."

"I'm fine." I sighed. "Oh, Mr. Devaney asked Jenn

and me to come up with a great way for him to propose to Frances. Isn't that sweet?"

"That is sweet," Trent said. "Those two deserve all the happiness in the world."

"I know."

"Do you and Jenn have a plan?"

"We're getting there." That reminded me. I needed to talk to Jenn about the ideas we'd come up with and what I'd learned about Frances. I said into the phone to Trent, "When will I see you again?"

"I'm sorry," he said again. "Business is always crazy on yacht race weekend. Are you free for dinner tomorrow?"

"Sure. I'd love to see you."

"I'll pick you up at eight. We can have a star-filled picnic."

"Sounds nice," I said with a smile. "Thanks for calling me."

"Thanks for accepting my apology," he said. "I know you want to know before our date what is going on with Paige. Can I stop by with the investigator around lunch?"

"Sounds perfect."

"Good. Good night, Allie. I love you."

My heart skipped a beat at his words. "I love you, too. I'll see you tomorrow." I hung up the phone and sat for a moment absorbing what just happened. Trent had said he loved me and I'd had the presence of mind to tell him I loved him, too. It was a big step. I was glad that he finally understood how hurtful it was to not include me in the investigation. Finally, things started to feel right again.

All I had to do was figure out who really killed Carin before Rex went any farther with Paige. Why did figuring out who killed Carin seem so impossible? Somehow, somewhere I had overlooked a clue.

# Chapter 18

"We've got some trouble," Jenn said to me the next morning.

I had just come up to the office to take a break from fudge making to make myself presentable for Trent and his investigator who were coming by for an eleven AM lunch.

"What's up?" I asked as I hung my chef's coat up on the coat tree by the office door.

"I just got off the phone with the yacht club." Jenn put her elbows on the top of her desk and her chin in her hands. She watched me as I pulled the office chair away from my desk and sat down. Our desks faced each other in the center of the room so that when we worked together we saw eye to eye.

"And?"

"The yacht club committee has decided it's best if we don't continue on the committee."

"What?"

"They don't like the bad publicity," she said.

"But we didn't do anything."

"They don't like the fact that you fished a body out of the bay and worse that the Jessops are basically withdrawing from us. No one has seen you with Trent since the incident."

"You would think that would be a good thing, since Paige is accused of Carin's murder."

"No, it's bad," Jenn said. "Apparently the Jessops have a lot of clout at the club. A rumor is going around that you are the one who is the eyewitness placing Paige at the scene."

"But that's ridiculous," I said. "In an hour, Trent is coming over with his investigator to let me know what is going on . . . to see if I can help them build Paige's defense."

"Well, the ladies at the club didn't know that," Jenn said. "I tried to tell them you two made up on the phone last night, but they didn't believe me."

"What about the chocolate centerpieces for to-morrow night's end of race gala?"

"Cancelled," Jenn said.

"What do you mean *cancelled*? The pieces are almost all done. Sandy has been working a week on them. Plus the pieces at the opening ceremonies were well-received. Sandy has three new clients because of the centerpieces and favors we had that night. And they saw me with Trent that night, which was after I dragged Carin from the water."

"Yes, well that was before Paige was arrested," Jenn said. "I couldn't argue them into letting us stay and taking the centerpieces. They told me we could keep the fifty percent down money."

"It's good-bye and good riddance?"

"Seems that way," Jenn said.

"That's just wrong." I wanted to stomp around but instead, drummed my fingers on the desktop. "Have you told Sandy?"

"I thought you should . . . since you're her boss."

"It's going to devastate her."

"You can still sell the pieces," Jenn suggested. "Put them in the shop window. People will pay good money for them."

I frowned. "Tourists, you mean."

"Yes, tourists, not islanders . . . but that's not altogether bad. It's the tourists who buy most of your fudge."

"Yes," I said with a sigh. "That's true. Is it only the yacht club?" I held my breath.

Jenn shook her head and frowned. "No. The Festival of Horse committee just called and asked us to step down from that as well."

"But we were going to make those great hollow horses. Sandy's been working on the molds."

"They claim that we've been hogging the social calendar this year and they want to bring in a more diverse group of volunteers."

"That's silly," I said. "Seriously. Some of the same people have been on these committees for years."

"Yes, but they are longtime islanders and they have a lot of money," Jenn said. "We are just now breaking into the island society. I'm surprised we've made the headway we have in the few short months since I've been here."

"Why would you turn down volunteers?" I asked, shaking my head. "Crazy."

"Well, if you're seeing Trent today, maybe that

will help squash the rumors and get us back on track."

"One can certainly hope." My desk phone rang and I picked it up. "McMurphy Hotel and Fudge Shop, this is Allie. How can I help you?"

"Hey Allie, it's Rex."

"Rex"—I tilted my head in curiosity—"why didn't you call my cell phone?"

"I'm at my desk doing paperwork and don't have your cell phone programmed. I was looking over my report on the bear trap incident and I wondered if you had any more insight into who might have done that and why."

"Oh, no, I still don't know." I sat back in my chair. It creaked and for a brief second I was reminded of Papa Liam sitting in this chair doing the same thing. It was a brief memory that warmed my heart and left me with a moment of grief over his passing.

"No other notes were found?" Rex said, breaking into my emotion. "No message left on any of the phones?"

"Well, I haven't talked to Frances in depth about it, but I don't think so. I'm sure if she had had any type of threatening message she would have told me."

"All right," he said. "Keep me updated should anything else happen."

"I will. Any clue as to where the trap came from?"

"I've sent it to the lab, but it's low on the list of things to go over. It might be a month or two before we find out anything."

"Huh," I said.

"It's not like a rape kit or a dead body," he said. "Those things take priority. This is more of a threat than an actual crime."

"So it would have been a bigger priority if someone had been hurt," I surmised.

"I'm afraid that's true, Allie," Rex said.

I could hear him run his hand over his face.

"What I can do besides assign it a case number and send the evidence to the lab is ask that we patrol your alley twice a day. Once in the evening and once in the morning."

"Okay. I guess that will have to do."

"Be careful, Allie. It's the best I can do right now."

"I understand. Thanks, Rex." I hung up and Jenn looked at me. "There's nothing he can do about the trap."

"What?"

"Since no one was hurt and there's no further evidence, he's at a loss," I said. "All he can do is send what he has to the lab where it will take a low priority."

"Because no crime was committed," Jenn deduced.

"Crazy, right? Anyway, he said to be careful and report anything else that comes up as suspicious or threatening."

"That's comforting." Jenn's tone was sarcastic.

"He's going to see that they patrol our alley twice a day. In the meantime, I'm going to suggest to everyone that we be very careful using the back doors. It means going out of our way, but it will be worth it if it keeps us safe."

"I say this is proof you are closing in on the killer." Jenn picked up a pen and absently tapped the end on the desk.

I shrugged. "Maybe. I can't figure out who it is or what the motive is." I pursed my lips. "The killer may think that someone I spoke to already told me everything and I'm close to putting it all together."

"Or maybe they just don't like your line of questioning," Jenn said.

"No one has liked my line of questioning," I said. "Even me."

Jenn laughed.

"Seriously, I have no clue who the killer is. I feel like I'm just going around in circles." I sighed. "Maybe I'll find out more in a few minutes when Trent and his investigator come by." I glanced at my watch. "They should be here any minute. I'm going to serve them coffee and snacks in the apartment. Can you keep things running here?"

"Sure," Jenn said. "I'm helping Frances turn over the rooms on the third floor. I'll tell Sandy the bad news about the yacht club and the horse celebration committee. She'll watch the fudge shop. Do you want her to do the twelve-thirty demo?"

"Yes. I don't know how long I'll be meeting with Trent." I stood and gathered up two pens and a legal pad of paper.

"Promise you'll tell me everything," Jenn said.

"I promise," I replied and left the office. I was so lucky to have Jenn as my second in command this season. It didn't hurt that Frances was practically on autopilot when it came to maintaining the hotel part of the McMurphy and I could trust Sandy to take good care of the fudge shop. It left me time to rest and to look at my business investment returns and strategy for next year.

I opened the apartment door and Mella met me. She wound her way around my legs and meowed for attention. I reached down and gave her long strokes from head to the end of her tail then hurried to the kitchen where I washed my hands, pulled out a tray, and started heating water in the teapot. I set out a plate of cookies and a small plate of fudge. Teas and coffee finished the tray and I placed it on the coffee table between the couch and the chairs. Mella draped herself across the window sill hogging the light.

There was a knock at the door.

I opened it to have Mal come bounding in as if she'd brought me the best present ever. And she did. Trent stood there in all his handsome glory— over six foot tall with dark hair cut in an expensive style. His square jaw, dark eyes, and patrician nose gave him the look of good breeding and centuries of wealth.

"Hi." That was usually all I could say whenever I saw him. He took my breath away and my brain basically fell to my feet.

"Hi, sweetheart," he said, reaching down to hug me and give me a good solid kiss on the lips.

I put my hands around his neck and enjoyed the taste of him, the weight and feel of his warmth against me.

Someone cleared their throat and Trent pulled away from me. Mal jumped up on me looking for attention as mine was drawn to a short man with a round jaw, sparse brown hair, brown eyes, and an equally drab brown suit.

"Right," Trent said. "Allie, this is Tom Hartman. Tom, Allie McMurphy."

"A pleasure to meet you," I said and shook his hand. "Won't you come in? I have tea, coffee, and snacks." I picked Mal up to keep her from jumping on me. She settled her head under my chin like a little baby.

"Sure," Tom said.

I held the door open for the two men as they entered the apartment. Trent always filled the room with his presence. Tom seemed smaller in comparison, but he was taller than me so he might have been five foot ten in height and medium build. If we were on the street or in a crowded restaurant, I wouldn't even notice him. He was that average. I bet that worked in his favor as an investigator.

"Please, have a seat." I waved toward my two wingback chairs and the couch.

Tom took one of the chairs. Trent sat on the couch. He wore black jeans, deck shoes with no socks, and a crisp white striped dress shirt with the collar open. Even with no tie, he somehow still managed to look dressed to kill.

I went to the counter and took out a dog teat. I set Mal down and ran her through her tricks before I gave it to her. Then I poured out three tiny cat treats for Mella. She had gotten up from her spot and bounced up on the bar to see if there might be something of interest in it for her.

"Thank you for coming," I said as I washed my

hands again, dried them carefully, and then took a seat beside Trent on the couch.

"I understand you've been asking some questions about the Moore case," Tom said and got out a small notebook and pen. "Do you mind going over what you've been thinking?"

I took Trent's hand. "No, not at all, as long as you let me in on what the police have in their case. I simply can't imagine what they have against Paige that isn't circumstantial at best."

"Why do you say that?" Tom asked.

"I've talked to everyone I know who might have known something about where Paige was that night. That led me to understand that she didn't have any motive. I looked for who might have motive and I followed through Carin's last day. There doesn't seem to be anyone with motive to kill her. I know the police have the murder weapon, but they can't put it in Paige's hands, can they?"

"They have a credible witness," Trent said.

"Who?"

"Harold Jones," Tom said. "Apparently Mr. Jones is an avid stargazer. He was out at three AM when he saw two women on the pier who appeared to be arguing."

"I don't understand," I said. "Is he saying he could identify one of the women as Paige?"

"Yes," Trent said. "He claims that Paige stepped into a circle of light and he saw her clearly."

"If he saw her hit Carin with the oar, why didn't he report it right away?" I asked.

"He claims that a meteor caught his attention

and when he looked back at the dock both women were gone," Tom said.

"Rex's case is built on the oar and this man's claim that he saw Paige arguing on the dock that night?" I asked.

"Yes," Trent said. "Apparently the DA thinks that, along with the public knowledge that there was no love lost between Paige and Carin, it is enough to convict."

"It's ridiculous," I said. "I learned that Paige and Carin were actually getting along."

"Yes, that's what Paige contends," Tom said. "I need someone who will collaborate that. Can you give me a name?"

"Yes, try Janet Biggs." I turned to Trent. "How does the prosecution explain Paige getting from the *Scoundrel,* which was out on the lake, to the dock and back?"

"That's where the oar comes in," Trent said. "They claim she had time to take a lifeboat, row ashore, argue with Carin, kill her, and row back."

"I know Paige is athletic, but it was dark and the waves get pretty high in the straits. I've seen the ferries get yanked about."

"The weather said it was calm that night," Tom said. "It was the first thing I checked."

"And if it hadn't been calm?" I asked.

"The DA thinks Paige may have had an accomplice," Trent said. "Witnesses say they last saw her in a cocktail dress and heels."

"I've got a couple who claim to have seen her sitting on the deck of the *Scoundrel* in that outfit at four AM. She supposedly got up and told them good night." He flipped through his notebook. "That was Tori Scott and her boyfriend Richard Allen. They had decided to take a walk on the deck before they retired that night."

"Paige was alone?" I asked.

"Yes." He reread his notes. "They said she seemed contemplative but okay. They couldn't imagine she would look like that hours after murdering someone."

"That's good, right?" I said.

"Yes, that's good." Trent patted my knee. "It would have been better if Reggie hadn't passed out on her that night."

I nodded. "I think he was drugged. I talked to him and he said he couldn't believe that he'd passed out after two drinks. I told him he should get tested to see if there was any drug left in his urine or blood. Sometimes there's residue."

"Who would drug him and why?" Trent asked, seemingly surprised by the idea.

"My theory is that whoever killed Carin did not do it on the spur of the moment. I think they planned it out carefully. I think they drugged Reggie and most of the people on the *Scoundrel.* I think they took the oar ahead of time and then put it back on the *Scoundrel* once the boat docked."

"That's stretching things a bit, don't you think?" Tom said with a frown. "How do you drug a boatful of people and not Paige? Also, it's clear that Tori Scott and Richard Allen were not drugged as they are very aware of their entire night."

I frowned. "I suppose that does seem odd."

"You're really reaching," Tom said. "If the killer

had an accomplice on the *Scoundrel* that night, why would they take the chance of not drugging everyone? What if Tori and Richard went on the deck earlier and were able to alibi Paige?"

"Yes," I said wryly. "I can see the flaw in that idea. They are sure they were awake and aware the entire night?"

"They were and so was the crew," Tom said. "The captain was aboard that night along with two servers and a bartender."

"Did the crew see anyone leave the boat?" I asked. "If Paige had taken a lifeboat and gone to the pier, someone would have seen it, right? I mean she would have had to untie it and lower it to the water. Then somehow tie it back to the boat upon return. Not to mention the time it would take for her to row here and back."

"She would have had to have an accomplice," Trent muttered.

"Exactly," I said. "If the killer didn't have an accomplice aboard, Paige wouldn't have had an accomplice either."

"She has a point," Tom said and made a note. "We need to find out if the crew noticed the missing lifeboat or if they noticed a lifeboat that was wet or untied and had obvious signs of use that night."

"That makes sense," Trent said. "Go back and interview the crew. See if anyone noticed anything out of order with the lifeboats."

"Got it." Tom got up. "Thank you, Miss McMurphy. Keep in touch."

"I will." I stood. "Shall I walk you out?"

Tom shook his head. "No. I can show myself out."

"Go out the front," I said when he headed toward the back door. "I've been threatened from the alley and I don't want anyone to get hurt."

He frowned. "What kind of threats?"

"Someone left an open baited bear trap at my back door. There was a note, suggesting I watch my step. The message was pretty clear."

"Hmm." He made a note then slipped his notebook in his breast pocket. "A threat like that is tough to pull off without someone seeing something."

"If you find someone," I said, "let me know. So far, no one has a clue how that trap got there or why."

Later that afternoon Jenn and I met at the coffee shop on the marina. I ordered tea and Jenn ordered iced coffee along with a plate of scones. The clerk gave us a number and we sat out on the tiny deck to catch the lake breeze and watch the yachts move in and out of the marina.

Our plan was to talk about Douglas's proposal to Frances, but being so close to the spot where I first saw Carin made me more uncomfortable than I'd thought. I watched the boats to see what size had lifeboats on the sides and what size craft must have had inflatables.

"Well, look who's here," Gail Hall said as she brought us our coffee order. She placed the tea and iced coffee down on the table along with our plate of scones, then picked up the cardboard number.

"Hi Gail," I said. "How are you?"

"I'm doing well. How about you? How are you holding up through all the hoopla?"

"I'm hanging in there. How's the painting going?" I noticed that her hands were free of black paint.

"The painting?"

"The dresser you were refinishing," I reminded her.

She laughed. "Oh, yes. As I said, it doesn't look as good as what they show you on television. I guess I'm not a good do-it-yourselfer, but I keep trying. I was thinking of stenciling a chair rail around the coffee shop next. What do you think?"

"Like vines?" Jenn asked.

"I think flowers are more Victorian," she said. "Maybe cabbage roses?"

"That would be pretty," I said.

"Pretty ambitious"—she laughed again—"considering how bad the dresser turned out." She winked at me. "You girls have a nice visit and enjoy your drinks."

"We will," I said and picked up my tea.

Jenn picked up her coffee.

"Here's to us," I said. "The best people we know."

"I'll drink to that." Jenn touched her glass to mine, then we sipped. "You talked to Frances's best friend, right? How was that?"

"Maggs is great," I said and drew my gaze to Jenn. She wore her hair down and it floated around her shoulders like a thick black veil, smooth and shiny in the afternoon sun. Her skin was tan and her body toned. She wore a white sundress with tiny flowers sprinkled on it and sandals. I still had on my McMurphy pink and white polo and black slacks. My hair was pulled back in the perpetual ponytail of a candy maker. I was lucky enough to remember to take off the hairnet before I left the hotel.

"So? What does she suggest for romance for Frances?"

"She thought the McMurphy would be great since they met there and work together there," I said.

Jenn grinned. "Of course it would be perfect! But we need two other ideas so that we can give Mr. Devaney choices."

"Well, Maggs suggested a moonlight carriage ride around the island and a candlelight picnic at Lover's Point."

"Oh, I like that, too!" Jenn's eyes lit up.

"Finally, she suggested the most obvious—that he rent the sunporch at the Grand Hotel and hire a tiny three-piece orchestra so they can dance and have a candlelight dinner for two."

Jenn sighed and put her chin on her hand. "All great ideas. I hope you know I'm going to use them should I ever get asked to plan an engagement again."

"Great," I said. "The thing to do now is to come up with menus and price each one so that he can see the entire picture. I know that when it comes to love, money is no object, but if we are going to be professionals . . ."

"I'll work up quotes," Jenn said.

"You should be careful about it because people talk. If anyone suspects this is for Frances, they will tell her."

"Oh, right." Jenn bit the inside of her mouth. "I didn't think of that. Good thing you're on the case. I'll make up some couple that called from Chicago. I can even tell Frances about it and see what she thinks."

I winced. "I wouldn't go that far. If she asks, tell her what you're working on like you do with the other things you propose."

"I get it." Jenn winked. "We have a no ask, no tell policy."

I rolled my eyes. "Just be careful, okay? We really need this to be a surprise."

"Should we have Sandy make a chocolate sculpture? Like a wedding cake or something?"

"Maybe an open ring box?" I suggested.

"Or a horse and buggy with *Will you marry me?* on a banner on the back?"

"Oh, this is fun . . . but we don't want to give too much away, too soon," I said.

"I'll ask Sandy." Jenn made a note. "She's great at these things."

"Maybe a champagne bottle?" I suggested.

"Or roses?" Jenn was writing fast.

"Let's hope that Frances is amazed and delighted and says yes."

"Oh, she will," Jenn said. "I'm certain of that.

Even if covered in sweat and sawdust, he asked her in the middle of the alley."

"That reminds me," I said. "We need to get someone to video the moment."

"What? How did that remind you of video?"

"Because I'm having a camera installed on the back of the McMurphy and a motion sensor light," I said.

"That's a great idea," Jenn said.

"Trent suggested it. He called the guy he uses for the stables and the bars. They're coming over tomorrow to install."

"Did you let Mr. Devaney know?"

"I sure did. He was excited and called the installation guy to find out all the specs and to make sure he had any gear they might need."

"That's Mr. Devaney, always on top of things," Jenn said.

"I know. He's the best. Let's give him and Frances a night to remember. They deserve it."

# Chapter 19

"Do you know Mr. Harold Jones?" I asked Frances the next morning. My date with Trent the night before was wonderful and I felt energized knowing that my love life was back on track. It made me want to help Paige even more.

"Harold Jones?" Frances pursed her lips and tapped a pen against her cheek. She sat perched behind the receptionist desk. Her black and white polka dotted reading glasses coordinated with the polka dots showing on the underside of the rolled-up sleeves of her black and red striped shirt. Her long black skirt was belted by a thick red patent-leather belt.

I had teased her that she looked like an older version of Minnie Mouse. She'd retorted that she didn't have the right shoes.

"Yes, Harold Jones," I said. "I was told he likes to star gaze and uses a telescope that he can focus on the water so he can see the boats and the pier."

"Hmm. I don't know a Harold Jones. There's an Irene Jones who comes to the senior center now and again. Poor dear is in a wheelchair so she doesn't get out much. Perhaps Harold is her son."

"Funny. You know everyone on the island. Why don't you know if Irene Jones has a son named Harold?"

"Oh, she is the stepsister of Cassandra English. Cassandra owns a big Victorian with a view of the straits. Irene came to live on the island a few years ago when her husband died. I don't know much about it except that Cassandra was kind enough to take her in and see that she gets the nursing care she needs." Frances frowned. "Now, tell me why you need to know about Harold Jones."

"The Jessops' investigator told me that Harold Jones is Rex's eyewitness. Apparently he was out stargazing and heard a commotion on the pier around three AM. He turned his telescope on the pier and saw two women fighting. One stepped into the circle of light from the lamp and he recognized Paige Jessop."

"He's saying he saw Paige kill Carin and didn't do anything?"

"No, he says he was distracted by a meteor and when he turned his lens back on the pier both women were gone. He didn't think anything about it until I found Carin's dead body. Then he went to the police to tell them what he saw."

"He knows Paige well enough that he can identify her through a lens? How far away was he?" Frances asked.

"I didn't get those details." I cocked my head to the side. "You make a good investigator."

"It doesn't make sense that he knows Paige and

I don't know who he is . . . unless he somehow works for the Jessops."

"That could be." I tapped my chin. "The Jessops own quite a few businesses in town. You and I don't go to the bars very often. I suppose he could work at one of them."

"I have friends who might know." Frances frowned again. "What? Are you surprised that seniors go to bars? Simply because my friends are old does not mean they are dead."

I waved my hands. "I didn't mean any disrespect. Papa Liam was always up for a drink or two. Can I have Cassandra English's address? Mal and I will walk up there and see what the view is like."

"Sure." Frances wrote down the address and handed me the notepaper. "It's a nice walk from here. I'm sure Mal will enjoy it."

I put Mal's harness and leash on and headed toward the back of the building. She was scrambling toward the door, happy to go out. The back door was held open by a rock.

"Be careful coming out!" Mr. Devaney shouted.

Oh no, I forgot I had asked everyone to go out the front. I slowed Mal down and took a careful step out. A ladder leaned against the side of the building. Mr. Devaney was holding it as a gentleman in overalls ran wiring along the gutter. The security guys were installing the motion sensor lights and the camera.

"How's it going?"

"It's going," Mr. Devaney said. "These gentlemen have their system of installation down pretty well."

"Yes, ma'am," a second man said as he leaned

over the rail of the deck off my apartment. "You'll be set up and rolling by dinnertime. From now on, you'll have a video record of anyone who comes and goes through the alley here."

"Thanks," I said.

"Our pleasure," he replied and went back to work.

I leaned toward Mr. Devaney. "Who will have access to that information?" It struck me that it was my back door and there were a lot of gossips on the island. The last thing I needed was someone like Charlene knowing everyone who came and went from my home and at what times.

"They will set up a closed circuit digital stream," Mr. Devaney said softly, "and a password protected site where the files will be stored. Every time the motion sensor is activated, the camera will record. The recording will be stored on the site. You can set up the password and grant access to anyone you wish. I put the system literature on your desk. They'll show you how to set it up before they leave."

"Thanks." I headed down the alley with Mal. She had waited patiently during the exchange. It was a relief to know that only I would have access to the videos. I'm certain the company would have the ability to get into the site should anything happen to me, but I was glad to know that no one would be monitoring my private life. There was safety and then there was privacy. A girl needed both.

The English cottage was on the highest point of the island that looked out over Main Street and the marina. Off the main road, the driveway was long and windy. I let Mal go. She picked up her leash and ran up the drive. My baby knew her tricks.

"Mal," I called after her and raced up the drive. "Mal come here."

She stopped halfway, looked at me, then turned and hurried up onto the front porch of the magnificent Victorian cottage.

It looked like something right out of a period movie It had two turrets and multiple pointy roofs with colorful gingerbread accents. Attached to the house was a rain roof for carriages to stop under to unload passengers before circling around to the carriage house and back down the winding drive. Made of all white gypsum, the drive shone in the morning sun.

The house was painted blue and white with accents of red. Beside windows that shone as if they were freshly cleaned were old-fashioned shutters that could be pulled over to protect the glass. Flowers danced in the carefully groomed beds. Evidently, a gardener went out daily to keep all the plants in shape. There was a hush about the place. The sound of the trees swaying in the breeze was very different from the busy bustle of Main Street where I lived.

I could have been transported back in time 150 years and still seen the exact thing. Sometimes the island struck me that way—as if it were a place where time stood still. Usually my cell phone would ring about then and pull me out. It was Mal who barked and wagged her stub tail as if to remind me that she had done her job.

"Mal!" I scolded and went up on the porch. "Come here."

She dutifully came straight to me. I bent over and slipped her a dog treat as I took the leash. A look around told me that the porch was empty. A glance in the beveled glass front door showed me the front hall was also empty. If anyone was about, they were out of sight—perhaps upstairs or in the back of the house.

I kept up my pretense though in case they could hear me. "Silly doggie. This is not where Frances lives." I straightened, taking note of the view of Main Street from the front porch. It was lovely. Mostly the tops of the buildings. I could see the flat top of the McMurphy right after the pointed top of the hotel behind and the rounded top of the pool house between. I turned to see if I could see the fort. Yes, there it was and the tops of the boats, but I couldn't see the pier or docks from there. At least not with the naked eye. But then the witness had said he'd had a telescope.

"Come on, Mal." I started down the stairs with her leash in my hands.

Suddenly she pulled away from me.

That was not part of our routine. "Mal?"

She raced down the stairs and around the far corner of the house.

"Mal!" I went after her only to discover a sunporch on the side of the home. On the porch was an old woman in a wheelchair. She was dressed in a lovely, lightweight, long-sleeved dress that fluttered in the breeze. Her white hair was pulled back into a bun on the top of her head. Her face was pale, but her smile lifted her cheeks and sparkled through her watery blue eyes. Mal stood on her hind legs on the side of the wheelchair. The lady made a slight patting motion with her hand and Mal was up in her lap.

"Mal!" I hurried over. I knew not everyone loved little fluffy dogs. I thought I had taught Mal to be more polite. "I'm so sorry."

"Don't worry," the old woman said and waved her hand as if to brush away my protest. She patted Mal on the head. "What a pretty little doggie. How nice to have visitors."

"Are you sure she's okay?" I asked as I faced the woman. I crouched down to look her in the eye.

She appeared to be all there. I could see the intelligence shine.

"She's fine, dear," the older woman said. "What did you call her?"

"Mal. It's short for Marshmallow. I'm Allie. Allie McMurphy."

"Hello, Mal." The older woman scratched her behind the ears. "Are you out on a walk this fine morning? Did you come all the way from Main Street?"

"She likes her walks," I said. "I'm so sorry."

"Please have a seat, dear." She pointed toward the white, wrought iron garden chair next to a matching bistro table. On top were a bright blue tablecloth, a set of white teacups, and a teapot. "I was having a refreshment. Would you like something?"

"Oh, no thank you," I said and took a seat. "Are you Mrs. English?"

"Oh, no, dear. Cassandra is my stepsister. I'm Mrs. Jones."

"It's a pleasure to meet you, Mrs. Jones," I said. "I'm relatively new to the island. I used to come to Mackinac every summer growing up, but I'm living here now and getting to know all the locals."

"That's right. Your grandfather died this spring, didn't he? I was so sorry to hear that. He was a jolly fellow."

"He had his moments," I agreed. "Did you know him well?"

"Oh, no. I've only been here with Cassandra for a year . . . but I did see him on occasion at the senior center when they had their monthly birthday lunches." Mrs. Jones leaned toward me. "I like to go for the cake."

"I like birthday cake, too," I said with a smile. "Mal seems to be really taken with you."

"She's a dear. She reminds me of my Fluffy. Fluffy was a bichon. She lived to be seventeen years old. Almost as old in dog years as I am now. She would have liked you, Mal." The old woman lifted Mal's chin and looked her in the button eyes. "Bichons love other bichons."

"Mal has a good eye for nice people," I said.

"And a good nose for the dead, I hear." Mrs. Jones looked at me. "You're the one who keeps finding the murdered souls."

"Oh, um, not on purpose," I said. "Angus Mc-Elroy keeps pulling out his lucky rabbit's foot around me. He's worried about the number of dead people I've found, but I swear I don't make it a habit."

She laughed and reached for her cup of tea. "It's okay. I don't hold it against you."

"Mal, get down."

"Oh, no, she's fine," the woman said and put her hand on Mal's back. "She's not begging."

"I don't let her near a table," I said. "She has to learn manners."

I went over and lifted Mal from her lap. "We are so sorry to interrupt your morning. We should be going."

"Oh, no, dear. You aren't interrupting." Mrs. Jones put two sugar cubes in her teacup and stirred. "I fully expected you to come around sooner or later."

"I beg your pardon?"

"You have been investigating that poor girl's murder. The one you pulled from the water." She took a sip from her teacup, her gaze filled with mischief. "It was only a matter of time before you found out my son Harold was the key witness. I was certain you would be coming by to check out his story."

"Oh." I sat down.

Mal wiggled in my arms.

"Right."

"What would you like to know, dear?"

I swallowed hard. "Well, I guess I wanted to know if your son truly is a stargazer. I'm sure the police have checked out his story, but I wondered how good the view was from your home."

"I see." She sipped her tea. "The telescope belonged to my stepsister's grandfather. It has been in the house for over a hundred years. It's on the roof near the first turret. There's a widow's walk there. The old man had it installed so that his wife could look for his ship when he was out on the lake. You see, he was a merchant and owned quite a few ships that moved through the lakes to Chicago and down the rivers. It was quite the waterway at the time. A lot of goods still move through the lakes. Sadly, it's mostly sand, gravel, and oil these days. We don't move manufactured goods this way much anymore."

"I see. Everyone knows that the telescope is there?"

"Oh, yes, it's quite a fact. I believe my stepsister's mother has a biography in the library where she talks about the widow's walk and the telescope." She eyed me over her cup. "Anyone with a library card would know it's there."

"Does your son use it?"

"You'd have to ask him," she said with a slight shrug. "I'm usually in bed by nine PM. He has a job at the Nag's Head that keeps him out quite late. And then, there's his new lady love. He doesn't think I know about her, but I do."

"Who is she?" I asked.

"Why would you want to know?"

"She might know if he was here that night looking at the stars . . . or not," I said. "She could corroborate his story."

"Funny. I wonder why the police didn't ask me that." She shrugged. "Perhaps they took him at his word. He's a good boy, my son."

"I'm sure he is." I patted her hand. "I bet he has a very good mother."

"I'm so proud of him," she said with a sigh. "His lady is a member of the yacht club. He told me he met her there. I remember how exclusive that club is and I'm glad to know he is with a woman of good breeding."

"Have a good day, Mrs. Jones. It was so nice to meet you." I put Mal down and tugged her onto the grass and away from the house.

"Thanks for the visit, dear," she called after me. "Come by again any time and bring your lovely doggie friend."

"Thank you," I called, waving back at her. I rounded the corner of the house and looked up. She was right. There was a widow's walk on the roof. I looked carefully and saw a long metal tube that could have been the telescope of so much interest. I had almost asked her if I could go up and look through it, but that would have been too forward. Besides, I was pretty darn sure that Rex already did . . . and at night. He wouldn't have left anything as important as Paige's life to a witness whose story wasn't checked completely. It would be too easy to defend with an he said-she said argument.

I frowned as we walked down the winding road. Harold Jones had a girlfriend from the yacht club. I glanced at the house. Mrs. Jones was right. The club members were very exclusive. Did they think Harold owned the English house? The man worked at the Nag's Head bar. He wouldn't be doing that if he had money . . . so why would a woman from the yacht club be dating him?

I heard Jenn's voice in my head. *He might be really*

*hot.* It made me laugh. Mrs. Jones was in her eighties. At his youngest, Harold Jones was in his forties. What hot forty-year-old worked at a bar on a small tourist island and then went home to stargaze?

It didn't add up. Maybe if I could figure out who his girlfriend was, I would have better insight into what his motives might be for testifying. Was the killer offering him money? That would make sense. If he wanted to impress a yacht club member he would need a lot of money. I hurried down the hill with Mal.

I needed to get back and do a fudge demonstration, then Jenn and I had a meeting with Mr. Devaney about the engagement plans. If I had time later in the afternoon, I might run by the yacht club and nose around a bit. I suddenly remembered that we were excused from the committee. That meant no entrance without a membership and I didn't have one. I blew out a long breath. I would have to wait until the race week closing gala. Luckily, Trent had told me last night we were still going. It might be the last time I'd get inside the yacht club for a while. I would have to find out everything I could without being too obvious. It was going to be tricky.

I had to have a proper plan if I was going to pull this one off.

# Chapter 20

"It feels strange meeting you girls here for lunch without Frances," Mr. Devaney said. He looked ruffled by the secrecy. It was pretty clear he didn't like it.

"Well, you wouldn't like being a spy, would you?" Jenn asked and winked at him.

He harrumphed.

We were seated in the corner of the Grander Hotel's bistro. It was the best place we could meet for lunch without any of the locals knowing. The Grander Hotel was brand new on the island and run by an outside firm. Most of the locals boycotted it out of principle. They liked the idea that the island hadn't changed from the Victorian era. The new hotel was fully updated, energy efficient, and a replica of a Victorian mansion.

It was the replica part they hated the most. Everything else on the island was original. People worked hard not to turn the island into a theme park, but we needed new emergency equipment and updates to the police and fire departments . . . and the developers of the Grander Hotel had deep pockets. In the end, the replica was built and the island's emergency responders had enough money to buy two fire trucks and hire two more police-men.

It was really a win-win . . . unless you were a local. Then you groused about it. As it turned out, most of the tourists were suspicious of the replica and preferred to stay in an original. That was good news for the McMurphy, as well as the other hotels. The added hotel space was filled by overflow and brought more people downtown to eat at the pubs and buy fudge.

I wasn't afraid to give them my money for one lunch. As far as I was concerned, the Grander Hotel did more good than harm to the island.

"What can I get you?" The waitress was dressed in full Victorian worker garb—long gray skirt and white leg-of-muffin sleeved blouse with an apron over it all, white hair cap.

We gave her our orders.

"What do you girls have for me?" Mr. Devaney asked.

"We have three options," I said. "We wanted to give you choices."

"How soon can these options happen?" he asked. "I don't want to wait weeks while you two create something elaborate."

"All three could be set up within a few days," Jenn said. "Of course, that will make some more expensive than others."

"I'm not worried about the cost," he said with a

wave of his hand. "I want to do it soon before Frances gets suspicious or some knucklehead lets her in on the plans. If it were up to me, I'd just ask her this evening over dinner, but I want this to be her last proposal. I want it to be as memorable as all the young kids are doing it nowadays." He paused and looked at us. "What?"

I grinned. "Like all the young kids are doing it?"

"I see those YouTube clips," he replied. "I'm up-to-date on trends. I'm just pretty sure a mob of dancers would scare the hell out of Frances. Let's not do that."

"Got it," I said. "No mob of dancers."

Jenn's eyes sparkled. "We don't want to give Frances a heart attack."

"She's stronger than you think, but that's off topic. Our first idea is a romantic dinner on the roof of the McMurphy with the island at your feet. Jenn and I would decorate it like a fancy terraced restaurant complete with fairy lights, candles, and soft music so that you two can dance." I paused and watched his expression.

Mr. Devaney had the best poker face ever.

"Okay, number two is a romantic moonlight carriage tour around the island where you would stop at Lovers Point. We would have set up a picnic dinner complete with candles, soft music, and views of the bridge."

"And the third choice?"

"The third choice is to rent the sunporch at the Grand Hotel and have a three-piece orchestra playing while you are waited on hand and foot by your own personal staff. They would be very discreet, of course," Jenn said.

"Well, I can imagine which one is the most expensive," Mr. Devaney said. He pursed his lips. "What do you girls think?"

Jenn and I looked at each other. We had discussed what to say should he ask our opinions.

"We think that any of these three would be memorable and romantic for Frances," I said.

"But you prefer one of them," he said as the waitress came with our drinks.

We waited patiently for her to leave. Even though we didn't know her, there was a chance she knew someone who knew us and word would get out. It would be hard enough to explain our lunch should anyone ask, but we had agreed upon a back story just in case.

"We think Frances would like the McMurphy option best," I said. "It's where you two met and is her home when she isn't at her apartment."

"Hmm," he said as the waitress brought our lunches.

Jenn and I let him think about it while we ate. Since he was a man of few words, I was on pins and needles wondering if the suggestions were anything that appealed to him. Our discussion turned to the security camera that was being installed on the back of the building.

"I wonder why Papa Liam didn't have one installed earlier," I said.

"It's a small island," Mr. Devaney said. "People

here don't lock their doors outside of tourist season and even then rarely."

"Right." I pushed my empty plate away. "The issue came up because I investigate murders."

Mr. Devaney shook his head. "I think it's a different situation when you have two young girls living alone versus an old man. Your grandfather knew people on the island. He was never more than a few feet away from friends. You girls are new."

I frowned. "We need extra care?"

"Let's say it's a different animal," he said.

"If you ask me, it's a good thing," Jenn said. "Well worth the money."

"I agree." He leaned forward. "I've decided on a proposal."

"Wonderful!" Jenn said and we all leaned in like conspirators.

"I want the rooftop one."

"Yes," I said with delight. "When?"

"When can you get it done?"

"Well, tomorrow night is the end of the yacht race week. The yacht club is having its final gala," I said. "If you can wait a couple days, the night crowds will dissipate and you won't be disturbed by pounding party noise."

"Fine. Let's do it the night after the gala." He put his hands on the table to stand. "You girls can do that, right?"

"Yes," Jenn and I said together.

I added, "We will need your help to get things up on the roof without Frances noticing."

"It won't be a problem," he said. "We'll tell her we are having estimates done on creating event space up there. It will account for any workmen that go up."

"Perfect," I said.

"I've got a plan of action right here." Jenn pulled out papers from her tote. She handed us each a copy.

"This is well thought out," I said as I looked down at the list of tasks that had to happen. Each task was assigned to me or Mr. Devaney or Sandy or Jenn.

"I'm a good project manager," Jenn said with a grin. "We'll meet again tomorrow to see where we are. It's going to be a lot of fun."

Mr. Devaney harrumphed. "It all depends on your definition of fun."

"Keep your eye on the prize," I said to him. "Frances is going to be so happy. It will all be worth it in the end."

"It better be," he said. "I'm counting on it."

## Raspberry Chocolate Chip Bars

### Ingredients

¾ cup butter

⅔ cup sugar

⅔ cup brown sugar

1 beaten egg

1 teaspoon vanilla

1 cup mashed raspberries

1¾ cups flour

2 teaspoons baking powder

½ teaspoon salt

1 cup dark chocolate chips

**Directions**

Preheat oven to 350 degrees F. Grease and flour a
13- x 9-inch pan.

In a medium bowl, cream butter and sugars until
smooth. Add egg and vanilla until combined.

Fold in raspberries. Stir in flour, baking powder,
and salt. Add chocolate chips.

Spread into pan.

Bake for 20-30 minutes until set. Cool.

Sprinkle powdered sugar on top and cut into bars.
Enjoy!

# Chapter 21

"Are you still going to the yacht club gala tomorrow?" Jenn asked me as we walked back to the McMurphy.

"Trent asked me," I said. "Unlike the opening night fund-raiser, this one is black tie."

"I know." Jenn sighed. "I had such high hopes of going, but after we were not-so-graciously kicked off the committee and handed our business hats, I have no way to go. Shane isn't part of or even interested in the social set."

"Neither am I," I said.

"But think of all the great networking opportunities," Jenn pointed out.

"You are the networker. I'm a fudge maker and for one, am so glad I have you. I wouldn't know half the people I've met on the island."

Jenn laughed. "I do get around, don't I?"

"Do you know Harold Jones?" I asked.

"Who?"

"Harold Jones," I repeated. "I think he works at the Nag's Head Bar and Grill."

"No, why?"

"He's the eyewitness who placed Paige on the pier the night Carin was murdered."

"Really. Hmmm. How did he see her and not say anything to the police at the time of the murder?"

"Well, he was stargazing from the widow's walk on Cassandra English's cottage. He claims to have heard an argument and turned the telescope on the pier where he saw two females fighting. One stepped into a circle of light and he recognized her as Paige. Then a meteor caught his eye and he focused on that for a moment. When he looked back at the pier both women were gone."

"That is oddly coincidental," she said.

"Apparently he stargazes every night after work," I said. "I walked Mal by the English cottage today to see what I could see."

"And?" Jenn's eyes lit up.

"I ran into Harold's mother, Irene Jones. She's old and in a wheelchair. Mal charmed her," I said.

"Of course she did. So Mrs. Jones told you about Harold?"

"Actually, she expected me to come around sometime," I explained, feeling the heat of a blush on my face. "The interesting thing is that she said Harold has a lady love from the yacht club. That's how he could recognize Paige."

"Very interesting," Jenn said. "Want me to do some digging?"

"Can you check Harold out? It's weird that he works at one of the few bars on the island that the Jessops don't own. Weirder still is that any member of the yacht club would be dating a part-time bartender."

"Maybe they're trying to piss off their parents," Jenn suggested.

"Or maybe Harold has a motive to point the finger at Paige that has nothing to do with the yacht club," I suggested. "Find out if he was fired by one of the Jessops' bars."

"I'm sure if he was, the Jessops have already looked into that," Jenn pointed out.

I frowned. "Yes, they have an investigator who is quite on top of things. Darn. Maybe his girlfriend has a beef with Paige. Maybe she's using him to frame Paige."

"He'd be at risk of perjury," Jenn said. "She must really be something if he would risk going to jail for her."

"Men have risked their lives for the woman they love," I said.

"I suppose that's true. Wouldn't it be nice to find a man who would do that for you?"

"Yeah," I said with a sigh.

"Do you think Trent would risk his life for you?"

"I don't know," I said and felt a moment of sadness. "We've only been dating a few months, but he did shut me out for days."

"And apologized for it."

"Yes, he promised to never do it again and then brought in his investigator to collaborate with me on the information I'd discovered."

"See. I bet he would take a bullet for you," Jenn said with cheer. "You watch. After you show up at the gala tomorrow night, we'll have more island business back."

"It's almost like when his grandfather died," I said. "The island folks really are loyal to the Jessops."

"You know that no matter how long we live here, the locals will always think of us as outsiders. Shane tells me they think of him as an outsider because he lives in St. Ignace."

"It seems a little silly, doesn't it?"

"Sometimes," Jenn agreed.

I turned the question back on her. "Do you think Shane would risk his life for you?"

"He darn well better," she said brightly. "I think I'm falling in love with the guy." Her expression softened at the mention of Shane's name.

"Oh, that's wonderful. Does that mean you might be staying in the area?"

She sobered up. "I have a contract to work in Chicago this fall. I signed it before I came here and met Shane."

"Long distance romances work for some people," I said and patted her shoulder. "It will be okay. You'll see."

"Of course it will." She brightened. "Isn't it nice to know there's a man in the world—someone besides your father—who would risk his life for you?"

"Yes," I agreed. "It is."


Jenn was a mastermind.

She spent the next morning in and out of the attic staging the rooftop proposal. She didn't want to set it up on the roof in case we had a storm overnight. She supervised people moving giant potted palms, a gorgeous bistro set, and more into the attic. One guy was working on a portable gazebo. The roof was waterproof and the sides could be open with long gauzy drapes that could be pulled closed for privacy or opened for a view. If there was rain, storm walls could be rolled down and zipped up, making a cozy nest. Fairy lights were planned for the ceiling as well as the railing around the roof.

We used the cover story of having contractors assess the roof and give us a quote for having events up there. Frances seemed unconcerned about the activity. I stayed in the fudge shop when she was at the reception desk and Jenn stayed with her when they refreshed rooms.

I tried to be calm, but it was fun to sneak up to the attic and see the plans all coming together. Sandy was in on it, of course, and was creating a chocolate centerpiece of delicate flowers for the table. Another worker installed weatherproof speakers. Mr. Devaney had given us a list of 1960s love songs that would play in the background. Jenn was amazed by his knowledge of music and spent two hours downloading music to create the background music for the night.

"You seem distracted," Frances said suddenly as she looked up from her computer.

"I'm sorry?" I said.

"You've been standing by the coffee bar with a mug in your hand staring into space." She pointed with her hand. "What's going on?"

I moved closer to her. "Nothing."

"It's the investigation, isn't it? Are you worried because you can't help Paige?"

I grabbed her excuse by the horns and ran with it. "Yes." I felt the heat of a blush hit my cheeks. I was never any good at lying and felt my heart pounding harder under her scrutiny.

"No one expects you to solve every murder, you know," she said.

"I know, but I want to help." I leaned against the reception desk.

"I did some asking around about Harold Jones. He is in his early forties and takes care of his mother during the day. He works nights at the Nag's Head Bar and Grill and is sometimes seen on the widow's walk of the English cottage late at night."

"I met Irene Jones yesterday on my walk with Mal," I said.

"Really? You didn't mention it." Frances looked down at Mal curled up in her pink doggie bed at the foot of the reception desk. "You didn't tell me you met someone new, either."

Mal untucked her nose and looked at Frances. I knew that look. It meant *Are you going to give me a treat or are you just chirping at me?*

"Mrs. Jones loved Mal," I said. "She had a bichon named Fluffy."

"Oh my goodness. I remember that dog. Irene would bring her when she came to visit one week out of every summer." Frances frowned. "The last time I saw that dog was 1972."

"Oh, wow. Mrs. Jones sure has a good memory. She spoke about the dog as if it were just last week."

"That happens as you age," Frances said. "Things that happened decades ago are clearer than where you put your glasses today."

"She told me that Harold has a lady love who is a member of the yacht club. Do you have any idea who that is?"

"Do you think a girlfriend is his reason for lying about seeing Paige?"

"It might be plausible . . . if the woman had a reason not to like Paige . . . or Carin for that matter."

"Do you think he might be protecting the real killer?"

"I'm not sure," I said with a shrug. "It's an avenue to go down. I also wondered if maybe he got fired from one of the Jessops' bars and was taking his revenge out on Paige, but I think Rex would have looked into that."

"Yes, my guess is that Rex would have looked into that," Frances agreed. "In a case of he said-she said, I imagine that Rex is all over any doubt the defense attorney can put up about Harold."

"Yes," I said with a nod. "That's exactly what I thought." I leaned my elbows on the desk and looked at her. "Any idea who Harold might be dating? Is there any gossip about a rich girl dating a bartender? Maybe a rich girl looking to push her parents' buttons?"

"Well, a rich girl in her twenties dating a part-time bartender in his forties would certainly be a rebellious act against someone," Frances agreed. "I haven't heard of anyone like that recently. You've been closer to the yacht club crowd these days than I have."

"Not anymore," I said. "They uninvited us from the committees and dropped us as a vendor when Trent made it clear that he wasn't letting me in on the investigation."

"They only put up with you because you were dating Trent?"

"It seems that way," I said. "Jenn thinks after I go to the gala with Trent tonight, the committee members might change their minds about taking us off the approved vendor list."

"Interesting," Frances said. "Mackinac Island has that small-town mentality. I could see why Jenn thinks that, but are you certain there isn't another reason you were removed from the approved vendor list?"

"What do you mean? We have a good product and we under-promise and over-deliver."

"I know that and so does anyone who has hired you," Frances said. "But it might simply be that they have removed you from the list because the committee feels you remind the Moores of their loss. You did drag their daughter's body from the marina."

I pondered that thought for a minute. "I hadn't looked at it that way."

Frances turned back to her computer. "Nothing is ever cut and dry, but being cut from the list of approved vendors might be a good reason to stop by the yacht club in the afternoon."

A smile spread across my face. "Yes, it just might." I took off my chef's jacket and dragged the hairnet from my hair. "Why don't you come with me?"

"What?" Frances looked up at me from over the top of her reading glasses.

"Why don't you come with me? You know the older members of the committee better than me. We'll go talk to the manager of operations. If you see any member of the committee in the club, you can find out much easier than I can why we were booted. I'm sure Eleanor would have a canned response, but you might be able to get something more concrete from an actual committee member."

"Huh. Okay," Frances said. "If I do go with you, who will look after the desk and the fudge shop?"

I glanced at my watch. "Megan comes in in ten minutes. She can watch both while you and I go to the yacht club."

"All right," Frances said with a nod. "Remember, I scheduled her to take over this afternoon because I have a hair appointment. We have to be done at the club in time for that."

"You have a hair appointment?" I asked with a raised eyebrow. Frances loved the fact that she was a free spirit about her hair. She rarely had regular appointments. My question had her blushing.

"Douglas gave me a spa certificate on my birthday." She patted her hair. "I'm going to get my hair and nails done for our date tomorrow night. I thought it would be a nice surprise for him."

"I think that's a wonderful idea," I said. "Which spa are you going to?"

"Astor's."

I felt my eyes widen. "In the Grand Hotel?"

"Yes." She blushed again. "I know it's extravagant, but I couldn't tell him to take it back."

"I think it's wonderful," I said. "What are you getting done?"

"A full half day of services," she replied, her blush deepening further. "I'm scheduled for the deluxe facial, then hair styling, manicure, and pedicure."

"Wow. That is so wonderful." I nudged her with my hip. "I'm jealous. You win the best boyfriend award."

She laughed nervously. "Yes," she agreed. "I do win that award. I'm about the luckiest woman alive."

"I don't know about that. If you ask me, Mr. Devaney is the luckiest man alive."

"You are such a doll," Frances said. "Now, go wash up. I need to get some things wrapped up before Megan gets here and I take off."

"It won't take me long. I'll just duck into the hall bathroom."

Frances frowned. "No, really, I don't need you to hover. I'm fine. I can finish up here without you."

"Oh." I acted surprised. "Have I been hovering? I'm sorry. Sure, I'll leave you to your work."

"Good." Frances looked back at her computer screen. "Who knows? Maybe we'll learn something of value at the club . . . something for Paige's defense. Wouldn't that give me something to think about while I'm having my half day of beauty?"

I laughed. "You're not supposed to think about anything but relaxing when you're at a spa."

"Really?" Frances's eyes twinkled. "I wouldn't know."

"Neither would I," I admitted. "But I think I read that in a magazine once."

"Well, I'm certainly willing to find out."

"Maybe one day, I will, too." I grabbed my cup

and moved up the stairs. A glance over my shoulder told me that Frances was really into her paperwork. I reached for my phone. A quick text to Jenn let her know that Frances was momentarily alone, but would soon be out of the building.

Jenn texted back that operation rooftop was on schedule. She was heading down to ensure Frances didn't head up.

The whole secret event thing was tricky, but I had high hopes that we would pull it off.

# **Chapter 22**

"Hi Eleanor," I said as I knocked on her open office door. "Do you have a minute?"

Frances stood a few steps behind me in the hall.

"Just a minute." Eleanor looked at me with concern in her gaze. "Things are crazy right now because of tonight's black tie gala."

I winced at my poor timing. I knew about the gala. I was going, so why didn't I realize that it would mean all hands would be on deck at the club.

"This is Frances Wentworth, my associate," I introduced her as we entered Eleanor's small office and closed the door. "Eleanor, Jenn Christensen tells me that the McMurphy has been pulled from the approved vendor list for the yacht club."

"Yes, that's true." Eleanor folded her hands on her desk.

"Can you tell me why?"

"What do you mean, why?"

"Was it shoddy work? Was it not delivering our

product on time? Did someone get left off the list of yachts that we recreated?"

"No, no, and no," she said, ticking off the answers on her fingers. She splayed her hands out in front of her on top of the paperwork on her desk. "The truth is, Allie, right now you're a political time bomb. On the one hand, you are the one who pulled my dear friend Carin out of the marina. When people see you or your work, they are immediately reminded of Carin's grisly murder by Paige Jessop. The other is the whole business of you dating Trent Jessop. Some people on the yacht club board think the Jessops should not be allowed in the club at all. Unfortunately, the Jessops are powerful enough that we have to allow them access. The one thing I can do is take you off the approved vendor list and keep you off the volunteer committees." She frowned. "I take it you are attending tonight."

"Yes, I am." I folded my hands over my chest.

"I wish you wouldn't."

"There's no reason why she shouldn't," Frances said.

"Of course she shouldn't and neither should any of the Jessops," Eleanor said. "Please, this night is about the end of another successful week of the grand yacht race. People should be celebrating the winners and teasing the losers. They paid five hundred dollars a ticket to see the trophy given out and to help raise awareness for this year's charity. If you go, it will put a damper on the entire night. All anyone will talk about is poor Carin and the audacity of the Jessops to attend when everyone knows Paige killed her."

"The last time I checked, people were innocent until proven guilty," I pointed out.

Eleanor stood. "It's not about whether Paige is guilty or innocent. It's about how she will put a damper on one of the biggest occasions of the year. I have put far too much work and time into this year's race week to have it ruined by Paige Jessop . . . or you, for that matter."

"Wow." I raised my hands in surrender. "Okay. Good to know how you feel."

"Does this mean you won't come tonight?"

I shook my head. "No. I'll be here."

"Really? Seriously? You can't skip it for my sake? Or even the Moores' sake?"

"Eleanor," Frances said. "You know as well as I do that if the Jessops don't come tonight, half the board will be relieved and the other half will be looking for someone to blame. The Jessops are huge fund-raisers for the club."

"Yes, well, sometimes it's not about money," Eleanor said sharply.

"What is it about?" I asked.

"Decency," she said.

"And you think it's decent to take away my business because I'm the one who found your friend and tried to save her?"

"Oh grow up, Allie," Eleanor said. "This isn't personal."

"Right," I said with disappointment and a touch of anger. "Good to know." I turned on my heel. "Come on, Frances. There's nothing more we can do here."

Frances shot a look at Eleanor that would have

withered the most unruly of students and then walked out of the office with me. As we turned down the long hall and passed the big kitchen, Frances put her hand on my arm.

"What?" I asked, following her gaze into the kitchen where two older women were taking a break at a small table near the back door.

"You go on." She glanced at the oversized watch on her wrist. "I've got twenty minutes before my appointment. I'm going to say hi to my friends."

"Thanks for coming with me," I said. "Sorry it was a bust."

"It's okay. All may not be lost yet."

I watched her walk into the kitchen. I wanted to follow, but if Eleanor was right, I wasn't exactly the most welcomed person in the club. Especially not to the staff whose reputation depended on how well tonight's gala went.


"You look stunning," Jenn said as I twirled in front of the full length mirror attached to my wooden closet door.

I was dressed in a backless, floor-length black dress with a scooped front neckline and long sleeves. I wore a simple string of pearls that had belonged to my grandmother. I wore it like a choker in front and let it drape down my bare back. Pearl drop earrings accented my lobes as my hair was piled high into a stylish updo that Jenn had spent an hour crafting.

"Are you sure I don't still smell like fudge?" I bit my bottom lip. Jenn had given me a makeover complete with cat-eyed style, black eye liner, and deep red lip.

"No one will care," Jenn said and crossed her arms satisfactorily. "In fact, you are so stunning, no one's going to be talking about Carin or Paige. All eyes will be on you."

"Oh stop it. You're making me nervous."

"No, seriously. You look like Audrey Hepburn."

"I do not," I protested. "But thanks anyway." I gave her a quick hug and a kiss as the apartment doorbell rang.

"Oh, he's here!" Jenn clapped her hands. "This has been the best day. First, I've nearly finished setting the scene for tomorrow's romantic proposal and second, I got to make you look like a Hollywood movie star."

"The only thing missing is you." I eyed her blue satin pajama pants and white cotton T-shirt. "You should be going."

"Oh, no," Jenn said as she went to answer the door. "The only way I go to these things is if I'm working it. Trust me. I'm glad for a day off on this one." She opened the door and Trent stood there in a black tuxedo.

His square jaw and dark hair made him look like the perfect *GQ* model. His eyes flashed at the sight of me.

"Wow." Jenn and I said at the same time as Trent.

"Jinks!" Jenn said, laughing. "Look at you two." She held the door as he stepped into the apartment with a small flower box in his hand. "You look like something out of a *Vogue* fashion spread."

"Oh, no," I said. "I don't think so. Trent maybe . . ."

"You look gorgeous," he said in a low sexy tone that made a blush rush right up my cheeks. "I brought you a corsage."

"It feels like prom," I said when he opened the box and pulled out a delicate orchid wrist corsage.

"Did you go to prom?" he asked me.

"No," I said with a shake of my head. "I was too busy apprenticing at a local chocolate shop."

"It's better to go to prom as an adult anyway." He winked at me. "We know what we're doing now."

*Oh, boy.*

There was a ping of a text message. Trent reached for his phone in his pocket and checked it. "Paige says to have fun."

"Oh, she's not going?" Jenn asked.

"She's wearing an ankle bracelet and is confined to the cottage. Shall we send her a selfie?" He pulled me close and held his phone up. "Smile."

I did and a second later the picture was on its way to Paige.

"We should go. Are you ready?"

"As ready as I'll ever be," I said.

"Wait!" Jenn ran into her bedroom. She came back out with a shimmering silk scarf. "Take this in case it gets cold later tonight."

"Thanks!" I wrapped it around my shoulders. The dress had sleeves but being backless more skin was exposed than you would think. "Good night."

"'Night kids. Have fun now!" Jenn waved us out the front door.

We took the elevator down to the lobby and stepped into the dim evening light.

"You two look gorgeous!" Megan said from her place behind the reception desk.

"Thanks," I said as we walked by. "Have a good night."

Trent had a horse and carriage waiting outside. It was a short walk from the McMurphy to the yacht club, but taking a carriage was best considering my four-inch stilettos.

"How's Paige holding up?" I asked once we were settled in for the short ride.

"As best could be expected," Trent said. "She's brave."

I noted the tightness in his jaw and put my hand on his arm. "I know. Your investigator is very good. We'll get this figured out. It all comes down to the eyewitness. If we can figure out what motivated Harold Jones to say what he said, we can find the real killer. I'm certain."

Trent patted my knee. "Let's hope that happens soon."

We arrived at the yacht club and stood in a line of carriages that delivered guests in dazzling designer attire. My simple gown was a loaner from an online company who rented designer gowns. Jenn had found it and had them overnight ship the gown to me. The shoes were mine—black patent leather stilettos that had been an investment for graduation from culinary institute last year.

Trent held out his hand and helped me out of the carriage. He leaned in and whispered against my ear. "You look fantastic. Are you ready for this? It won't be easy."

"I'm glad to be by your side," I replied and gave him a long look to emphasize my words.

He smiled that charming, perfect smile of his that I swear had to be practiced and yet knew it wasn't. He slipped my hand into the crook of his arm and walked me up the red carpet and into the yacht club.

Music swirled at just the right volume. The air was scented with expensive perfume and fresh flowers. We were greeted by Richard Blake, the president of the yacht club, and his wife Amelia, who were hosting the evening's gala. As Trent shook hands and exchanged pleasantries, I could tell from the look in their eyes that they were on the fence about whether we should be there or not. I knew it was because they didn't want a scene. While he was welcomed, I was tolerated. I deduced it was partly because I wasn't of moneyed elite and partly because they had hoped I wouldn't come. As Eleanor had mentioned, I was a reminder to everyone that Carin Moore was dead.

The evening began with cocktails and canapés in the front parlor. I smiled and made small talk, mostly staying by Trent's side. That said, I wasn't passive. I could hold my own there. I spent the time looking at the female members, trying to figure out who might be dating Harold Jones. I had the feeling that if I knew who he was seeing, I could trace back to why he'd said what he'd said about Paige.

As people entered, I kept an eye on who had dates and who didn't. My thinking was that Harold's girl might show up unescorted. An hour and a half into the cocktails, I saw no one who didn't have a date. Trent had introduced me to several new people. Most had known Papa Liam and expressed their sorrow at his loss this spring.

"He was a fine man," Mr. Butterworth said. "I played cards with him often."

"You have to admit he was a card fiend, wasn't he?" I asked.

"More like a shark," he said and winked at me. "Not that anyone objected. Good man, your Papa. He was a good man. Now if you will excuse me, I see an old friend I haven't seen since last year's races." Mr. Butterworth patted me on the shoulder and moved on.

One of the servers came in holding a bell and hit it with a rubber hammer.

"Time to go in to dinner," Trent said.

I looked around, disappointed that I wasn't able to deduce who Harold Jones might be seeing.

As Trent escorted me to our table in the far corner, I saw several of the ladies leaving their shawls and heading toward the restrooms. "Please excuse me," I said, draping my shawl on the back of my chair. "I need to powder my nose."

Trent nodded and took a seat as I made my way through the crowd. It seemed surreal to use that old phrase, but I wasn't going to tell him that I needed to go to the restroom to see if I could pick up on any good gossip.

The line extended into the lounge area full of couches, mirrored walls with vanity counters, and small stools so women could either rest or sit and fix their makeup. I sat on a stool behind the crowd and took out my compact. The talk was mostly of the yacht race winners and losers as well as welcomes and quick hugs of old friends. And then I heard the conversation I had been waiting for.

"I cannot believe that Paige Jessop killed Carin Moore. I thought they had buried the hatchet last fall."

"I know," said a blonde in a long red Valentino gown. "Paige told me that she and Carin had more in common than anyone else. It's why Carin had said they should join forces."

"I know they worked on the Christmas fund-raiser for the Chicago Police Widows and Orphans campaign. It was quite the success."

"Well, they certainly wouldn't have argued about boyfriends. I spent a weekend with Carin last month. She was over the moon about this new man in her life."

"Really? Who?"

"James Jamison," the blonde said. "They met at the fund-raiser. His family is eyeing him as a candidate for Congress. In fact, Carin said he has his eye on the ultimate prize."

"The White House?"

"Yes." The blonde and her friend stepped forward in the line. "It's why Carin buried the hatchet with Paige. She wanted to bring the Jessops in on Jamison's campaign."

"Well, I can see that. What a force to have the Moores and the Jessops backing you."

I caught a glimpse of the other woman in the mirror. She was a brunette in an emerald green print gown that looked as if it might be Dolce & Gabbana.

"Having Paige Jessop accused of murdering Carin really puts a split between the families and their friends. Poor James not only lost his girl-friend, but all the backing the Jessops could have given him."

"Do you think Carin's murder was politically motivated?" the brunette asked.

I paused with my lipstick half raised toward my lips and held my breath. Here was an angle I hadn't known about. I wondered if Rex knew about it. Certainly Trent and Tom would have told me if they had known about it.

"Oh, I doubt it. Politics are murder, but there are easier ways to split the two families than to kill Carin," the blonde said. "There are so many skele-tons in the closets."

"True. That's what happens when families have generations of history behind them," the brunette said.

They stepped closer to me as the line slowly moved.

"I wonder what Eleanor thought of Carin and Paige becoming friends," the blonde said.

The brunette's eyes grew wide and she gave a giggle. "I bet she was beside herself."

"Carin was her only friend," the blonde said. "Without her, Eleanor is nothing but the opera-tions manager of the yacht club."

"Manager of the club with a bartender boy-friend." The brunette shook her head. "That's no way to social climb."

"She spent her whole life riding Carin's coattails. I don't know what she'll do now," the blonde said.

"Find someone else to glom on to," the brunette said. "The smart thing to do would be to marry her way up. I'll have my mother warn all the eligible bachelors to beware."

"As if they would be attracted to that."

Both laughed as they walked past me into the stall area.

I finished my lipstick, washed my hands, and returned to my table.

"Are you okay?" Trent asked.

"Yes, I think I'm okay."

"Good." He patted my hand.

The waiter bent near me and asked if I would like red or white wine. I opted for white and looked over the crowd to see if Eleanor was visible. I finally spotted her near the front of the room in a strapless column dress of royal purple. Her hair was in an updo and she looked quite nice. I'd always thought of her as Snow White pretty with her black hair and pale skin, but on closer inspection, her eyes were a little too close together. Her mouth was a little too thin.

I watched her work the head tables like a pro, laughing at something Richard Blake said. Careful to touch each one just enough to be flirty but understated. I wondered if she was Harold Jones's lady love? I thought Mrs. Jones meant that he was dating one of the patrons. It never occurred to me that he was dating someone who worked there. It made sense. More sense than a part-time bartender in his forties dating a daughter of the yacht club set.

I watched her work her way around the head table. It was her job to keep the board happy, and she was doing it well. The music was perfect. The waitstaff on point. The cocktail hour could not have been better. The only bad thing was the empty table where the Moores and their friends would have sat. A black runner had been placed over the center and the plates turned over, signifying that the table was left empty out of respect.

As Eleanor queued up the president to move to the podium and begin his opening remarks, I thought about telling Trent what I had learned in the bathroom. I decided to wait since it was better not to rely on gossip.

I watched as her eyes teared when Richard Blake called for a moment of silence. After the meal, I would hunt her down and ask how did she feel about Carin and Paige's friendship and why hadn't she told me they were working together on James Jamison's campaign. I would also ask her point blank if she'd had anything to do with Harold Jones's testimony. If anything felt off about her explanations, I would tell Tom, not Trent.

Suspicions were one thing. To get to the truth I had to find proof.

# Chapter 23

"Very nice event, Eleanor," I said as I hunted her down after the auction.

"Thank you," she said with a curt nod of her head. "It would have been even better if you had had enough respect for Carin and for me not to come tonight."

"No one seemed bothered by my being here," I said.

"That's because you're with Trent. At least Paige had the good sense to stay home."

"She's on house arrest. No way would she have come with an ankle bracelet keeping track of her every move."

"She should be in jail for what she did, not allowed the comfort of her family home."

"I heard a rumor that you are dating Harold Jones. Is that true?" I asked loud enough for two older women to turn their heads in our direction.

"I don't know what you're talking about," Eleanor said and stepped outside onto a side porch away from the prying eyes inside.

"I heard two women talking in the restroom. They said you were dating a bartender on the island. Harold Jones is a part-time bartender at the Nag's Head."

"I don't understand what that has to do with me." She turned on her heel to come at me with anger in her gaze and her hands balled into fists at her side.

I resisted the urge to step back. "Harold Jones is the eyewitness who placed Paige on the pier that night. If you are dating him, he may be lying because he thinks you would want him to lie."

"Why in the world would I want him to lie?"

"Because he thinks Carin—your best friend— and Paige were enemies," I said. "But they weren't, were they?"

"This is crazy," she said in a low whisper. "First of all, I would never date a part-time bartender. Secondly, I didn't tell anyone to lie about Paige being on the pier that night."

"Would you be willing to take a lie detector test about that?" I asked.

"No, I would not." She crossed her arms. "Lie detectors are an invasion of my privacy and I will not stand for anyone to assume that I am not telling the truth."

"Come on, Eleanor. You knew that Carin and Paige were becoming fast friends and yet you led me to believe they were still feuding."

"You're new to the island," she said and raised her nose in the air. "Don't think because you are dating Trent Jessop that you know more things about Carin and Paige than I do."

"You knew they were becoming friends. You knew that Carin wanted the Jessops to support James Jamison for congress."

"You have no idea what I know," Eleanor said.

"Why don't you enlighten me then," I said, raising an eyebrow.

"Paige Jessop killed Carin in cold blood. She bashed her head in with a lifeboat oar and then left her to drown in the water of the marina."

"Why would she do that, Eleanor?" I pressed. "Because Carin beat her at homecoming queen? That was ten years ago."

"Reggie wanted Carin back. Paige and Carin fought the afternoon she was killed. We broke it up. Janet told you that. After that, Paige had enough time to preplan Carin's murder. Paige used Ronald Lorrie to lure Carin away from her party that night. Ronald asked Carin to wait for him on the pier, but he never showed. Instead, Paige picked up the oar and bashed Carin in the head, dumped her into the water, and then rowed back to the *Scoundrel*. Everyone knows Paige did it. Everyone knows why."

"No," I said. "Everyone does not know it. Yes, they fought that afternoon, but not hard enough for anyone—least of all Paige—to want to murder Carin. Certainly not enough to preplan it. In fact, it is just as likely that you lured Carin away from the party that night."

I saw a spark of fear in Eleanor's gaze and knew I was on to something. "You did, didn't you? It was you on the pier that Harold Jones saw through his lens. That's why you are dating him. You want him to tell everyone it was Paige, but it was you."

"I don't know what you're talking about. Carin was my best friend." Eleanor's back went straight. "I'm going in now. I'm working. I don't have time for this nonsense."

"It's not nonsense," I said and followed her to the door. "You were mad that Carin and Paige were becoming friends. In fact, it was something you said to Paige that sparked the fight that afternoon, wasn't it?"

"I have no idea what you mean."

"You told Paige that Carin was hitting on Reggie."

"I saw it with my own eyes."

"What you saw was Reggie comforting Carin," I said.

"He was holding her in his arms," Eleanor cried. "When I came around the corner, they stepped apart like a pair of guilty children caught with their hands in the cookie jar. Someone needed to let Paige know."

"But Carin was your best friend. Why betray her? Why tell Paige?" I put my hands on my hips. "Was it your attempt at driving a wedge into their budding friendship?"

"I don't like two-timing men," Eleanor said. "I told Carin that and I told Paige that. It had nothing to do with Carin and Paige's so-called friendship."

"Really?" I said. "Or is it that you don't like losing the social status you got from being associated with Carin?"

"Now who's being ridiculous?"

"Come on," I said as she turned her back to me. "Carin was a mean girl yet you spent your entire life doing whatever she said. Even as she put you down for dating Harold Jones. Even as she told you your hair wasn't right. Your schooling wasn't good enough. You still stayed with her because you wanted to be part of the in crowd. With Carin and Paige joining forces, that left you out with nothing but a job as operations manager of the yacht club."

She turned on me. "I'm the director to one of the most prestigious clubs in the area. I have access to some of the wealthiest, most influential people in Michigan, Wisconsin, and Illinois. I think that's much more important than operating an unimaginative fudge shop."

"My ambitions aren't in question," I said. "Yours are. If Rex asks Mrs. Jones who her son's lady love is—"

"She'd better say Eleanor," a heavyset man my height said as he stepped out of the dark shadows of the patio. "I don't like what you're implying, Ms. McMurphy. Just because you think you've solved a few murders does not give you the right to cast aspersions on my girlfriend."

"You're Harold Jones?"

"Yes." He was bald on top with a ring of dark hair around the sides of his head like an old-fashioned monk. He had small brown eyes and a wide nose that looked as if it were broken once or twice in a bar brawl. His meaty hands were fisted. He wore a short sleeved Hawaiian shirt, worn blue jeans, and tennis shoes. He stepped between me and Eleanor. "I don't like where you're going with this line of questioning."

"You've been watching a lot of cop shows," I said.

"And you are lying about seeing Paige on the pier that night."

"Yeah? Prove it." He put his hand on Eleanor's waist. "Don't worry, baby. Everything's going to be all right."

"Don't touch me," she scolded him. "Not here. We had an agreement. Until the trial is over, we're not going to be seen in public together."

"I know, baby. That's why I was waiting out here in the shadows for you. But then I heard what this fudge maker was saying and well, I had to step in."

"Because I'm on to the truth, aren't I?" I said, my eyes growing wide. "You were on the pier that night, weren't you, Eleanor? You were the one who killed Carin and then covered it up."

"You have an amazing imagination," Eleanor said. "I'm sorry, but you've crossed a line."

"Do you want me to take her out?" Harold asked.

Eleanor looked me up and down. "Yes, take her out to the middle of the straits and dump her. With any luck, her body will wash up on shore after Paige has been convicted of killing Carin."

"What?" I looked at Eleanor. "Are you threatening me?" I took a step toward her.

Harold wrapped his big hand around my arm and pulled me back.

I did what any girl in my situation would do. I lifted my skirt and stomped my four-inch spiked heel into his instep.

He gave a sharp howl and I kicked him in the groin. He doubled over in pain and I ran inside.

The lights were low. Most people had gone, but a few die-hards were still on the dance floor.

A quick glance around told me that Trent was in the far corner talking to Richard Blake. I lifted my skirt and ran toward him.

He looked up and spotted me. His face went suddenly grim and he made a beeline to me. "What is it?" he asked as I put my arms around him and buried my head in his shoulder. "Are you all right?"

"I am now," I said, out of breath and trembling.

Eleanor came through the door, pointed a finger at me, and screeched, "Call the police. Allie McMurphy just assaulted a man. I saw everything."

# Chapter 24

"Is he going to press charges?" I asked Rex as I sat in a small interrogation room at the police station. Trent's jacket over me helped to stop my shivering. I hugged my waist.

Trent had not been let back into the room with me. He'd insisted on calling in his lawyer, but I knew Frances would call in her cousin, the man who had handled my previous run-ins with the law.

Once Eleanor had made a scene, the lights had gone up at the club. Harold Jones had come limping in, his face red and his eyes watering. I could see he was hopping mad.

So was Trent for that matter. If two of the young guys hadn't stepped in to hold him back, we both might have been in custody on alleged assault charges. Richard Blake had had someone call the police and made everyone wait where they were until Rex could come and sort everything out.

We all went down to the police station and Rex had escorted me into this tiny room. I was lucky he didn't handcuff me. As it was, my shoes were taken into evidence. It seems I'd taken a nice chunk of skin out of Mr. Jones's instep. Unfortunately, that was evidence that could prove I did indeed attack him.

"The real question here is why?" Rex asked as he paced in the space between the table and the door.

"I told you. I discovered that Eleanor and Harold are dating and thought it was suspicious. The only witness to put Paige at the scene of Carin's murder was dating Carin's best friend. After the gala ended, I asked her about it."

"And why didn't you bring your suspicions to me?"

I sighed. "Because I knew you would just say it was hearsay. That I needed proof."

"And you thought you would simply walk up to Eleanor and ask her if she was the one framing Paige for Carin's murder?"

I looked at Rex. "You know Paige is being framed?"

He smirked. "I'm not stupid. I had to act on the information I had, but that didn't mean I wasn't working on other leads. You are right. I don't have a solid case against Paige . . . or anyone else, for that matter."

"Huh. If you had told me, I would have been more forthcoming with my investigation."

"I can't tell you." He ran his hand over his face. "You are not a professional. Telling you would severely damage any case I could build against whoever is the killer."

"Please tell me you have Eleanor in custody."

"No, I don't. She did nothing wrong."

"She told Harold to take me out to the straits

and dump me." I pointed in the direction of the lakes. "He grabbed my arm and started to pull me away. If I hadn't acted, I would be out there right now and no one would be the wiser."

"Listen. We're taking statements from everyone in the area," Rex said. "Someone had to have seen him grab you."

I frowned. A purple handprint had developed on my forearm. "He grabbed me."

Rex scowled and a flash of anger appeared in his eyes. He was a sight to behold. He turned his back and walked carefully to the door. "I'll have Shane document the bruise." Rex left me in the room.

There was a commotion down the hall. A door slammed and I jumped.

Officer Heyes came in with a paper cup filled with coffee. "Hey. Rex said you might need a warm cup. I put cream in it. Do you want sugar?"

"No, thank you." Another door slammed and I jumped again.

"Don't let that bother you," he said, his voice calm. He handed me the cup. "I'm going to stay here with you until your lawyer comes, okay?"

"Okay." I took the cup and wrapped my cold fingers around it, inhaling the scent of the thick brew. "Smells like you could stand a spoon up in it."

Officer Heyes lifted half his mouth in a quick wry smile. "Cop coffee. It's all we have."

"I like it strong." I took a sip. It was as strong as espresso.

Officer Heyes answered the knock on the door. Shane stood in the hallway with his crime scene kit in his hand.

"Come on in," I said. "There's a party going on in here."

"You look like you've been partying," Shane said and gave a low whistle. "Nice dress."

"It's a loaner so you can't have it for evidence. I can't afford to buy it and I really doubt the county can either."

"I see." He put his kit on the table and opened it. Once gloves were on, he pulled out a camera. "I'm going to start by looking at your hands and arms for defensive wounds."

"Okay." I put down the coffee and held out my hands.

He took pictures of the red manicure that Jenn had given me earlier in the evening. When he motioned with his hand, I turned my palms up.

"No obvious cuts," I said.

Shane glanced at me through his thick glasses. "There usually aren't."

"I do have this bruise where he grabbed me." I pushed up the sleeve and Shane took shots of the bruise—a palm and five finger marks showed as deep purple welts—and my other forearm. He asked me to place my forearm on the table beside a measuring stick to document the size and shape of my bruise.

"You pulled away," he said as he took pictures.

I nodded. "I took a self-defense course in Chicago when I was living downtown. We were taught how to use the weakness of the attacker's thumb to pull away. I then stomped on the instep of his foot with my heel. He let go and I turned, gave him a kick in the groin, and dashed away."

"I see," he said judiciously.

"I didn't mean to do real harm," I went on to explain. "Only to get away."

Shane put down his camera. "I'm going to take scraping from under your nails."

"Okay," I said. "I don't think I scratched him."

"It's all part of the process. Please hold out your hands."

I did. They shook as he slipped paper under them and used an orange stick to gently scrape anything that had gotten caught under my nails.

There was another knock at the door. It was Trent with a man in an Armani suit in tow.

"What are you doing?" Armani Man asked.

"Collecting evidence," Shane said without so much as blinking. "I'm a neutral party. She didn't say anything to me. Ask Officer Heyes."

Trent and Armani Man looked at Officer Heyes who shook his head. "I brought her coffee and am keeping her company until you got here." He held his hands up in surrender. "I'm going now. Take care, Allie."

"Thanks." I held my breath as Shane asked me to stand.

"Coat off please," he said.

I handed the tux jacket back to Trent. He looked all sexy and undone in rolled up shirtsleeves and untied bow tie.

Shane took more pictures of me, front and back, then asked for pictures of my feet and legs. I was lucky that he didn't insist on taking the dress . . . although he did swab it. Then he packed up his kit and left without a word.

"I'll tell Jenn you said hello," I said to his back.

He didn't even stop.

"He's trying to remain neutral," Armani Man said as he took a chair across from me.

Trent draped his jacket back on my shoulders and tipped my hand over to see the bruise on the underside of my arm. A muscle ticked in his jaw, then he looked at me. "Allie, this is Brent Childs, your attorney."

"Hello, Mr. Childs." I shook his hand. "I'm sure I don't need you. This was an act of self-defense."

"Until we know that no charges will be filed, I think I'll stick around," he said. "Why don't you tell me in your own words what happened?"

I related the scene the best that I could remember.

Trent pulled a chair up next to mine and put my hands between his to warm them. "You told Eleanor outright that she was more likely to have murdered Carin than Paige?"

I shrugged. "It seemed like the thing to say. I wanted to shock her into telling me what really happened that night."

"Instead, she told Harold Jones to drown you?" Mr. Childs asked.

I nodded. "Yes, she actually did. I was stunned. I mean, I was there as your date, Trent. What was she going to say when I came up missing? I'm certain someone saw us step outside together."

"Eleanor is a master manipulator," Trent said. "You should talk to Paige about her sometime."

"Did she tell you that she killed Carin?" Mr. Childs asked.

"No"—I shook my head—"she didn't. She said I was in the way and needed to be handled."

"She said you needed to be handled?" Mr. Childs asked.

"Something like that," I said.

"I'm afraid something like that won't hold up in a court of law." Mr. Childs sat back. "This may turn into a case of he said-she said."

"Won't Eleanor corroborate Harold's statement?"

"We can have her tossed out as a hostile witness," Mr. Childs said.

"Wait. I'll have to go to trial?" I turned to Trent. "I was grabbed with the intent to kidnap and I'm the one who will have to go to trial?"

"It will depend on the evidence." He rubbed my back through his jacket. "It's going to be okay. Mr. Childs is a very good lawyer."

"I can't afford to go to trial," I said, trying to keep the panic from my voice. "Seriously, I can't. And I really can't go to jail. I have the McMurphy to think about and the staff and the rest of the season and Mal and Caramella and Trent . . ."

"Nice to know I was on that list somewhere," he said with a low chuckle. "Even if I was last."

"Stop teasing me," I said with tears gathering in my eyes. "This is serious. I did everything right. I got away. There's a bruise to prove he grabbed me. What am I missing?"

"Eleanor is saying you attacked her. That Harold grabbed you to stop you before you could touch her. Then you took your anger out on him," Mr. Childs said.

"But that's a total fabrication," I said.

"We know." Trent put his arm around me.

"There seems to be a lot of fabrication going around lately," Mr. Childs said.

"It's all Eleanor," I said. "I'm certain she and Harold Jones are framing Paige."

"The problem is we need proof," Trent said. "I'll get Tom on it. If your theory about Eleanor is correct—"

"It is," I said, more certain than ever before. "Why else would she be accusing me of attacking her?"

"There has to be evidence," Trent said quietly.

"Thank you for bringing the connection between Eleanor and Harold Jones to light," Mr. Childs said. "We can use that as a negotiating point for Paige."

"See?" Trent leaned me against his chest. "What you did tonight was a good thing. Let me worry about your court costs and such. It's the least I can do considering what you've been doing for Paige."

A thought occurred to me. "Who was the bartender on the *Scoundrel* the night of the murder?"

"Why?" Mr. Childs asked.

I looked at Trent. "Do you know who it was?"

"I believe it was Scott Thomas. Why?"

"Bartenders tend to hang out with each other, right? I mean, it's a small island. Even if they don't work at the same bar, they would connect just to keep their options open. Plus they have things in common."

"Okay," Trent said. "What are you getting at?"

"I suspect that Reggie and the others on the *Scoundrel* were drugged that night, causing them to pass out early."

"And Paige to not have an alibi," Trent said.

"Yes," I said with a nod and then looked at Mr. Childs. "Harold Jones is a bartender at the Nag's Head Bar and Grill. He could have had access to the alcohol that was served on the *Scoundrel* that night."

"That's really a stretch," Mr. Childs said.

"Not so much of a stretch," Trent said. "When we hire a bartender for a party on the boat, they usually bring their own stash. If Scott is friends with Harold there might have been an opportunity for him to spike the booze."

"I'll have Tom check it out," Mr. Childs said.

"That makes Carin's murder premeditated, doesn't it?" I asked.

"If there's a connection, then yes," Mr. Childs said.

There was a knock on the door and Rex stuck his head into the room. "You're free to go."

We stood.

"Are they pressing charges?" I asked.

"I've advised them that we have collected evidence from both sides and at first glance I don't see anything that proves criminal assault . . . either way." He crossed his arms over his chest.

"But they tried to kidnap me," I said.

"And they swear you attempted to assault Eleanor and did assault Harold," Rex said. "I'm declaring there is too little evidence to charge anyone with a crime. That's a good thing, Allie. Go home. Get some rest."

"Come on." Trent put his arm around my waist. "Let me walk you home."

We stepped into the hallway and I stopped in front of Rex. "They tried to get rid of me because I suggested that Eleanor has a stronger motive to kill Carin than Paige does. How do you know they won't come after me again?"

"Because you told everyone here about your suspicions," Rex said. "Hurting you now would only make them look guiltier. Go home, Allie. Get some rest."

Trent walked me out of the admin building. He shook Mr. Childs's hand and the attorney headed back to his hotel. My shoes were still in EVIDENCE so my feet were bare. Officer Heyes came out of the station with a pair of disposable flip-flops in hand.

"Miss McMurphy, I forgot to give these to you inside. You're going to need something on your feet if you're walking home."

"Thanks," I said and slipped them on.

Trent shook his head.

In the soft street lighting, I could make out a grin on his face. "What?" I asked.

"You. Only Allie McMurphy would not think twice about walking out of a police station barefoot while wearing a designer gown."

I had to giggle. "Truthfully? I forgot the gown was designer."

"Come on. Let's get you home before anything else can go wrong."

## Spicy Fudge Pudding

### Ingredients

⅔ cup sugar

⅓ cup dark cocoa

3 tablespoons cornstarch

½ teaspoon of cayenne pepper

Dash of salt

2¼ cups milk (Do not use skim milk. Whole milk makes a creamier pudding.)

2 tablespoons butter

1 teaspoon vanilla

### Directions

Mix the first five ingredients in a medium sauce pan. Slowly whisk in milk. The cocoa will float to the top, but it will mix in.

Cook on medium heat, stirring constantly until the pudding boils. You will see little volcano like plops. Boil for one minute and remove from heat.

Stir in butter and vanilla. Dish into four pudding dishes. To prevent skin from forming, cover with plastic wrap.

Chill until cool. Enjoy!

# Chapter 25

The next morning the dress was carefully boxed and set out for the package delivery guy to pick up. I had gotten about five hours of sleep and when I came downstairs, Sandy was in the fudge shop making the first two batches of fudge. I grabbed a cup of coffee from the coffee bar and headed inside the fudge shop to look over the day's work.

"You had an eventful evening," she said when I walked into the kitchen.

"How do you know?"

She grinned. "Small island. It's hard to keep secrets."

"Unless you're a killer," I muttered.

"Even then," she said with a straight face.

I watched her stir the boiling liquid base for the next tray of fudge. "Today is a big day for Douglas and Frances. Do you think we've been able to keep that a secret?"

"She might suspect, but she'll be happy."

I sipped my coffee in silence while the radio

played soft tunes. Once the fudge was ready to be poured, I put down my cup and helped her lift the giant copper kettle and pour the boiling liquid onto the cooling table. We worked in tandem, stirring it with paddles until it cooled. I added pieces of nuts and berries, then folded it into a long loaf and cut it into one pound pieces and placed them on a tray.

Sandy washed the kettle and began the next batch. The contrast of the everyday morning compared to the excitement and glamour of the night before was stark. I thought about what Eleanor had said about being just another unimaginative fudge shop on a street where there was fudge on every corner.

The thought made me smile. This was my heritage and the life I had chosen. I would rather be in the McMurphy making fudge than on any one of the yachts in the harbor or buildings in Detroit or Chicago where people lived and worked indoors, rarely going outside.

I found something comforting about living in a place where my family had lived for over one hundred years. They'd crafted something that made memories for generations before me and for generations to come. While I might not be rich and famous, what I did still made a difference in the magic of a little kid's life or the magic of a pair of senior citizens who suddenly found themselves in love again.

Jenn and Mal came bounding down the stairs at seven AM. One hour before Frances was set to come in to work.

"Good morning, ladies. Are we ready for the big day?" Jenn grabbed a cup of coffee, adding flavored syrup, sugar, and cream. "I've got a sharp schedule to keep if we are going to pull this off. Sunset is roughly ten o'clock. Mr. Devaney is going to pick her up at eight-fifteen. They are going to ride Jessops' best carriage around the island. Then end up at the McMurphy where they will head up to the roof for cocktails and sunset. Right after sunset, the waitstaff will light the candles and the fairy lights and dinner will be served with dessert around ten thirty. Then he will ask her to dance to his song and when it is done, he'll go down on one knee and ask her. I've got cameras in two corners to catch all the special moments. Susy next door will edit the film down into a keepsake five minutes." Jenn glanced at her watch. "Today's weather is perfect with no rain in sight. The wind will be slight, giving the sheer curtains a soft billowing effect while leaving the view of the lake and the stars." She sighed. "Perfection."

"What's perfection?" Frances said as she came in from the back alley door.

Jenn jumped. "Oh . . . the weather. I was just saying how the weather is going to be perfect tonight."

Mal barked and jumped up to twirl. Frances pulled a treat out of the treat jar and gave her a reward for being cute. Jenn sent me a look that said she knew she almost got caught.

I looked at my watch. "You're here early."

"I was up," Frances said with a shrug.

"How was your day of beauty?" I asked.

Jenn looked from me to Frances and back.

"Mr. Devaney gave her a spa day for her birthday," I explained. "Frances went yesterday."

She took off her hat and ran her fingers through her hair. She sported new blond highlights and a fresh cut. "It was fun."

"Oh, love the hair," Jenn said and went over to look at the highlights. "Who was your colorist?"

"Kendra Goering," Frances said. "She put in low lights and highlights. I feel like a princess."

"Frances had her nails done, too." I walked over to lift Frances's hand. "French tips are very nice."

"She wanted to do silver glitter," Frances said, "but I thought it was a bit too much for a woman my age."

"Pedicure, too?" Jenn asked.

"The works, along with a relaxing facial," Frances said. "I slept so well I was up early."

"I heard you have a big date tonight." Jenn wagged her eyebrows. "Is he taking you anywhere special?"

I turned and looked at Sandy in the fudge shop. She shrugged. If I looked at Jenn, I'd give away my surprise at her question.

"Oh, nothing too fancy, I hope," Frances said. "It's really not our style."

"But you're going to dress up, right?" Jenn asked.

Frances shrugged. "I don't know. Maybe."

"I can help you pick out something nice," Jenn volunteered.

"She does a great job," I said. "She dressed me for yesterday's gala."

"How did that go?" Frances asked.

"I thought you would have heard," I said.

Frances and Jenn turned to stare at me.

"Heard what exactly?" Frances asked.

I felt the heat of a blush rush over my cheeks. "Nothing." I checked my watch. "Won't you look at the time? Mal needs her walk." I grabbed Mal's leash from its hook beside the mailboxes and put it on her.

"Allie, what happened?" Jenn asked, her hands on her hips.

"Nothing too important. I'm fine. Everyone is fine."

Mal was happy to be leashed and pulled me toward the back door of the McMurphy.

"Just if you hear anything, take it with a grain of salt. Okay?"

"Allie . . ." Frances called after me.

"Be back in a bit." I waved goodbye as Mal and I raced out of the McMurphy and down the alley before anyone could follow. I wanted to pick up my pup and kiss her, but she was intent on finding the right patch of grass for her business. I cleaned up after her and thought about last night.

Trent had said that bartenders take their own booze when they work a party on a boat—sort of like caterers take their own food when they have a gig. That meant the bartenders had to have a liquor store or a distributor to buy their booze from. I texted Jenn, figuring she would know. She planned parties and often times bartenders were staffing an open bar.

Me: Jenn, do you ever hire bartenders for your parties?

Jenn: Yes, sometimes. Why?

Me: Do you buy the liquor or do they?

Jenn: If the venue has a liquor license the venue provides the liquor. If it is on a picnic area or boat then I usually go through McGriff's.

Me: McGriff's?

Jenn: They cater open bar, which includes the liquor and the staff, set up and tear down.

Me: Where is McGriff's?

Jenn: On Main Street next to The Island Bookstore.

Me: Thanks.

Jenn: Why?

Me: Following a hunch.

Jenn: Be careful. We need you for Frances's big night.

Me: Mal has me covered. I added a smiley face emoji. ☺

I tugged on Mal's leash. "Come on, Mal. We have a store to visit."

Most of the stores on Main Street didn't open until ten. I glanced at my watch. It was just after nine. I took a chance anyway and headed to McGriff's. It was closed. I walked Mal around to the alley behind. The back door was open so I stepped over the threshold. "Hello?" I called.

"Be right with you," a husky male voice called back.

Mal found an interesting smell next to the

Dumpster just outside the door. I tugged her toward me. She pulled back. When she got interested in something, it was not usually a good sign.

"Can I help you?" A big burly guy with sandy hair came around the corner wiping his hands on a cloth.

"Yes, hi. I'm Allie McMurphy. I run the McMurphy Hotel and Fudge Shop."

"Alex Hicks. I run McGriff's Liquors. What can I do for you?"

"Well, I'm going to redo the McMurphy's roof as an event space. Since I would rarely need a bartender, I don't want to get into the whole liquor license thing. My friend Jenn Christensen told me that you hire out a full-service bar complete with liquor, bartender, set up, and tear down. Is that true?"

"It's one of the things we do," he agreed.

Mal tugged on the leash as she nosed around the Dumpster. I tugged back. "Sorry, my dog seems to be interested in something in your Dumpster."

"Must be yesterday's chicken sandwich," he said.

"Right, okay. I was wondering if your catering service used bartenders from the island or off island."

"Does it matter?" he asked with a shrug.

"I like to hire local," I said with a quick smile.

"Sure. Yeah. Most of the guys freelance with me. We don't talk about it too much because they are usually in competition with each other. Some of them work for the Jessops and some not. But yeah, I hire locals."

"Great." I said. "Do you have a business card or a price list I can take with me, Alex?"

"Oh, sure. Come on in. I've got a price list on my desk."

I yanked Mal's leash and practically dragged her away from the Dumpster. We followed Alex down the dark hallway and into the tiny back office. The light was on. From the software displayed on his computer screen, I could tell he'd been doing inventory.

"I use that inventory software, too," I said conversationally.

"Yeah, it's pretty good once you get the hang of it." He turned and handed me a flyer and his business card. "This lists all our services and prices for this season. Things might go up next season. I heard talk about an increase in minimum wage and how tips might be cut out and straight salary required on these guys." He leaned in closer. "Frankly, these guys make more in tips than they could bring home in salary after taxes. I don't see how the government is going to be able to make their life better."

I took the papers and glanced at the standard packages. "How do you keep your inventory right if you have different guys doing different packages?"

"Oh, it's easy really. I pull what is needed for that day's gig and put it in a box with the bartender's name on it. All they have to do is pick up their box and off they go. They barkeep until the booze is gone or time is up."

"What do they do with any leftover liquor?"

"Honey, there's no such thing as leftover liquor." He chuckled.

"Right." I walked toward the door, stopping on the threshold and turning back to Alex. "One more thing."

"Sure."

"Do you watch the boxes after you put them out?"

He frowned. "What do you mean?"

"I mean, do you keep an eye on the boxes and make sure that the guys are picking up the right box and no one is tampering with the boxes."

"Look, I trust my guys, okay? I inventory the boxes. They know they have to double-check the boxes against the order before they leave. If there's a discrepancy, we deal with it before it ever goes to the client."

"But you don't watch the boxes," I confirmed.

"Like I said, I trust my guys."

"So any one of your guys could trade bottles— say substitute cheaper vodka for the vodka you put in the box—and you would never know."

He frowned again. "Well, now if I caught them doing that, they know I'd fire their butts fast. Plus I'd make sure they didn't work on the island again. I have a reputation to uphold."

"Thanks, Alex." I shook his hand. "It was nice to meet you." I raised the papers. "We'll be doing more business next year once the roof space is finished."

He smiled. "Great. You can count on McGriff's."

I could count on McGriff's to provide an opportunity for Harold to have drugged people on the

*Scoundrel.* He could have easily slipped a drugged bottle of vodka or whiskey in the box that Scott took on board. But how would he know that Reggie would drink that drink and not Paige?

Mal stopped me at the Dumpster one more time. I sighed. "What is it, girl?" I looked inside the Dumpster. Contrary to Alex's comment about chicken, all I saw were boxes. Then I noticed the handwritten names on the boxes. Did the bartenders bring their boxes back here? That would be too easy, wouldn't it? I dug around a little bit, but there was no way I was climbing into the Dumpster.

Under the top layer of boxes was a box marked SCOTT FOR THE SCOUNDREL. I didn't want to touch anything in case there was evidence inside. A simple look around showed me a mop drying against the back of the building. I grabbed it and used the handle to push the top boxes away. Opening a flap of the box marked SCOTT, I saw empty bottles inside. My heart pounded. This could be it. *Evidence!*

I put the mop down and dialed Rex.

"Manning," he said in his sexy authoritative voice.

"Hi Rex. It's Allie."

"Is everything okay?"

I couldn't help my wry smile that he would assume I was in trouble every time I called. "Yes, everything is okay. I'm calling because I think I may have more evidence in Carin Moore's murder."

His tone turned to scolding. "Allie, you need to let this one go."

"I can't. Eleanor and Harold made it personal last night when they tried to kidnap me."

"Allegedly," he pointed out.

"That's your word not mine. But I didn't call to argue. I'm in the back alley behind McGriff's. Mal was sniffing around the Dumpster."

"Not another murder."

"No," I confirmed with a sigh. "But there is a box with words *Scott* and *The Scoundrel* handwritten on the side. Inside are empty bottles. I think you should call Shane out here to collect them. There might be evidence inside one of them that Reggie and the others on the *Scoundrel* were drugged that night. Harold and Scott work freelance bartending for McGriff's and Alex told me he boxes up the inventory for each job. It sits for the bartenders to pick up. Harold could have slipped a tainted bottle into the mix. No way for Scott to know. The bartenders simply check that they have the requested inventory in the box and they go to the gig."

"Allie—"

"Please." I cut him off. "I know it's a long shot, but just check it out. Mal sniffed up the box. She's been right a hundred percent of the time."

Rex sighed. "Fine. I'll come collect the box myself and get it to Shane. Even if we find drugs on the bottles, there is no way to prove that Harold put them there."

"Unless you find his fingerprints on the bottle," I said.

"Allie, this isn't television. There are other reasons that his fingerprints might be on the bottles."

"Are you coming down?"

"I'll be there."

I hung up the phone and frowned. Rex was right. It was a long shot. I sighed and put the mop back where it was when I noticed Mal nosing around the wheel of the Dumpster. "What is it?"

I got down low and looked around. Behind the wheel was a syringe. My heart beat a little faster. Was this the evidence that would prove Harold had drugged those on the *Scoundrel*?

When I stood, I saw Rex coming down the alley. "All right," he said, putting on evidence gloves. "Let's take a look at this Dumpster."

"Yes," I agreed. "Thank you. And you might want to bag the syringe that's behind the wheel."

"What?" His eyes narrowed.

"Mal said there was something near the wheel." I squatted back down.

Rex did the same and got out his flashlight. "Do you see what I see?"

"A syringe," he said evenly.

"Yes," I said. "An easy way to place a drug into a bottle of alcohol."

"I'll bag it, but there's no guarantee it has anything to do with Carin's murder."

"I know," I said with a nod. "But it might."

# Chapter 26

I spent the rest of the morning making fudge and trying not to think about the evidence I found and whether Rex had sent it to Shane yet. Even if there was proof that Harold drugged people at the party so that Paige didn't have an alibi, it still didn't prove Eleanor killed Carin.

Plus the murder weapon was an issue. How do I put the oar in Eleanor's hands? How do I put Eleanor at the scene? It was pretty clear to me that Harold lied about who he saw on the pier that night.

Jenn popped her head into the fudge shop as I was washing the last dishes of the day. "You're on."

My assignment was to keep Frances occupied for the rest of the afternoon while Jenn put the finishing touches on the rooftop. At five, she was going to go home with Frances and help her pick out an outfit. I was certain that would give away the entire surprise since she'd never helped Frances dress for a date. Jenn disagreed.

I let her win. She could charm the pants off anyone. Even if Frances became suspicious, in the end she would be happy that Jenn dressed her. The whole thing was being videotaped.

I put away the last dish. "Okay, I'm done here."

"What are you going to do?" Jenn asked.

"I'm taking Frances out for a coffee," I said. "Megan's in, right?"

"She just got here."

"Super." I wiped my hands on the lint-free dish towel, took off my chef's jacket, and walked out to the lobby. "Frances, Megan's here. Let's take Mal for a walk and go get a coffee."

"Splendid idea." She hopped off her stool. "Megan, the Hansons are the last to check in. They called to say they expected a late check-in. If they don't make the last ferry, call them and let them know we'll hold their room one more night, but their credit card will be charged for both nights if they aren't here by noon tomorrow."

"Got it." Megan's eyes were bright with intelligence.

I assumed Jenn had told her what was going on, but she acted as if she didn't know. She was good . . . very good. I hoped she would come back next year.

Frances leashed Mal and I hung my chef coat up and grabbed my wallet and my phone. We stepped out into the early afternoon crowd. The numbers of tourists were down by half since the race had ended yesterday, making it easier to walk down

Main Street. We headed toward the marina and my favorite coffee shop.

"I got wind of what happened last night," Frances said. "I'd love to hear it from your own mouth."

"Well, I was almost arrested for assault."

"That's crazy," Frances said as Mal proudly led us down the street.

"You and I both know I didn't do it. In the end, the evidence was inconclusive. Rex told me to go home and told Harold Jones there wasn't enough evidence to press charges."

"Harold Jones," Frances said. "We're to believe you assaulted Harold Jones? My friend Grace said that Harold is six foot two and two hundred and forty pounds."

I raised an eyebrow. "He's a big guy, yes."

"What did you do to him?" Frances asked, her gaze filled with laughter.

"It's a story," I said as we crossed Main Street and walked to the end of the marina.

"Do tell. This should be interesting."

"Let's get some coffee first. Or do you want tea? Scones?"

"Yes," Frances said. "Chia latte and cherry scones. Mal and I will find a table outside."

I went in and ordered the drinks and scones. Gail wasn't working. I glanced at the bright yellow walls and imagined stenciled cabbage roses. They might just work. When I came out, Frances had found an empty table with an umbrella and was facing the lake. I sat across from her and faced the marina. I handed her the tea and scone, then opened a bottle of water and poured some in a paper cup for Mal.

"I'm waiting for the story," Frances said.

"Okay." I leaned my arms on the table and wrapped my fingers around my cup of coffee. "It all began when I overheard two women talking in the yacht club bathroom about Eleanor, Carin, and Paige."

"Who were the women?"

"I'm not sure." I drew my eyebrows together. "They were very well dressed and looked to be in their early thirties. One was a blonde and one brunette."

Frances sipped her tea. "They could be anyone."

"I think they went to school with Paige or Eleanor. They seemed very familiar with the whole dynamic of Paige and Carin. In fact, they were talking about how surprised they were that Paige killed Carin."

"Why?"

"Paige and Carin had made up at the Christmas fund-raiser and were working together on Carin's boyfriend James Jamison's run for Congress."

"Now there's a bit of gossip I hadn't heard before."

"Probably because he's running in Illinois. I don't think he is from Mackinac."

"I agree. There aren't any Jamisons on the island."

"From the discussion I overheard, it didn't take much to figure out that Harold Jones was dating Eleanor and—"

"That meant he had a motive for telling the

police that he saw Paige on the pier that night, Frances interrupted.

"Yes," I said.

"How did this almost get you arrested?" Frances pinched off a bite of scone and fed it to Mal.

"After most of the people had gone, I confronted Eleanor about the connection between her and the eyewitness in Paige's murder case. When I started talking, she stepped outside in what I can only assume was an attempt to keep our conversation private."

"What did she say when you told her what you knew?"

"She said I was mistaken. Then Harold Jones stepped out of the shadows and joined us on the patio."

"Wait, Harold Jones was waiting outside the yacht club?"

I nodded. "Yes. He said he was waiting for Eleanor to be done working so he could walk her home."

"That's a strange dynamic," Frances said. "They're dating and she didn't invite him to the dance?"

"I don't think she wants anyone to know they are dating. It ruins his credibility as a witness. When I told Eleanor that she had more of a motive to want Carin gone than Paige did, she ordered Harold to take me out to the middle of the lake and dump me."

"She did not!"

"She did," I said. "I thought she was joking, but Harold grabbed me. I was so surprised. Long story short, before he could haul me off, instinct kicked in. I followed my self-defense training without really thinking about it. I dug my heels into his instep and then kicked him in the groin and ran back inside. Lucky for me, Trent was there to keep them from doing anything further. Then after the police arrived, Eleanor had the gall to say I assaulted Harold."

"That's crazy."

"I know it's crazy," I said. "But he had a chunk of his instep missing from the force of my heel and was limping. Someone called the police and Rex took us all down to the station."

A small smile teased Frances's face. "Rex Manning is a man of action."

I shook my head. "I guess. Anyway, in the end, evidence was taken and Rex told us to all go home as he couldn't see anything criminal. I had bruises on my arm showing Harold had grabbed me so even though his instep was mashed we were both bruised. It became a he said-she said thing."

"Well, good for Rex for taking your story seriously. They tried to kidnap you, for goodness sake," Frances said with a scowl on her face. "You could press charges." She slipped Mal another bite of scone.

I shrugged. "It would be my word against theirs. It's okay. I got away. Now they can't do anything to me or it will look suspicious."

"Do you think it was Harold who put the bear trap on your doorstep?"

"I'm not sure." I sipped my coffee. "I was narrowing down suspects before last night. I don't think I gave much thought to Eleanor as the killer until

I realized that if Carin and Paige joined forces, Eleanor would be left out. Think about it. Eleanor has spent her entire life doing whatever Carin wanted. In return, Carin brought Eleanor into the social elite. But when Carin and Paige got together . . . well, they had more in common. They both live and work in Chicago. Carin's boyfriend runs in the same social circles as Paige and Reggie. Well, one of Carin's boyfriends anyway."

"One of Carin's boyfriends?" Frances lifted an eyebrow. "Not Reggie."

"No, Ronald Lorrie said he and Carin were having an affair, that Carin was thinking of leaving James for him."

"No," Frances shook her head. "Carin would never leave a political force like James Jamison. They say he might someday be in the White House. She had big plans."

"Plans that left Eleanor out in the cold," I said. "From the way she treated Harold, it was clear that he is the one in love, not Eleanor. She could hardly stand to look at him."

"Maybe it was Eleanor Harold saw on the pier with Carin that night," Frances suggested. "Maybe he was using his testimony to blackmail her into dating him."

"That would be an interesting twist," I said thoughtfully. "But that still leaves the problem of the oar."

"The murder weapon?"

"Yes." I grabbed a scone. One bite and I understood why Mal begged for the soft buttery treat. The cherries added just the right amount of sweet and tart. "How do I get it in Eleanor's hands? I mean, it says *Scoundrel* right on it and has Paige's fingerprints on it."

"Did you ask Paige about that?"

"No, but I imagine Rex and her legal team did already. My asking isn't going to help. I'm trying to think outside the box. With Paige as a suspect, no one is looking anywhere else." I studied the boats docked at the marina. "I've started Rex thinking about Eleanor, but without any real evidence there isn't any reason to charge her instead."

"How has the new camera system been working?"

"Okay," I said with a shrug. "I've mostly caught Caramella coming and going, and Mr. Beecher on his twice daily walks. A few people coming home late from the bars. Nothing sinister."

"That's a relief," Frances said.

I eyed the boats in the marina some more. "You've lived here all your life."

"And?"

"You must know about boats."

"I do," Frances said with a nod. "Not the yachts of course. I never cared to run around with that crowd. But I can sail a small boat and I can use an outboard motor."

"What do you know about oars?" I fiddled with my cup. "I mean, seriously, I didn't even think oars were needed on a yacht."

"Some are purely decoration like the ones along the dock here. Others are kept on the lifeboats," Frances said. "I can imagine it would be easy to take one and not have anyone notice it was missing.

It's not like they inventory the safety gear every time they go out on the water."

"They should," I said.

"Yes, they should, but I imagine they don't. That night was a party night. They weren't going that far."

"I'm sure Rex questioned the captain and crew about it." I put my elbow on the table and my chin in my hand. "That would be one of the first things I would do."

"Except I'm not certain the *Scoundrel* is big enough to warrant a crew," Frances said. "It could just be one of Paige or Trent's friends that captained the *Scoundrel* out that night. You should ask Trent about that."

"Wow, I will. I sort of think of it like that old movie *Overboard* where they had a captain and crew."

Frances laughed. "I do love Goldie Hawn movies, but the *Scoundrel* isn't that big."

"Everyone says the murder weapon came from the *Scoundrel* because it has the name painted on the handle," I said. "What if someone painted it on to make it look like it came from there?"

Frances winced. "That's a lot of preplanning," she pointed out. "There are more effective ways to kill someone. Think about it. If you were preplanning a murder, why wouldn't you use poison or a gun? Even a knife is more likely to kill than a boat oar."

"True," I said. "Unless you are trying to make it seem like a crime of passion."

"Still, an oar turned sideways so the edge hits the

right place on the back of the skull to kill her? That is not premeditated. That's anger."

"If it wasn't premeditated, how did the oar get in the hands of the killer? How is it that so many people on the *Scoundrel* were passed out? That no one can recall seeing Paige during the window of opportunity the killer had to kill Carin?"

Frances had another question. "What if the killer was on the *Scoundrel* and didn't want anyone to know they were slipping off to meet Carin on the dock?"

"You mean someone other than Paige?"

She nodded. "Yes. Who was at the party that night?"

"Good question," I said. "Let me text Trent and see if he can send me a list of guests."

"Maybe the answer has been right under our noses all along."

"Wouldn't that be something?" I hit SEND on my text to Trent. "Now, what's the big deal about tonight's date?"

Frances blushed. "It's our three month anniversary."

"Oh, sweet," I said. "You celebrate your anniversary each month?"

"At our age, we never know how many days we have left," Frances said. "We try to celebrate as many anniversaries as possible."

"What a great way to look at life," I said. "We all need to celebrate more of the little things. Do you know where you're going?"

"No," Frances said with a shake of her head. "But he did ask me to dress semiformal. Jennifer is going to come home with me at five and help me. She promised to do my makeup so that I look great." Frances leaned in closer. "I want to look good should we go to the Grand and the photographer wants to take our picture."

"That would be a great memento." I made a mental note to see if we can't get a still photograph to go with the video.

"I'm excited," she said, her gaze sparkling in the afternoon light. "I feel like a teenager again. Who knew we could find love at our age?"

"I think you can find love at any age," I said. "If you look for it hard enough. In fact, most of the time it's right under our noses."

"Yes," Frances said with another nod. "The answers to life usually are."

# Chapter 27

I handed Frances off to Jenn and went upstairs to my office. I'd asked Trent to have Paige go over the list of party invitees and mark through anyone who hadn't gone and add anyone who was not on the original list. He'd texted back that Rex had asked for the same thing early on in the investigation so they already had a copy on hand.

I downloaded the list to my laptop and printed it out. I studied it carefully. Several of them simply had a plus one marked by their name. It was important to know who all were there. I made notes of who I knew and who I didn't know. All told, twenty-five people had been aboard. The boat had been captained by Trent's friend Peter. That was the extent of the crew. A catering staff and bartender had also been aboard. I frowned. The list wasn't telling me anything.

I gave up and went up to the rooftop to see how things were progressing without Jenn. She had said all was well and I believed her, but still I wanted to check it out. Frances had been so cute about her date tonight. I'm not sure she suspected the proposal, but I was happy to help make it special.

It had me wondering why Trent and I didn't celebrate our monthly anniversaries. I'd never really thought of it. We'd been together eight weeks . . . or was it ten? I laughed at myself. No wonder he didn't include me in his sister's investigation from the start. We weren't as serious as Frances and Mr. Devaney. The next thought had me stopping halfway between the roof and the attic. *What would I do if Trent asked me to marry him?*

White sheers billowed prettily in the breeze. The sky was a royal blue, creating a stunning backdrop for the gazebo. Soft music played through the speakers hidden behind four large palms. I knew video cameras were also hidden in two of the palms and would be activated with a remote by Mr. Devaney, giving him total control of what was recorded and what wasn't.

I smiled at the thought of when he might turn it off.

"Everything is set and ready," Sandy said. She had two big pillows in her hands.

I tilted my head and raised an eyebrow at the pillows.

"Editing," she said solemnly. "First you put out everything you think you want, then you edit back. What you leave out is just as important as what you put in."

"Right." I nodded. "Makes sense. At their age,

I don't see them getting down on the floor and sitting on pillows."

"The chairs were plenty," Sandy said. "Plus more room for dancing."

"It's going to be a wonderful evening." I held the trap door open for Sandy as she climbed down with the pillows. When I headed down a thought struck me. *Maybe it wasn't as important who was on the invitation list for the* Scoundrel *that night as it was who was left off the list.*

I headed back to my desk where the list sat and scanned it briefly front and back. If Carin and Paige had made up and were becoming fast friends, why wasn't Carin invited to the party?

I sent a text to Trent.

> Me: Why wasn't Carin Moore invited to Paige's party the night she was murdered?

Trent texted back. Let me ask Paige.

I waited a minute and drummed my fingers on my desk.

He finally texted back. Carin had a campaign committee meeting she'd planned to attend via Skype.

Wait. If she was part of a Skype committee meeting, why was she wearing a silk cocktail dress?

> She was wearing a cocktail dress when I found her. Who else was having a party that night?

> It was yacht club week. Everyone was having a party that night. Trent answered.

Except you and me. I texted back wryly.

We don't need a yacht race to celebrate.

I texted a smiley face emoji, but my mind was still on Carin's murder. If Paige and Carin had joined forces to support James Jamison's political campaign, who else had joined in? Eleanor? Mrs. Jones? I needed to get my hands on a list of locals who may have contributed. Maybe Carin left the Skype call to attend a political party.

Trent, can Paige provide me a list of James Jamison's political supporters? The local ones?

He texted back. I'll have her e-mail it to you. Am I still dropping by around ten?

I texted back. Oh yes. You don't want to miss this.

He sent me a heart icon, which made me smile. This gorgeous, sexy, wealthy man had said he loved me. It made me want even more to prove his sister's innocence.

## **Easy Almond Butter Fudge**

### Ingredients

1 cup almond butter
1 cup butter, melted
1 teaspoon vanilla
½ teaspoon almond extract
¼ teaspoon salt
2 pounds of powdered sugar

**Directions**

In a microwave on low, melt butter. In a large bowl, mix almond butter, melted butter, vanilla, almond extract, and salt.

Sift in powdered sugar, stirring until thick. This may take more or less powdered sugar to get the texture you desire.

Dump into a wax paper–lined 8-inch baking pan. Pat the top smooth. Using a butter knife, score into 1-inch pieces. Chill until firm.

Use the edges of the wax paper to take the fudge out of the pan. Remove paper and break into scored pieces. Drizzle with chocolate sauce.

Enjoy!

# Chapter 28

The list of political contributors was short and mostly the names I expected—people with the most wealth and power on the island—except one. I frowned at the name and the substantial amount that she had contributed.

Gail Hall, the coffee shop owner, had contributed twenty-five thousand dollars to the Jamison campaign. She didn't seem the type to have that much money. I checked my watch. It was eight fifteen. Time for Mr. Devaney to pick up Frances for their romantic carriage tour of the island.

Jenn sent me pictures of Frances wearing a black sequined top with a floaty chiffon tea length skirt and black pumps. Her hair was tucked into an updo with baby's breath in it. She looked gorgeous. I also received phone pictures of Mr. Devaney in a black suit, white shirt, and red bow tie. He'd picked Frances up in a white Cinderella carriage and they slowly took the trail around the island that started at Main Street. Later they would return to the back of the McMurphy where he would help her up the flower strewn steps to the roof.

Everything was set. Mal was freshly bathed and had a red bow attached around her neck. Caramella was also groomed with a red ribbon and little bell around her neck . . . much to her chagrin. I was dressed in a black cocktail dress and three-inch black pumps. In exactly an hour, Jenn and Shane would be here. Trent would come. The four of us would have cocktails in the apartment and wait for Mr. Devaney to signal that she said yes and they were ready for us all to come up and bring champagne.

I looked at the list and I looked at the time once more. The coffee shop didn't close until nine PM. I could go get some éclairs and ask Gail about her contribution to the Jamison campaign and still be back by nine.

Really, I had nothing else to do but wait. I grabbed my clutch purse, gave Mal a treat, and texted Jenn as I left the McMurphy.

Going for éclairs at the coffee shop. Be back well before nine.

I stuffed my phone in my clutch purse and headed off as fast as I could in heels. I knew better than to check my phone when I heard it ding that a text had arrived. Jenn would be chiding me. But really, the coffee shop was a half a mile from the McMurphy. I doubted I would be in too much trouble if I stopped by and bought dessert.

"Allie McMurphy," Gail said as I entered the empty coffee shop.

"Hi Gail," I said with a smile. "I hoped you were still open."

"You know we close at nine, but since yacht week is over, there's little business after seven."

"Do you have any of your éclairs left? I thought I'd pick up a dozen for dessert."

"Sure." She pulled out a bakery box and folded it. "Chocolate?"

"Yes," I said.

The shop was quiet. I could hear the splash of the waves against the pier and the distant sound of a foghorn.

"Do you live above the shop?" I asked to make conversation. After all, I lived above my shop and the coffee shop had two stories.

"Yes. I like being right on the water." Gail grabbed a bakery tissue from the box and opened the glass door and started to count éclairs as she put them in the box.

"You must have a great view," I said, chattering as I tried to bring up the question I had come to ask. "We have to go on the roof of the McMurphy to see the lake. My apartment has a nice view of the alley and the pool house behind."

"Too bad for you," she said as she put in thirteen éclairs.

She smiled at me. "A baker's dozen." A baker's dozen was when they added extra for free. She closed up the box and moved to the counter.

"Thanks." I said as she closed up the box and moved to the counter. "Listen I was wondering . . ."

"Yes?" She rang up the éclairs at fifteen dollars.

"I saw that you contributed quite a bit to the Jamison for congress campaign." I tilted my head and opened my purse to dig out a ten and a five-dollar bill.

"Yes," she said.

"Why? I mean he's running for congress in Chicago, right?" I handed her the money.

She took it and opened her register, placed the bills carefully in the bin, and then looked at me. Her brown gaze had turned strangely cold. I took a step back.

"Carin had promised me if I gave that amount to the Jamison campaign she would ensure that the marina zoning committee renewed my lease for another five years."

"Oh." I sent Gail a small smile. The hair on the back of my neck rose when she didn't close the register drawer. "I would have donated, too, if I thought it meant I could keep the McMurphy."

"The committee turned down my renewal," Gail said, her gaze growing dark. "They want to tear down the historic shops and put up condos."

"Well, they can't do that." I picked up my box of eclairs and took a second step toward the door. "The historic committee won't let them."

"That's what Carin said." Gail closed her register with a bang. "But she lied. It seems it takes more than my life's savings to buy the historic committee."

"That's horrible."

"Yes, it is, but not enough to make Carin sorry. I wondered how long it would take for you to figure me out." She pulled out a gun and aimed it at me. "Drop the eclairs."

I swallowed hard. The glint of light on the gun was terrifying. I raised my hands. "I didn't have you figured out. I . . . wait. You had black paint on your hands the morning I pulled Carin from the water."

Her expression was grim. "I stenciled *Scoundrel* on the oar. But you figured that out, didn't you?"

I winced. "I knew that oar was not an original. It didn't make sense. Let me guess. There are only two on the manifest, but there were three on the boat."

She didn't say anything.

So I had to ask, "How did you get Paige's finger-prints on the oar?"

"That was pure luck," Gail said. "I put the oar on the deck. Paige must have picked it up and moved it."

"And drugging everyone?"

"I had nothing to do with that. I overheard Harold bragging about the prank he pulled and used it to my advantage. I confronted Carin on the pier that night when I'd overheard the committee talking about building condos where my shop is. She couldn't have cared less that I gave her my entire life's savings. She shrugged and said that was a risk I took."

"So you grabbed an oar and hit her as she walked away."

"I was so angry all I saw was red. The next thing I knew, she was in the water. I thought, good. Let her ruin her dress and have a headache in the morning. That darn dress probably cost what I had given to the campaign." Gail shook her head.

"But you'd painted the oar before you brought us coffee the morning I pulled Carin from the marina."

"I saw you jump in and got worried. I pulled the oar out of the back room and stenciled it with *Scoundrel*," she said. "It was still drying when I brought you coffee."

"You hid the oar until the *Scoundrel* came in and then managed to toss it on the deck without being seen."

"No one notices you if they are used to seeing you on the pier. It was a simple matter of rowing over, tossing the oar, and rowing back to the coffee shop."

"And they arrested Paige," I said.

Gail shrugged. "The Jessops are rich enough that they would be able to see that Paige didn't go to jail for long. The cops wouldn't look anywhere else. I was out my life savings, but I had my revenge."

"Until I started looking."

"Until I heard you were poking around. Then I got nervous."

I frowned. "You put the bear trap on my doorstep."

"I warned you to back off."

My hands were in the air, but I took a step back so that I was in the window of the shop. All I could do was hope that someone was out and about and would see me standing there with my arms up. "You could have killed my pets."

"I doubt it. Your dog is too smart and a cat . . . well, a cat isn't going to get caught in a trap."

"You shouldn't have done it," I said. "It only made Rex suspicious and kept me looking."

"I hate to burst your bubble, but Rex is as much a part of the political scene here as the Moores and the Jessops. He wasn't going to do anything about a bear trap he couldn't trace."

I tried to keep her talking. "You can't shoot me. People will figure you out. If you let me go, I won't say anything. I just came for éclairs."

Gail smiled. "Don't be silly. If I let you stick your head out of the door you'll be screaming bloody murder. No, we're going to go out the back and down to the water. You're going to kill yourself and leave a note that you were the one who killed Carin. That you did it because Trent asked you to, but you couldn't live with yourself."

"No one will believe that," I said.

Gail shrugged. "Maybe not, but they aren't going to have any idea it was me." She waved the gun toward her back door. "Go. Don't try anything heroic or your body might be lost at sea."

"You can't shoot me here," I said. "There will be blood evidence."

"I have a lot of bleach," she said. "I'm not too worried about blood. Now go out the back."

"No." I held my ground with my heartbeat pounding in my ears. "If you're going to shoot me, you are going to have to do it here. In front of your windows. Then you're going to have to figure out how to clean up the mess."

A flash of pure anger rose in her gaze. "I'll

simply burn the place down," she countered. "Your death will be accidental and I'll get insurance money."

"People won't believe you."

"They will because they'll want to. They want this property for condos, remember?" She held the gun out straight. "Good-bye, Allie."

The door was kicked open with a bang.

"Freeze! Police!"

The sound of four guns being cocked filled the air.

Gail's eyes narrowed and for a brief moment I thought she might shoot me anyway. Then she raised her hands in surrender.

"Put the gun on the ground!" Rex ordered.

Gail slowly put the gun down, not taking her gaze from me. I shook from head to toe with my arms in the air.

"Get down on the ground," Rex said.

I fell to my knees along with Gail. Two policemen grabbed her and pushed her down, cuffing her.

Officer Brown came toward me. "Are you all right, Allie?"

I nodded. "Yes. How did you know to come?"

"Jenn Christensen called Rex," Charles replied as he helped me to my feet.

My knees were still a little shaky.

Jenn burst through the door as Gail was hauled away. "Allie, are you okay? I called Rex the moment I got your text."

I tilted my head, confused. "All I texted was that I was going for éclairs."

Jenn put her hand on her hips. She looked

ridiculously fierce in a black body-conscious dress and spikey heels. "You never go out for éclairs this late. I figured it was code for you knew who the killer was. Why else would you leave us during this big night?"

I sent her a wry smile and shrugged. "I wanted éclairs?"

Jenn snorted inelegantly and I laughed.

"What happened?" Rex asked.

Shane came in the coffee shop with his crime scene kit in hand. He put down the kit and put on gloves.

"Um," I started to say when my knees buckled with relief.

Officer Brown caught me and pulled out a chair from a nearby table.

"Thanks."

Jenn stood over me. "This could have waited until tomorrow."

I winced. "I had a question. I thought it was an easy question."

"What was the question?" Rex asked me.

"I wanted to know why Gail gave twenty-five thousand dollars to James Jamison's political fund. He's running for congress in the Chicago district."

"And Gail's answer?" Rex asked.

"She said that Carin had promised to influence the board against putting condos up where the coffee shop is . . . if Gail donated to Jamison's campaign."

"But the board passed zoning for condos here," Jenn said.

"Gail confronted Carin that night when Carin was waiting for her lover on the pier," I said.

"Where did she get the oar from the *Scoundrel*?" Jenn asked.

I looked at Shane and Rex. "I bet if you check the inventory there were three oars not two on board when you searched. Shane, check the paint on the murder weapon. The morning I pulled Carin from the marina, Gail brought us coffee. She had black paint on her hands. Tonight, she told me she had stenciled *Scoundrel* on the oar."

"What about the drugs found in the alcohol at Paige's party?"

"A prank," I said. "Harold bragged about it after the *Scoundrel* left the marina that night. Gail overheard him and that's how she knew Paige wouldn't have an alibi. It wasn't premeditated. Stenciling *Scoundrel* on the oar was an afterthought."

"And you're okay?" Rex asked.

"Yes." I raised my hand to stop Shane. "There's no reason to take this outfit into evidence."

Jenn laughed. "Let's hope not. We have an engagement to celebrate."

"Crap," I muttered and looked at my watch. It was 9:15. "Did we miss it?"

Jenn checked her phone and chuckled. "Mr. Devaney texted." She showed us her phone.

**She said yes.**

We all cheered.

"Wait. There's another text," Jenn said with a twinkle in her eye.

"What?" I asked.

Jenn read it aloud. "'Don't come up.' it says. 'C U in the morning.'" She grinned and raised an eyebrow. "Looks like they want their privacy. He's turned the video cameras off."

"Why is Mr. Devaney texting Jenn?" Rex asked. "I didn't think he even had a cell phone."

"He asked us to help him pop the question to Frances," I said. "Jenn is our point person. We were all supposed to meet them on the roof to celebrate."

"It's why Shane is wearing a suit coat," Jenn pointed out.

"I wondered about that," Rex said. "Plaid suit coat. Not a bad choice for you, Shane."

"It's not plaid," Shane said and a blush rushed up his neck. "Is it?" He glanced from the sleeve of his jacket to me. "Jenn picked it out."

"It's not plaid." I frowned at Rex. "It's got faint lines is all. Brown looks good on you. Goes well with your glasses."

"Never fear"—Jenn kissed him on the cheek— "your girlfriend has good taste."

"Yes, she does," Rex said. "You girls can go. This won't take long for Shane to process."

"We'll save the champagne for tomorrow," I said.

"That's the best idea I've heard yet. Come on, girlfriend." Jenn linked her arm with mine. "Let's go find Trent and give him the good news."

"Thank you," I said to Rex and Officer Brown. "For coming to my rescue. For a while there, I was afraid I was going to end up in the marina like Carin."

"You have too many friends here to ever let that happen," Jenn said.

I felt the warm glow of happiness and relief. Deep inside, I knew she was right. No matter what, I had good friends who would ensure I was safe and sound. And now we had Frances's engagement to celebrate.

Life couldn't get much better.

# Acknowledgments

It takes a village to create a book. I want to acknowledge the people of Mackinac Island Tourism Bureau, the wonderful booksellers at The Island Bookstore, and all the professionals who have let me reach out and bug them with silly questions about Mackinac Island until I get it right. Any mistakes are purely my own. Special thanks to my editor Michaela and all the copy editors, assistants, production folks, and readers at Kensington Books. Thanks, too, to my agent Paige Wheeler, who keeps me on track and helps me make a living doing what I love. Finally, thanks to the readers who keep buying my books, sharing my stories, and allowing me to be a part of their lives. You all *rock*.

Join Allie, Mal, and their friends
in the next Candy-Coated Mystery

### *Oh, Fudge!*

Coming from Kensington in 2017
Turn the page for a preview excerpt . . .

# Chapter 1

The Mackinac Island Butterfly House didn't open until ten, but I had a message from Blake Gilmore, the current manager, that she needed to see me about a possible tour group staying at the McMurphy. I walked my puppy, Mal, around the back of the Butterfly House looking for an open door. I saw movement in the greenhouse and figured Blake was watering plants or checking the butterflies.

"Hello? Blake?" I called as I opened the back door and stepped into the tropical humidity of the glass building. Mal tugged on her leash pulling me through the lovely winding, lush trail of the greenhouse that contained the live butterfly collection.

Suddenly I heard a short scream. My heartbeat sped up and Mal and I ran toward the sound. I stopped short at the sight in front of me. "Tory?"

Mal tugged at her leash, but I held her back.

In front of us was my California cousin, Victoria Andrews, kneeling over a woman. Tory held the handle of a gardening spade in her hands. The rest of the spade was stuck firmly in the chest of a woman I didn't know. The woman's jeans-clad legs were oddly angled. Her hands spread out, but empty. A pool of blood blossomed from beneath her checkered blouse.

"Tory, what's going on?" I couldn't tell if she was pushing the spade in or pulling it out. When she saw me, she let go of the handle and held up her hands as if I were the police and had just said, "Freeze." Her blue eyes filled with fear. Her long, blond hair was pulled back in a low ponytail, but a streak of blood caressed her cheek. Her bow-shaped mouth trembled and her tanned skin looked ashen.

"Tory? What's going on?"

She stood and wiped her bloody hands on the front of her jeans. She was trembling from head to toe. "It's not what it looks like." Her California accent was clear through the tremble in her voice.

Mal dragged me toward the scene.

"No," I said, tugging her back as I took out my cell phone. "Tory, sit down," I ordered as I pointed to a nearby bench. "You're in shock." I dialed 9-1-1 and eased my cousin over to the bench.

Mal jumped up beside her to comfort her and ended up with blood on her white fur.

"9-1-1. This is Charlene. What is your emergency?"

"Hi, Charlene."

"Allie McMurphy. This can't be good. Where are you? I'll send Rex over there right away."

"Thank you," I said. Rex Manning was my favorite lead policeman on Mackinac Island. "I'm at the

Butterfly House. Tell him to come around to the back. We're in the greenhouse."

"He's on his way," Charlene said. "You said *we?*"

"Yes, It's me, my cousin Victoria, and—"

"Another dead person?"

"Well, she certainly looks dead," I said. "I haven't touched her."

"Then how do you know she's dead?"

"Well, there's a hand spade sticking out of her chest and she's not moving." I wasn't going to tell Charlene that my cousin might have been the one to put the spade there. Not until I had all the facts. "Let me check for a pulse."

I skirted around the pool of blood and put my fingers on her neck. She felt warm, but there was no heartbeat. I shook her shoulder. "Are you okay?"

Her eyes simply stared lifeless into the skylights.

"She doesn't respond to verbal cues and I didn't feel a pulse."

"Enough said," Charlene said. "I swear we've never had this much trouble until your Papa Liam passed. God rest his soul."

It was then that Tory moaned. "I think I'm going to be sick."

"Charlene, I've got to go." I hung up the phone. I carried doggie-doo bags with me whenever I walked with Mal. I pulled one from my pocket and handed it to Tory. "Breathe into the bag. I think you're hyperventilating."

"It's not breathing that's a problem," Tory said before she turned her head and emptied her stomach into the bag.

I put my hand on her back as she heaved. "It's going to be okay."

Mal put her paw on Tory as if to say she wanted to comfort my trembling cousin.

"What happened? Did you stab her? Was she attacking you?"

The woman appeared to be middle-aged. Her feet were ensconced in gray and pink walking shoes. Her black hair, including the streak of white hair along the left side of her face, was pulled back into a neat ponytail. She had high cheekbones, thin lips, and wide-open brown eyes that stared at the sky.

"No, no she wasn't attacking me," Tory said, lifting her head from the baggie. "I didn't kill her. It's Barbara Smart. I was supposed to meet her here this morning to continue our discussion about a possible wine tour excursion. I found her like that."

"But you had your hand on the handle of the spade." I had to point out the obvious.

"I wanted to help her. I thought if I pulled it out I might be able to do CPR, but as I tugged more blood came out and I was afraid I was only making things worse. Then you came in. Did I hear you correctly? She didn't have a pulse?"

"No, she didn't," I said. "Didn't you check for one?"

"I know it's the first thing you're told to do when you take a CPR class, but I didn't. I panicked and knelt down and shook her shoulder. I thought I heard a moan so I tried to take the blade out. That's when you got here."

"Did you see anyone?"

"No." Tory hung her head. "You and your dog were the first live people I've seen."

"Wow, okay. So what time was your meeting? Was Blake supposed to be here? After all, she manages the Butterfly House."

"Barbara and I met with Blake last night. Blake had another meeting this morning, but told us we could meet here to finish the details of the tour."

"Wait. You were here last night?"

"Yes."

"And you didn't call me? It's before the ferries come so you had to have stayed on the island last night. Why didn't you let me know you were coming? We have room at the McMurphy. You could have stayed with me."

She gave me an angry look. "I didn't think I was welcome at the McMurphy. You own it, not me—even though our great-grandfather started it."

"What?" I straightened away from her. "Papa Liam always said your dad didn't want anything to do with the McMurphy even after my father moved us to Detroit. It's the only reason I took it over."

"Listen, can we talk about this later?" Tory said. "Barbara's lying there dead."

"Sure, but we will finish this conversation. Where are you staying?"

"Dad still owns a cabin on the far north side. I'm staying there."

"What's going on?" Officer Rex Manning walked in through the back door. His black police boots crunched on the soft mulch that was the winding trail between the raised beds. "Charlene says you found another body?"

"Hi, Rex." I stood.

Mal jumped off the bench and raced over to beg him for a few pets.

He reached down to pat her and noticed the blood on her paws. "Sorry kid, can't touch you when you have evidence on you." He looked up at me with his flat blue gaze. "What happened?"

He wore a perfectly pressed police uniform. As usual, he'd taken his hat off the minute he entered the building, showing off his shaved head and square jaw. The man had the build of an action movie hero and the attitude that went with his good looks.

"I had an early appointment with Blake," I said. "The front door is closed until ten so I came around back. I saw movement in the greenhouse and thought it was Blake so I came in. I heard a scream and rushed toward the sound to find my cousin Victoria kneeling over the woman with the garden spade in her chest." I pointed at the body.

"I see." Rex walked over and checked the pulse point at the dead woman's throat. He glanced over at Tory who had put the doggie-doo bag down by her feet and had her head between her knees. "This woman is dead," he announced and picked up her wrist. "She's still warm. I don't think she's been dead long, but we'll have to wait for the coroner's report to know for sure." He stood and went over to Tory. "Tory Andrews?"

Tory looked up at him. "Hi, Rex."

I frowned. How did they know each other?

"It's been a while," Rex said as he squatted down

to look Tory in the eye as she hung her head. "I thought you were in California."

"I am." She took a deep breath, then blew it out slow. "I mean, I was . . . up until yesterday."

"You have blood on you. Can you tell me what happened?"

Mal tried to nudge herself between Rex and Tory. He gently pushed Mal back and sent me a look that silently told me to take care of my pet. I scooped up my evidence-covered pup and took a step back, knowing that the EMTs were most likely on their way along with the county CSI guy, Shane Carpenter.

"I was supposed to meet Barbara here this morning, but when I arrived she wasn't in the office so I came out here looking for her." Tory put her head between her knees again. "I heard a noise and came this way. I saw her lying there and knelt down to shake her."

"Is that how you got blood on you?" He was calm and there was kindness in his tone I hadn't heard in a while.

"Yes," Tory said. "I was going to pull out the shovel. When I put my hands on the handle more blood came out so I stopped. Then Allie came in. She got me to the bench."

Rex looked at me. "Did you see anyone else?"

"No." I shook my head.

Just then Blake came around the corner. "What's going on? I saw Rex's bicycle parked out front. Wait!" She froze in place and put her hands over her mouth. "Barbara?" It came out as a shocked whisper. Her knees buckled.

Rex and I got to her at the same time and each took an elbow and helped her slowly to the bench.

"Barbara? Oh, Barbara! What happened?" She glanced from me to Rex to Tory.

"I found her like this," Tory said.

Mal put her front paws on the bench seat and looked from one distressed woman to the other as if unsure how to comfort them both.

"Is that a spade? Who would do such a thing?"

"We'll find out." I patted Blake on the shoulder.

She was an older woman in her midfifties with light brown hair highlighted with blond streaks that shimmered in the daylight. Her face was round and pretty. Of average build, she could pass for younger. Today she wore a pair of jeans, sneakers, and a white polo shirt with the Butterfly House logo monogrammed on the left breast.

George Marron and Walt Henderson came in through the door with a stretcher between them and their EMT bags in their hands.

"What do we have?" George was the lead EMT on Mackinac Island. He had long, black hair that was pulled back in a single braid, copper skin, and high cheekbones of his Iroquois ancestry.

"Dead body," Rex said in a low tone. "She's probably been gone about forty-five minutes to an hour, but we'll have to wait for the coroner to find out for sure."

"Cause of death seems pretty clear." Walt was a tall thin man with gray hair and a hawklike nose. He had sharp features and dark brown eyes. His skin had the weathered look of a fisherman . . . or at the least someone who knew their way around the water.

"Tory Andrews," George said. "When did you get back on the island?"

"Hi, George," Tory said, trying to sit up straight. "Sorry, I can't." She grabbed the doggie bag and heaved again.

George let go of the stretcher and went over to Tory. He checked her pulse and eyes. "You're in shock." He waved for Walt to bring a blanket over, then slung it around Tory's shoulders. "Are you hurt?"

"No." She shook her head.

"There's blood. I should check."

"It's Barbara's," Tory said and closed her eyes. "I tried to take the spade out of her chest, but I couldn't."

"Okay. Well, let's take you back to the clinic and get you checked out just in case. Okay?" George looked at Rex, who nodded.

"I'm fine, really," Tory said.

"You should go," I said. "They can give you something to settle your stomach. Besides, the crime scene guy will want your clothes. You're covered in evidence."

"Come on," George said and helped her to her feet. "Allie and I will take you to the clinic."

"What about Barbara?" Tory asked as she glanced at her friend one more time.

"Walt and Rex will take good care of her." George said.

"Come on, Blake," I said, tugging her to her feet. "Come with us. You look a little shocky yourself."

"I can't leave Barbara," Blake said with tears in her brown eyes.

"It's okay. Rex is with her." I locked my arm with Blake's. "Tory can really use our comfort right now. Right?"

"It is better if you ladies stick together," George said as he walked Tory out the door.

Shane stopped us on the way out. He wore his navy blue CSI jacket and ball cap. His horn-rim glasses emphasized his concerned eyes. "I hear you've found another crime scene."

I shook my head. "Not me this time. My cousin Tory did." I pointed toward her and George.

"Tory Andrews?" Shane's face burst into a wide smile. "When did you get back on the island?"

"Yesterday," I muttered. "She just didn't tell anyone."

"I had meetings," Tory said.

I frowned. "Gee, Tory. Everyone seems to know you."

"They should. I went to school with all of them up until senior year when Dad moved us out to California. Unlike you, Allie, I'm not a Fudgie."

I bit back a retort as Shane made his way into the building. After all, Tory had just found a woman lying dead in a pool of her own blood. That kind of shock did things to people. I looked at George who simply shrugged at me.

"Poor Barbara," Blake said, bringing my attention back to the poor woman who clung to me. "Poor Barbara. She didn't deserve to die."

I patted Blake's arm. "No, she didn't."

"Who could have done such a thing?" Blake asked. "Barbara wouldn't hurt a flea."

"I didn't know Barbara," I said, "but no one deserves to die like that."

"I've got to put up a sign." She pulled away as if to go back into the crime scene. "I've got to let everyone know that the Butterfly House is closed. I've got to let Barbara's family know."

"The police will take care of her family." I gently guided Blake back toward the ambulance. "You need to take care of yourself. Trust me, you've had a shock. You should go to the clinic and get checked out."

George helped Tory into the ambulance—one of the few motorized vehicles allowed on the island for safety purposes.

"Let George help you," I said.

Mal nudged Blake as if to let her know that she was not alone in her sorrow.

"Thank you. It's so upsetting," Blake said as I helped her up in the ambulance.

Mal jumped up with them.

"It is okay if Mal goes with you?" I asked George.

"She should be quarantined until any evidence she's carrying is collected," he said. "Are you staying?"

"I should give my statement and see if there is anything that Rex or Shane needs," I said.

George nodded and closed the doors on the ambulance. "We'll take good care of these girls. You can pick Mal up after Shane gets his evidence."

"Thanks." I waved them off as he slowly drove away. I turned and looked at the trail to the Butterfly House entrance. What a terrible thing to happen in such a fun and beautiful place. First thing was to put a note on the door. The next was to go back inside and see what I could do to help figure out who would do such a terrible thing. Last was to figure out why my cousin Tory didn't feel that she could stay with me.

Was she hiding something? Was it something that had to do with the dead woman on the floor of the Butterfly House?